EYES IN TH

BOOK (

SITE ALPHA

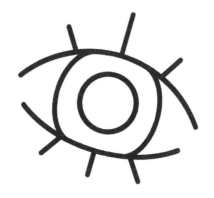

This book contains varying degrees of the following:
Adult Language, Adult Situations, Violence, Suicidal References.
Please read safely and responsibly.

EYES IN THE DARK
BOOK ONE: SITE ALPHA

Copyright © 2022 by Neal Romriell

Editing Services Provided By Ashlynn Wittchow

Line and Developmental Edits Provided by Avery Romriell

Cover / Interior Art and design by Tye Smith

PAPERBACK ISBN: 979-8-9860492-0-5
HARDBACK ISBN: 979-8-9860492-1-2
ELECTRONIC BOOK ISBN: 979-8-9860492-2-9

What Folks are Saying About *Site Alpha*.

"Site Alpha is a masterfully crafted page-turner with a cast of animated heroes you'll love, and duplicitous villains you'll love to hate. Showcasing his talent for action and intrigue, Romriell pulls you into the story on a visceral level and doesn't let you go until the last page." – **G. Barker, Award Winning Author of *Life After***

"Site Alpha latches the reader from the very first word and pulls us into a world parallel to reality, where trained secret agents work to protect cryptid creatures from discovery and exploitation. With each new page, I opened my heart to the characters in peril and became more invested in solving the ultimate riddle of the story; what legendary creature is targeting other cryptids?

Neal Romriell tackles this suspense-filled plot by infusing hilarious quips to lighten the mood, leading to an impressively balanced debut that will leave you wanting more of his awesome fantasy world that exists right under our noses, but just beyond our reach." – **R. Weber; Author of *The Painter's Butterfly***

"Site Alpha is easily my favorite new title. I'm a big cryptid fan and I love shadowy organizations. The way Neal characterizes these creatures is exciting and I just want more. I can't wait to see where he takes the story next." – **Matt Clark, Co-Host of The Rough Craft**

EYES IN THE DARK
BOOK ONE:

SITE ALPHA

CONFIDENTIAL: FILE #8108-6840

Table of Contents

A Note From The Author

Thank You for taking some of your hard-earned time to read my debut novel, *Site Alpha*. My hope is that you'll enjoy reading it as much as I enjoyed writing it.

Music plays an incredibly important role in my life, and that importance extends to my writing as well. While writing and editing *Site Alpha* I listened to hundreds of hours of music. I'd pick songs based on the mood of the scene I was writing, sometimes listening to the same group of songs on repeat for days as I hammered out a chapter.

In the spirit of my love for music, I've prepared some playlists on Spotify™ based on the main and secondary characters of this book. Once you've read *Site Alpha* and found a character (or characters) that you love, I'd encourage you to search out **Neal Romriell** on Spotify™ and check out the playlist I designed based on some of the music I was listening to when I wrote them. (You may even discover some information about those characters in the playlist descriptions)

Once you've had a listen to your favorite character's music, look me up on my website **www.nealromriell.com** and let me know if you agree (or disagree) with the choices. If you happen to have discovered a new song or artist, I'd love to know about that as well!

Again, thank you for reading *Site Alpha*.

Neal Romriell – April 7th, 2022
South Carolina

I'd like to dedicate this book to my wife Tonya and my daughters, Rae, Sarena, and Avery. Had it not been for their love and support, Site Alpha would never have been completed. They gave of their time and talents to help me get through the hardest moments, and have remained my first, and truest fans.

I love you girls.

Chapter One:

The Same Team

Red...

It wasn't usually a color she liked. But as Chuck looked down at the tiny splatters of blood, nicely rounded after dropping from her throbbing nose onto the mat, she thought about giving the color another chance.

Pulling her hands off her knees, she straightened herself and regretted it as a wave of dizziness swam over her. She reached up to check her nose. Unpleasant, but not crippling pain told her it probably hadn't been broken.

Greg stood across from her in the ring, soaking up his moment in the sun. She'd underestimated the recruit's speed, and her nose paid the price by absorbing a jab. Reaching back and tightening her ponytail caused a fresh shot of pain to radiate from everywhere on her face at once.

Normally a recruit wouldn't be fighting their training agent. But Greg's abilities far surpassed his fellow recruits, and he'd accepted her offer to spar seemingly without thinking about it. Now she wondered if maybe she should have thought about it more herself.

"Again."

She raised her hands, clenching them into fists.

The corners of Greg's mouth curled up in a smirk. "You sure you don't want Doc to look at that? It might be broken." He turned to flash a smile at the other recruits standing outside the ring.

Adrenaline caused the pain in her nose to disappear. Greg could fight, but his pride would be his downfall. She tensed as his head turned. The second his eyes left her, she exploded forward.

"Ugh!" he grunted as she sprung at him. She struck high then low, leading with a left hook followed immediately by a low leg kick. His speed continued to impress her as he blocked the hook cleanly. He absorbed her kick, holding onto enough balance to keep his legs under him.

1

Greg feigned a jab, hopping to his left at the same time. She switched her stance as he put space between himself and the ropes. Chuck pressed her advantage relentlessly, throwing an uppercut to try and take the wind out of him.

He backed off, then reversed his momentum rapidly. She tilted her head, the breeze from a high kick cooling the sweat on her temple. An impressive move, but overly aggressive. He was trying too hard now, wanting to put an exclamation point on his performance.

The image of that smirk flashed in her mind as she anticipated his next attack. He pulled back his right hand, setting up a straight jab. She faked a leg sweep, backing him up just enough for the incoming strike to miss. This put her face within striking distance of his left hand. Predictably he took the bait.

Too late, Greg realized she'd shifted her weight. His left hand, cocked to deliver the finishing blow, couldn't get back fast enough to block the strike coming in at face level. A tingle went up the length of her arm as her elbow smashed with a satisfying *THWACK* into his cheek. She wanted to cave in the smug little bastard's face, but at the last second she changed her strike angle. It probably didn't reflect well on a teacher if they maimed a student.

He spun slightly as he went down on one knee, both hands covering the injured side of his face. She stood over him, hands still clenched, muscles taut. Despite the last-second sparing of Greg's nose, she felt more wound up than she would've liked. The noise of the other recruits caused her body to relax.

Rita, who'd been recruited into the Family as a doctor, had already made her way onto the ring apron. Chuck would typically applaud the trainee's quick reaction to seeing a fellow agent go down, but Rita couldn't be given too much credit. She and Greg were hooking up.

For his part, Greg recovered quickly, shrugging off the outreached hand Rita offered him. He stood, his hands dropping to his sides. Chuck winced involuntarily. His left cheek was smeared with blood. A cut under his eye dripped a red trail down the side of his face and onto his neck. Greg's face showed pain and anger. Needing to de-escalate the situation, she dropped her own hands.

"Everything okay, Agent?"

Sally DeRosa's voice cut the tension between Chuck and Greg like a knife. They both turned to face her.

DeRosa was currently Site Alpha's only certified field agent. As such, she evaluated how well Chuck did with training the recruits.

Wiping away a rivulet of blood from her nose she nodded. "All good here."

The other recruits—Marcy, Josh, and Jess—stood next to DeRosa. To the common person passing her on the street, Agent DeRosa might not have left much of an impression. Her average height frame peaked in a rounded, well-tanned face. Brown, darting eyes kept your attention away from the chestnut colored, shoulder length hair that had started to carry an occasional grey streak.

"Really? Because it looks like you two just beat the shit out of each other."

Chuck looked back at Greg. He stood stoically as new lines of blood ran down his cheek. A pang of guilt twisted in her stomach. Pride had caused her to go at him harder than necessary. Not that long ago she'd been a recruit. Extraordinary circumstances had placed her in a role usually filled by much more seasoned agents.

DeRosa motioned for them all to gather up. "We're on the same team here people. Out in the field, a wild Chupacabra, or Batsquatch isn't going to pull punches. You'll need to be able to defend yourselves. Some of you"—she fixed her stare on Greg—"have arrived better equipped to do so. However"—she turned slightly to gaze at Chuck—"now that you are part of the Family, your responsibility is to learn from those that have gone before you. Just because you *can* do harm, doesn't mean you *should*."

Chuck could almost hear the collective feet of the group shuffling ever so slightly. Experience and rank gave DeRosa well-earned respect among the recruits. She didn't often insert herself into training sessions, but in this instance Chuck was grateful she did. Greg had gotten to her today, a mistake she didn't intend to repeat.

"Charlotte, Greg, I want both of you to check in with Doc. The rest of you clean up and report to Agent Moseby." DeRosa held out two fingers towards Chuck and Greg and motioned them towards the medical wing.

The other recruits hurried off to gather their gear. Rita put a hand on Greg's shoulder, then retracted it quickly as she noticed Chuck looking at them. The young woman hurried out of the ring, leaving the sparring partners facing each other once again.

"What the hell?" Greg hissed through clenched teeth, likely not wanting it to carry to DeRosa. He poked at the cut, beads of fresh blood rising and standing out in stark contrast to the darker, almost dried blood caking his cheek.

She pointed to her nose. "I could ask you the same question." They fell silent, waiting as DeRosa, along with the recruits, headed for the exit.

"How bad is it?" He poked at the cut again, anger rising in his voice. "Shit! It's going to need stitches, isn't it?" Pretentious to a fault, Greg scowled.

Of course, that's why he'd be mad. Media Day, or as some of the older members of the Family called it, Rec Day was of great importance to the recruits. It was the day they got to go off site and spend a bit of time, back in the real world. Butterfly bandages and bruising were probably not the look Greg wanted in his upcoming Insta posts.

Chuck had never cared all that much about what strangers on the internet thought of her, but Greg, and most of the other recruits did. She probably owed him an apology. "Listen, I'm sorry about cutting you like that."

"Whatever."

He moved through the ropes and jumped off the ring apron. She jumped down herself, shadowing his pace. A knot of anxiety tightened in her chest. These recruits were hers. For good or for bad, DeRosa would evaluate her on how well she taught this batch of newcomers.

She'd gone straight from being a recruit, to training them. If not for the Fitchburg Incident, she—and certainly DeRosa—wouldn't be in this position. Chuck was punching above her weight class, and she knew it. Gaining the respect of eighteen-year-old recruits was challenging, when you were only twenty yourself.

As she followed Greg out of the gym and towards the medical wing, the anxiety only grew stronger. She'd never really understood people, especially among her peer group, who thrived on drama. As such, she had a habit of tiptoeing around confrontations, which ultimately only spiked her emotions more, and left her feeling insecure about her decisions.

He didn't look back or make a comment during their walk. They traveled the sunless halls of Alpha in silence. The artificial light created by the decades old lighting gave the entire place a strange, almost horror movie vibe. Chuck still hadn't quite adjusted to living most of her waking hours forty feet underground.

A set of double doors separated the medical wing from the rest of the facility. Greg reached them first and stepped through, making no attempt to hold one for her. She caught the door as it swung shut, a new wave of consternation welling up within her. She was about to say something when a crash rang out from within the reception area, stopping both in their tracks.

Chapter Two:

Doc

"Damn it!"

Doc's baritone voice echoed down the hall as the noise began to quiet. Greg moved first, his long strides quickly outpacing her own.

A string of half-mumbled, half-grunted words joined a chorus of fresh crashes and clangs. The whole symphony reached a crescendo as she rounded the corner of the entry hall into the brightly lit medical wing. Greg had stopped, a minefield of spilled Q-tips and tongue depressors blocking his way forward. She saw Doc's balding head bobbing up and down behind an old hospital bed.

Doc haphazardly placed a variety of objects, including surgical instruments and a stethoscope, onto the bed. The primary noise culprits appeared to be bedpans, several of which were on the floor. Greg stood and watched, seemingly unsure what, if anything, he could say.

Chuck cleared her throat as gracefully as possible. "Need some help, Doc?"

A bedpan rattling onto the bed answered her. Doc leveraged his arm, hand still firmly clutching the bedpan, so he could raise himself up.

Doc's eyes looked perpetually sleepy to her, especially when he didn't have on his gold-rimmed glasses. Regardless of how tired he looked, Doc seemed to be assessing everyone and everything around him constantly. His free hand darted up to the pocket of his lab coat. Out came the glasses, which he placed on the bridge of his nose.

Doc let out a chuckle. "It looks like Mr. Roberts here is the one who needs help."

Greg, a statue up to this point, seemed to suddenly remember why they'd come here in the first place. He raised a hand to his injured face and winced.

Doc squinted. "Looks like you took a pretty solid shot there slick."

Still gripping the bedpan, he swept his hand from left to right over the bed like a game show assistant displaying all the fabulous prizes you could win. "Well, either take a seat and wait for me to clean this up or lend me a hand so you can leave sooner. It doesn't make much difference to me."

Chuck began scooping up the Q-tips while Greg helped Doc tidy his stack of equipment. As she moved about the room, it occurred to her that her nose might be hurt worse than she'd realized. Usually, the medical wing smelled like every other hospital she'd ever been in, a stale, weighty smell, with a not-quite-bleach undertone to it. Except today it didn't.

She tried to inhale, and a searing pain burst out from between her eyes. She glanced at Doc, perturbed he wanted them to help him clean up before attending to any injuries they might have.

It took time to deal with the entire mess. Several chairs and a couch were set around the reception area. The medical wing included an ER and infirmary, behind which individual offices and observation rooms were located. The space was laughably huge, considering only one or two people ever manned it at any given time. There were two other doctors besides Doc, and three nurses who rotated shifts.

She had to carefully pick out several Q-tips from the elevator doors, located across from the ER. Oversized to accommodate stretchers and gurneys, the elevator allowed access to Warehouse 3 located above the medical wing.

Greg helped Doc push the bed, now laden with clutter, into the ER. They returned a few seconds later, Doc apparently satisfied that the mess had been cleared, if not actually cleaned up. He directed Greg and Chuck towards the set of doors which led to the long room serving as Alpha's infirmary. The two of them sat down across from each other on adjacent beds as Doc strode in between them, donning a pair of black surgical gloves.

"Ladies first!" Doc announced, pulling a spinning stool out from a slot built into the wall and squatting down on it. "What seems to be the problem, Agent Barnes?"

He grabbed a compact flashlight from a drawer, shining it directly into her eyes. Chuck had to look away as the pain previously hiding behind her nose now spread.

"It's my nose, Doc. I just need to make sure it's not bro—"

Doc's gloved fingers suddenly sprang up and hooked her by the nostrils. Pain erupted, and she felt blood start to flow again from high up in her nasal cavity. "Jesus, Doc!" she blurted out, or at least attempted to.

As quick as they'd gone into her nose, Doc's fingers retreated, replaced with two long wooden Q-tips. They were covered in a slimy substance, the smell of which caused her stomach to flip flop. She batted away his hands, the assault on her senses overwhelming her. Doc let out a chuckle as he admired his handiwork.

"Nope, not broken! Give those a minute. They'll reduce the swelling." He swiveled as he turned his attention towards Greg.

She liked Doc well enough, but his bedside manner left a lot to be desired. He'd been a combat medic in his previous life. But based on most of the stories she'd heard him tell, he hadn't fixed up that many soldiers during his time. Instead, he'd treated hundreds of civilian casualties, many of them children. Hopefully, his treatment of those kids had been more gracious.

Doc was a bit of an anomaly, having joined the Family after retiring from the military. By his own admission he'd come to Alpha mostly because of its proximity to several great golf courses. During the week he spent his time attending to humans and cryptids. Then on the weekend, he'd play golf and drink, one probably more than the other.

"One of your compadres get a little overzealous, did they?" Doc asked Greg as he began wiping away the caked blood. Greg's eyes darted across the space and locked onto her.

Doc looked over his shoulder and gave a nod of recognition. "Charlotte, you did this?" He pointed a thumb in her direction. "And I bet you did that to her?"

Greg winced as Doc squirted a syringe of saline into the cut to clean it out. "You must have some talent if you got one in on Charlotte here, sport. She's one of the best damn hand-to-hand fighters I've seen in my time with the Family."

Greg's countenance seemed to soften a bit at those words. Whether Doc had told Greg the truth or not, she couldn't say, but she appreciated his attempt at relieving some of the tension in the room.

A small pile of soiled bandages and cloths formed on the bed next to Greg. With a final wipe, Doc pushed himself back, adding yet another red spotted cloth to the pile. "You two hang tight a second. I'll be right back."

Doc got up and headed for the offices at the back of the infirmary. The double doors barely made a sound as he disappeared through them.

Chuck hadn't recovered from the assault on her nose. Reaching up, she touched one of the wooden spikes hanging in front of her mouth. As she gave it a wiggle, a feeling of being watched came over her. She turned her head slightly to find Greg staring at her.

Another of his queer little smirks had replaced the pissed-off expression he'd been wearing ever since they left the ring.

She let out a sigh. "What?"

"Not to be an asshole, but that is not a good look for you," he replied.

He attempted a smile. In trying to keep the left side of his face from moving, he created an expression that looked half-Botox patient, half-madman. She rolled her eyes, surprised the pain she'd been feeling had suddenly disappeared.

Greg's next words came out quickly.

"Hey, I'm sorry, you know, for punching you in the face. I guess I got kinda amped up. Doc's right about you being good. I thought, maybe if I could get in a few hard shots, you know, maybe it would impress the others."

She hadn't really been expecting an apology and getting one caught her off guard. She sat a moment, trying to formulate a response. "Hey, I—I should apologize too. It's been a while since I've taken a punch that squarely. Have ah, you ever competed, as in before joining us?"

"I did in school, yeah. I never really got into the traditional sports like football or basketball. I started wrestling in middle school, but when I discovered what Mixed Martial Arts entailed, I went hard at it. I guess I liked the feel of punching and kicking people." He made a face. "I'm not unstable or anything—I just got tired of rolling around on the ground most of the time."

She raised an eyebrow. "You're good." That dumb smirk crept

back. "But you also leave yourself open when you get so aggressive." She flashed a smirk of her own. "You'll need to work on that. Out in the field a cut on the face would probably be the least of your worries if things go sideways."

He nodded, then looked down at his hands. He flexed them a couple of times, examining the blood on his fingers. After a brief pause, he looked back up at her and asked, "Did the Family teach you how?"

"How what?"

"How to fight? You know, where did you learn to fight like that?"

Greg had never really been one to hold a conversation with her on the best of days. Civility in this large of a dose, including asking non-rhetorical questions, had been basically unheard-of up to this point. She paused again, unsure of which direction she wanted to take the conversation.

"Oh, with my cousin. She started taking Muay Thai classes when I was in eighth grade. We were practically sisters, so I started going too."

It had become easy over the years to omit the part about her cousin being assaulted. She began taking self-defense classes the day after her assailant walked out of court with little more than a slap on the wrist. Chuck originally tagged along as a show of support, before finding that she enjoyed the art.

She was grateful to see the doors swing open at that moment. The conversation stalled with Doc's return. He moseyed up to them holding a black jar in one hand, and something that resembled a chew toy for a dog in his other. He placed them on Chuck's bed. "Let's see here," Doc pulled the Q-tips out of her nose. Fresh, not-grotesque-smelling air rushed up her newly unblocked nasal cavities. Doc bent down at an odd angle to shine his little flashlight up her nostrils.

"Oh yeah, all clear."

He almost casually discarded the Q-tips onto the biohazard pile. He reached a hand into one of his pockets and pulled out a strange looking green glove. For starters, it was very thick. Secondly, it glistened with an odd sheen, almost like it had been coated in something. The glove reflected light like a puddle of gasoline.

Greg shifted a bit on his bed, putting some distance between himself and the refuse pile. He craned his neck trying to get a better look at what Doc was doing.

"Umm, what is that for, Doc?"

The glove now firmly on, Doc pulled a pair of safety goggles out and put them on. "Charlotte, you should probably stand back."

She frowned, not moving. She didn't know how to feel about the odd glint she could now see in Doc's eyes. Stuck between stepping back and stepping forward, she raised her voice. "Doc?"

He made a shooing motion, then picked up the dog toy.

"Okay son, I'm going to give you this to bite down on. I'll have your face looking good as new in no time, but the process will… hurt a bit." He handed the object to Greg. The recruit turned to look at her.

"Doc." she said more firmly.

Turning to pick up the jar, he only winked in response—which was not as comforting as he appeared to think it was.

Greg was still looking at her as if asking what he should do. Chuck shrugged.

"That cut is in a tricky spot, son, so I need you to listen. When I tell you to close your eyes, you close them real tight. You hear me? Don't open them till it's over."

"Till what's over, Doc? You're not giving me stitches, are you?" Greg's smug façade had disappeared, his voice now tinged with worry.

"Oh no, no stitches," Doc replied. He motioned again for Chuck to back up. Although she trusted Doc, her instincts were screaming at her to step in and stop whatever he had planned. She stood, taking two steps, but no more. Doc turned his full attention to Greg now as he held up the black jar.

"I snuck this bad boy out of one of the R&D labs at Delta," he said, twisting off the lid. Even standing a few feet away, Chuck's eyes watered. A smell like summer roadkill emerged from the jar. Greg retched and turned his head away. Even Doc, safety goggles in place, winced and outstretched his arm to try and put some space between his face and the smell.

"Hot damn! It's even worse than I remember!" Doc had to choke the words out. Greg turned pale, and leaned away from scent. The cut, longer than Chuck had realized, stood out red and angry on his blood-drained skin. Doc retracted his arm, bringing the jar back in close to him.

"Ah, see, the sensation goes away pretty quick."

He was right—her eyes were still teary, but they no longer stung. The color had already returned to Greg's face. He blinked away tears and started to stand up.

A push from Doc's gloved hand landed Greg's ass squarely back on the bed. Doc shook his head, saying something under his breath that Greg clearly heard but she could not. Greg spared Chuck a sideways glance and lodged the chew toy between his teeth.

Doc nodded, then turned slightly to deliver another *get back* look to her. Chuck gave him three steps before stopping. Doc nodded and turned back to Greg.

Doc dipped two of his gloved fingers into the jar. "Whatever you do, son, don't open your eyes until it's over." He withdrew his fingers, revealing a thick pink sludge sticking to them. The substance had tiny blue flecks that seemed to be generating their own light. Greg closed his eyes, and Doc reached out, smearing a line of the substance down the length of the cut.

Chuck barely had enough time to wonder exactly what was supposed to happen when Greg suddenly spit out the toy and began to yell. The sound gave her goosebumps. The pink line sparked and spat little puffs of smoke. She stood transfixed as the substance turned black, then crumbled away like used charcoal.

Chuck had seen some weird stuff in her time with the Family, but what she'd just witnessed might have topped them all. Doc gave a "Whoop!" as he removed the now smoking glove and replaced the top of the jar.

"It's gone!" she blurted. Greg's head was drenched with sweat, and his hands were shaking, but the cut had disappeared. No scar, no angry blotches, no bruising, nothing.

Doc beamed as he shoved a plastic tub into Greg's chest. The recruit immediately threw up. The vomit was the same color as the sludge. Doc pulled away the tub and scraped the trash pile into it.

"Charlotte, there's some ginger ale in the cooler over there. Grab a can for Mr. Roberts, would you? I'll go throw this all out and be back."

Greg looked like he might have passed out. His head slumped

forward, chin nearly touching his sternum. Chuck hurried over to the cooler, grabbing a bottle of water for herself as well as the can of soda for Greg. As she returned he raised his head and wiped some of the moisture away from his eyes.

She popped the can's top before handing it to him. "You good?"

He took a sip, stuck out his tongue, then tried again. "Yeah... I guess," he looked up at her, eyes questioning. "What was that?"

She honestly had no idea what to tell him. Instead of responding, she stepped past him and grabbed a surgical tray, then held the shiny surface up in front of his face. A moment of confusion turned suddenly to realization, his free hand touching the spot where seconds ago there'd been separated skin. He looked up at her, and all she could really think to do was nod.

The doors rattled as Doc came back into the room. Chuck stepped aside as he walked up to Greg and examined his cheek. "How are you feeling, son?"

"Good, I guess. Uh, Doc, what did you put on me?"

"To be honest, I'm not entirely sure. I think the active ingredient is mermaid excrement," Doc laughed as Greg frowned. "Whatever it is, you'll be looking pretty for the girls tomorrow," he pantomimed taking a selfie as Greg touched his cheek yet again. Chuck wondered if he understood the favor that had been extended to him.

Doc took the can from the recruit's hand. "Now you two should probably get going. I suspect you'll want to clean up before dinner."

A short time later she and Greg were passing back through the training facility. He stopped to get his bag, previously forgotten. As he picked it up, he turned to her. "Thanks for not going easy on me. I shouldn't have been such a dick about it, you're just doing your job."

That gave her pause. The fact this was her job still didn't exactly feel real, even after more than two years.

Chuck smiled, grateful for how the afternoon turned out, despite the rocky beginning. "I mean, kicking your ass isn't exactly in the job description, but I appreciate the sentiment. How about in the future we keep the hits below the neck?"

Greg shrugged and held the exit door open for her. "I think I could get behind that." He flashed her another of his goofy smirks. "But I'm still not going easy on you."

"I'd expect nothing less."

Chapter Three:

Media Day

In the movies, secret societies and covert government agencies always have immaculate bases hidden behind mountain top waterfalls or sewage treatment plants. Their operatives all have bright white teeth, perfect hair, and cool sunglasses. As she studied the crudely drawn Mothman with the extremely exaggerated phallus which had been carved into one of the stall doors in the locker room, Chuck suspected that in real life, such groups had more in common with the Roger's Family than with their movie counterparts.

She'd finished relieving herself several minutes ago, but Rita and Marcy were giving Jess grief about her bra size. At four-fifteen in the morning she didn't think she could muster joining in on that conversation.

She gave the graffiti a good once-over, slightly jealous of the men who probably weren't out of bed yet, then grudgingly got up to start getting ready herself.

Emerging from the stall she was greeted with near matching smiles as all three of the recruits turned towards her in unison. The whole thing almost looked comical, and more than a little creepy. She returned a smile of her own and took her place at the next mirror available. The conversation had turned to K-Pop, and battle lines were being drawn.

"Whatever, I'm a BTS stan and you bitches can kiss my well-rounded ass!" Marcy declared after Chuck and Rita both expressed their distaste for the genre.

Jess, whose Korean heritage made her, as she put it "*an expert on the subject,*" rattled off a bunch of band names. She swiped her finger right or left after each to denote the good from the bad.

"Who do I have to kill to get some water pressure around here?" Rita complained as she messed with the faucet in front of her.

"I'll take shitty water pressure any day over the dead fish smell in here," Jess bemoaned as she touched up her mascara. Marcy mumbled something through the toothbrush in her mouth which Chuck couldn't quite make out. In her mind it was a comment on Jess being the source of the smell.

Sadly, the observations concerning the smell and water pressure were spot on. Alpha had been the very first major base the Family built. A huge plaque hung in the cafeteria noting the site had gone online in 1970. Over the years additions and upgrades had been made, but most were cosmetic. Phantom scents, unreliable water pressure, and even mysterious sounds were all part of life at Alpha.

Being an agent, Chuck had her own apartment, and could have technically prepped for the day there. She specifically chose not to, as the other women tended to be a bit more *real* on these mornings, helping her to learn extra tidbits about them.

Jess stepped back from her mirror. "You wanna hear some dopey shit? My dad is *still* pissed at me for not going home at Christmas. I got a letter, as in a handwritten, physical letter, from him telling me my mom was still brooding about it. My mom works too hard to brood about much of anything, let alone me." She frowned, zipping up her hoodie emblazoned with a bright yellow pitchfork on its back.

Shrugging up her shoulders, Jess continued in a mocking, deep voice, "All *your* mom does is sit in the study, playing piano all day. She really misses you." She let her shoulders drop and reverted to her normal voice. "She's not mad at me, she's just trying to avoid his grumpy ass. I'd be shocked if he's even home enough to have noticed." Jess didn't talk about her parents often, but Media Days tended to be an exception.

"He'd shit a brick if he knew the truth about what I'm doing out here," Jess concluded.

Rita checked her teeth. "I wish my stepdad wouldn't talk to me. My little brother hates him, so I guess he thinks that impressing me will get him in better with our mom."

"Ladies," Marcy interjected, "can we discuss our daddy issues later please?" Jess and Rita both raised middle fingers in her direction. "That stuffed French toast is calling my name," she continued, rubbing her stomach which let out an audible growl.

"Yeah, let's get going. Agent Moseby likes to rub it in my face when the guys beat us to the van," A glint in Jess's eye caused Chuck to immediately regret her choice of words.

The recruit raised her eyebrows. "I wish Tilly would rub something in my face!"

Always classy, Jess rarely passed up a chance to make sexual references, especially concerning Tillman Moseby. Not that Chuck blamed her exactly. Tillman was good looking, which contrasted somewhat with his nerdy awkwardness. Jess had been flirting with the tech trainer for nearly five months now, and Chuck doubted he'd even taken notice of it.

"Sorry, Agent Barnes!" Jess grinned. "I wish *Agent Moseby* would rub something in my face!"

She put her hands up as if to defend an incoming punch. Marcy and Rita laughed in unison. Chuck pointed at Jess, who mouthed *sorry*, still grinning from ear to ear.

Josh and Greg entered the locker room, already in their Sun Devil gear. Greg tried to coyly grab Rita's ass as he walked by. The yelp that escaped her lips ensured there wasn't anything all that coy about it.

"Come on ladies," Chuck called. The other women fell in behind her, leaving the guys to finish up whatever minor preparations they still had planned.

They reached the elevator, and she checked her watch. They had about ten minutes before the van would pull into the warehouse. If history were any indication, Tillman would arrive at this very spot in about eight minutes.

Ideally the whole group would be leaving Alpha and on the road by five-thirty. Any later and you'd hit a snarl of traffic entering Phoenix. If they didn't encounter too much construction they could reach Tempe by seven. Their normal routine involved stopping at the IHOP located directly across from the campus.

Chuck had enjoyed many a breakfast there during her time as a recruit. Honestly, it was one of the better perks of getting to be a trainer. Spending time off site didn't hurt either.

Everyone took a step back as the elevator doors groaned open. They crowded in, and she smiled as she heard the men coming down the hall while the doors slid shut. Tillman wouldn't have cause to gloat today, though he'd probably slept longer than she had, which made the victory ring a bit hollow.

The elevator deposited them in Warehouse 2 of the Rice Lake Home Goods Distribution Center. The facility, known to the Family as Site Alpha, sat snugly against I-17, near the small Phoenix suburb of Adobe.

Unlike the other above ground buildings that made up the complex, Warehouse 2 held actual stuff you would think to find in a warehouse. Supplies for cleaning, maintenance, and about a dozen other departments filled row after row of shelving.

The women huddled close together as they waited for the van to arrive. The warehouse was warmer than the temperature outside, but not by much.

Marcy looked at Rita who stood shivering. "Bad day to wear those," Marcy deadpanned. Rita had on shorts that didn't even make it to the bottom of her hoodie.

"Girl, I'm from Boston." Rita's accent came through much more pronounced than normal.

"What, people from Boston can't be cold?" Marcy pressed.

Rita pulled the hoodie up to her navel. "Back home the high today will be like in the thirties. That won't even be the low here. I'm not covering an ass this fine just because it's fifty degrees!"

Chuck had seen Rita's recruitment tapes. The Bostonian's interviews were filled with *yes ma'ams* and *sirs*. They showed a prim and proper girl from New England, who'd been cheer captain while holding straight A's. As a future doctor within the Family, Rita would be a member of the CIT, or Cryptid Involvement Team. The group performed a range of medical duties for cryptids and humans, both living and dead.

It usually took some time for recruits to get comfortable once they arrived on site. Not Rita. Before day one ended she'd been walking around like she owned the place. She started hooking up with Greg on the second or third day. In truth Chuck didn't know what in God's name Rita saw in him. The name alone should have been a turn off. Seriously, who'd ever been sexually attracted to someone named *Greg?*

Ding!

The elevator doors opened. Chuck wrinkled her nose when

only Greg and Josh exited. At nearly the same time, a side door of the warehouse began sliding away. The headlights of a van bathed the back recesses of the cavernous facility in light.

"Agent Moseby said he'll be up in a second, something about backup batteries," Josh said as they approached. She nodded and again checked her watch. Only a couple minutes past five, still good on time. Marcy's mention of stuffed French toast now had her thinking about breakfast.

She shielded her eyes as the van pulled up next to the group. As her sight adjusted, she was glad to see their old driver Walt had returned. Like Doc, Walt had come to Alpha mostly for the golf. She knew he'd been an agent at one point, but an accident forced him to retire from active duty.

The Family often employed former members of the military as on-site security personnel, and as a double shot of luck, today they'd drawn Ed. He hopped out of the passenger side and pulled out a clipboard. A security member escorted the group whenever they went off site. While mostly there for show, it wasn't unheard of for a recruit to try and slip away during these excursions.

"Hey Walt! Welcome back," she waved past Ed at him. Walt waved back, smiling.

"And hello to you, Ed. Back on mornings?" She thought he'd been working at night while his wife was doing overnight shifts at Mayo Clinic Hospital.

"Yes, ma'am. You solo today, Agent?" Ed flipped through sheets of paper, probably looking for the day's attendance list.

"No, Agent Moseby is just running a bit late. He should be up soon." Ed nodded, the paper he'd been looking for apparently found.

Walt leaned across the cab of the van. "Hey, Ms. Charlotte! Guess who's going to be a father?"

She gave the driver a knowing wink. "Walt Johnson, you're too old to be chasing toddlers!"

"Not me!" Walt waved his hands, then pointed to Ed.

"Congrats, Ed. Do you guys have a due date?"

Ed shook his head, smiling. "Not yet. We only found out a week ago." He pulled a pen out of his pocket, ready to get on with the task at hand.

Ding!

The recruits began pulling out their IDs as the elevator opened again. Tillman stepped out, a rolling suitcase in tow containing the recruits' phones and other gadgets.

Tillman had a pair of sunglasses resting on top of his black hair. His almond-colored eyes lit up as he spotted Chuck walking towards him, a grin stretching across his face.

She placed herself in his walking path. "Took you long enough."

Tillman held up his hands in surrender. "Sorry, sorry. I forgot about removing the battery packs from their chargers last night."

Chuck reached out and adjusted his ASU tie, so it didn't look crooked. "What's all this about? Are you meeting someone at the coffee shop today?"

He looked down at the vest and slacks combo. "What, can't a guy change things up once in a while?"

"You look like a hipster that forgot his fedora."

Tillman frowned, giving his outfit another look. "Noted." He turned to the group. "I'll have to hand out your phones at IHOP, guys. We should get checked in and going if we're going to beat the traffic."

He gave them a big smile. It was met with a chorus of curses and shoulder slouches. Tillman took it all in stride.

Tillman Moseby took most things in stride. He'd been a child prodigy before joining the Family at only fifteen years old. They were the same age, but Tillman outranked Chuck, as he'd already been promoted to full agent status as part of the Phantom Kangaroos, the Family's technology wing.

Most of the Kangaroos were hackers, who oversaw a host of initiatives meant to keep the Family's dealings a secret from the world at large. Tillman's primary focus was the recruits and their social media imprints.

Chuck had always found the Kangaroos' name odd. Evidently it came from a cryptid that had been rumored to exist, but never actually captured—sort of a play on the group's role within the agency. She didn't even know how many of them were stationed at Alpha, as they were notoriously reclusive workaholics.

"Okay, line up!" Ed yelled over the complaints "Let's get this—"

A shrill digital sound, like an old dialup modem but worse, cut Ed off. At the same moment Chuck felt her watch vibrating.

She lifted her arm, knowing what she would see there. Bright red letters spelled ALERT across the watch's screen. A pinhole light at the top of the display strobed brightly. She turned her head to Tillman; his watch was doing the same thing.

"Oh shit, does that mean what I think it means?" Rita asked, annoyance evident in her voice.

Red lights accompanied by a siren suddenly filled the warehouse.

Jess kicked a pallet. "They couldn't have waited another thirty minutes?"

Chuck was already heading for the elevator as she heard Tillman's voice raising over the blare of the alarm. "Sorry guys, looks like Media Day is cancelled."

Chapter Four:

Trapped

Red...

That was the last color I saw before the darkness overtook me. Those Rogers bastards tricked me, somehow. Upon waking I found myself inside this metal hell with hardly enough room to move my arms.

How long have I been here? It has been years at least, though time means little to one free to roam the world without fear of death.

And yet, when all you can see is the inside of a too small box, time suddenly becomes maddening.

Oh, to jump and run through the streets of a crowded metropolis again! To lounge about on the rooftops in the summer sun or stalk the drunken and foolish through the alleyways by the darkness of night.

My own wanderlust was my undoing. The sights and smells of the great city of London had become suffocating and stale. I wanted new playthings, new puppets whose strings I could pull in exciting and different ways. I thought New York would be such a place, and it was, until I encountered the insufferable Rogers Family and their likeminded supporters.

How long have I clawed at this accursed metal prison? They must have bewitched it. It's the only reason I can muster for its resistance.

The confinement afforded me has caused my body to weaken. My sinew aches, my joints cry out to bend. The fire that burns in my breast needs neither air nor fuel and my body persists without food or water. Yet for all the things I can do without, there is one resource I crave. One commodity above all that I desire. To speak, to converse, to interact with another, any other. This neglect poisons my mind.

I have no knowledge of where I am located. For some time after awakening in this infernal container I had the sensation of movement. Seeing as they imprisoned me in New York State, I can only assume they have taken me west, but how far, or how long they carried me, of that I have no idea.

At the journey's end my prison must have been dropped down a fissure or cliff. I felt myself, or I should say my metal coffin, falling briefly and then crashing down upon some firm surface.

How long ago was that now? Long enough that I have imagined a thousand ways to make those that put me here suffer. Long enough to have seen their deaths in my mind's eye over and over. Long enough that I will take no pity, show no mercy.

Should I ever escape and feel again the touch of wind on my face, or the smell of a rose. If the day comes where I escape, there will be no place safe for the Rogers. My rage will be unbridled, and my revenge absolute.

Chapter Five:

Red Alert

The elevator shook as it descended. Halfway down, Tillman turned to her. "I wonder if this is another of Hines's drills."

"On Media Day and at five in the morning? That would be kind of a dick move on the part of the Chief, wouldn't you say?"

Tillman shrugged, but his thought did have merit. In her two plus years with the Family, Chuck had only seen a handful of actual red alerts.

She snuck a look at Tillman's outfit, admiring it, and by extension, him. At six-foot-tall, he had a few inches on Chuck—which all went to his limbs—but he always wore clothes that managed to make him look smaller somehow.

"Sorry I called you a hipster."

"Nah, you're right. I mostly wanted an excuse to wear a tie."

Her stomach rumbled and she let out an inadvertent sigh. "Gonna be a protein bar on the run kind of breakfast I guess."

"Damn, you're right. IHOP's going to wonder what the hell happened to us."

Thankfully, as they stepped out of the elevator their watches fell silent in unison. Still dressed for their day out, and with Tillman's tech box in tow, they made their way towards the command center. Turning the last corner, Chuck pulled out her key fob, running ahead of Tillman so she could swipe hers first. Dragging his case, he was still a couple of steps behind her as she passed the card in front of the panel. The green light flashed, and she winked at Tillman while holding the door for him.

"The kids were disappointed, I'm guessing?" DeRosa said, surprising Chuck as she entered the room. The senior agent sat alone at the long table which dominated the room.

Chuck gave her a nod. "You could say that."

She took a seat next to DeRosa. While much of Alpha felt old and outdated, the Command Center showed off an impressive array of tech. The large table had built in monitors and hologram projectors. A multitude of monitors and displays lined the walls on all sides. The chairs even adjusted automatically, based on signals sent from the user's watch.

Tillman looked at DeRosa. "You get any details yet?"

DeRosa shook her head and looked at her watch. Suddenly the door directly across from their group slid open. In walked Chief Agent Garret Hines, followed closely by a retinue of staffers and Senior Kangaroo Deputy Smalls. Smalls had a phone pressed against her left ear while trying to work a tablet with her right hand. They all appeared rushed and tired.

"I wonder what made Delta think things should run smoothly with a single field agent?" Hines asked the room in general. He worked his way around the chairs until he stood at the head of the long table.

Hines sat while motioning the rest of them to do the same. Only his secretary and attaché remained standing. Tillman looked up as Smalls, who hadn't said a word since entering, took a seat next to him.

Hines turned to DeRosa. "Morning, Sally." His broad shoulders were hunched forward, always appearing to bear an invisible weight. He ran a hand through his salt and pepper hair before he continued. "Barnes, Moseby, sorry to cut your skip day short, but this is kind of an all-hands-on deck situation. It just happens we don't have many hands right now."

Tillman already had a laptop on the table. He clicked away rapidly at the keyboard, probably getting himself up to date. Not for the first time, Chuck felt a bit out of place. This was the first urgent event she'd participated in that wasn't a drill.

Hines picked up a small remote and proceeded with the briefing. "About an hour ago we had a Mogollon whose bio tracker showed a sudden increase in heart rate and breathing. Less than five minutes later the creature's vitals flat lined." Hines clicked the remote, bringing up a satellite image of a wooded area.

Smalls took over the narration. "Subject A001883's tracker shows it stopped moving at approximately these coordinates." She began typing on her tablet one-handed as she continued to hold her phone to her ear. "We believe the exact location to be within this search area." A red circle appeared, overlaying a central section of the image.

DeRosa looked at Hines. "We called a red alert over a body retrieval?"

"No, Agent. We called a red alert over this." He clicked his remote and the image shifted slightly while zooming in closer.

Though grainy, Chuck could clearly make out the back half of a Jeep parked near a dirt road. It took her a second to realize what that meant, and a grunt from DeRosa seemed to confirm her suspicion.

DeRosa scratched her head. "Yeah, that's a pretty good reason."

Smalls spoke, the phone still at her ear. "I'm sure you all are thinking the same thing we are."

The Griffins.

DeRosa stopped looking at the screen and turned towards Hines. "I thought we had a pretty good handle on their operatives in this region."

"We did too," replied Smalls without looking up.

Tillman hit a few keys on his laptop and a screen built into the table came to life. "The make and model are consistent with our intel of the closest known group." The screen changed to display a large map of northern Arizona. A long red line traced a path from a location outside Prescott to the site of the Mogollon's signal.

"Any idea how many there might be on site?" DeRosa gave a sideways glance towards Smalls, but kept her head turned to Hines.

"Not currently. Mogs are big and from what we can tell the body hasn't moved at all yet. Whoever's there may be waiting on reinforcements," Hines replied.

DeRosa synced her watch with the display on the table. "I'm not all that keen on going in blind boss."

"I'm not either, Sally. But Delta wants boots on the ground ASAP. We're the closest boots so..." Hines paused and rubbed his eyes. "We haven't had a Griffin poach one of our charges in years. The proximity of the vehicle might mean it was a chance encounter and not an actual hunt."

"What if it isn't the Griffins?" Chuck spoke the question out loud without really meaning to.

Hines nodded in her direction. "Good question, Agent Barnes. Even more reason to get a team out there. Sally, you and Agent Barnes, Agent Moseby, and one of the Security team need to be wheels up in less than twenty minutes. We've already mobilized a chopper. Your assignment is to evaluate the situation. The need for cool heads cannot be overstated. Civilian, Griffin, or otherwise, your mission is to deal with any human presence and retrieve that Mog body."

She glanced over at Tillman. The Kangaroos didn't go out into the field all that often. On the rare occasions they did, it was usually to upgrade or repair tech. Most of them were content to observe the subjects under the Family's care from afar.

Tillman was an exception to that rule. He liked going off site and typically took Smalls' place on runs she should have been doing by station. He looked Chuck's way and gave her a wink.

"Have we not picked up on any other signals in that area? Cell phone, sat phone, anything?" There was more than a hint of skepticism in DeRosa's voice, and rightfully so.

The Griffins were to the Family what a group of professional poachers might be to a big game warden on a protected wildlife reserve. The Yin to the Family's Yang. Much like the Family's own agents, Griffin operatives often traveled in groups and kept in frequent contact with their more senior officers. Considering this location looked remote and the Mog hadn't yet been moved, it was reasonable to assume whoever had killed it would be working hard to get some backup in case the creature had been chipped.

Hines looked across the table at Smalls.

Finally looking up from her tablet, she faced DeRosa. "We have not identified any signals transmitting from this location other than the chip. That doesn't mean there isn't one, simply that we have yet to detect it."

Hines rubbed his temple. "I'm sorry, Sally, but it is what it is." He stood, probably to stop any arguments before they started. "Now you and your team need to get going."

He started towards the door. Those already standing moved aside to let him through. Smalls, still on her phone but no longer fussing with the tablet, also stood.

"The van leaves in twelve minutes." Hines nodded to DeRosa, then slipped through the door with his posse in tow.

"Four of us aren't enough to move a Mogollon, Deputy, especially a dead one," DeRosa's gaze stayed fixed on the smaller woman.

"Take one or two of the recruits then. They'll probably enjoy going off site," Smalls replied offhandedly.

"I'm not a babysitter, damn it! How about you call up Momma Rogers and tell her to get me some help, instead of sending rookies into the field?"

Every eye in the room turned towards the senior agent.

Even by DeRosa standards, the statement was surprising. Calling the Family Matriarch *momma* would probably get DeRosa suspended were she assigned to any other site. Tillman stood comically frozen in place at the comment.

Smalls' mouth dropped open slightly, and her face flashed a deep shade of red. DeRosa stood her ground, continuing to stare daggers at the Deputy. Smalls lost the staring contest as she blinked and shook her head. Her color slowly returned to a more natural look. "Take Roberts then. I hear he has a hell of a right jab." Smalls somehow sounded defeated and disgusted in the same breath. She pivoted and stomped out the door.

Chuck had only a second to contemplate if the reference to Greg's punching ability had been a dig at her before DeRosa slammed a fist on the table. "Sons of bitches! They turn command and go all politician."

She spun in her chair, waving both Chuck and Tillman towards the door. "Let's get going. Charlotte, I want Nelson and Lamont ready and in the warehouse in ten minutes."

"But Smalls said—" Tillman stopped short as DeRosa raised a pointed finger towards him. "Ahh, gotcha, no Greg." Tillman gave them a wave as he headed out.

"No way in hell I'm bringing that undisciplined little shit out on a real assignment." And with that Chuck and DeRosa were heading back towards the recruits' living quarters.

She'd seen DeRosa mad before, but this was different. Not that she didn't understand why the senior agent would feel the need to lash out on occasion. DeRosa had a chip the size of a kettlebell on her shoulder.

Prior to DeRosa arriving, some of Alpha's regulars shared stories about her with Chuck. DeRosa had been called a liar, a coward, even a deserter—all by people hovering near the top of the Family's food chain. She'd supposedly been transferred to Alpha to get her far away from Delta, which served as the hub for all the Family's operations.

For an extra kick in the ovaries, Alpha had its total number of agents scaled back. This left DeRosa leading a group of four recently graduated agents, Chuck included, and not much else.

The other three rookie agents had been pulled to do cold weather training in Canada until mid-April—making Sally DeRosa and Chuck Barnes the only two trained and deployable agents covering most of New Mexico, Arizona, Nevada, and Utah. Admittedly the sector tended to be the one of the quietest in America. But she couldn't escape the feeling that a lot of the decisions were made expressly to try and force DeRosa into saying to hell with the whole thing.

She and DeRosa split shortly after, not a word spoken between them since leaving the command center. Chuck stopped by the dorms long enough to order Marcy and Josh to get ready. Sprinting to her own quarters, she stripped off the college garb and donned her field uniform in record time. She laced up her boots, grabbed her go bag, and headed out.

Chuck found Tillman standing next to the elevator's door. His grey field gear looked so much cooler than her drab green. He flashed her a smile and held up a foil-wrapped object.

"I thought this would be better than a protein bar."

In one fluid motion, she reached out and grabbed the gift. Her stomach rumbled as she freed the breakfast burrito from its packaging. The scent of bacon, eggs and cheese was heavenly.

Ding!

"You're welcome," Tillman laughed as the elevator opened. Chuck could only nod as she took a bite of her unexpected treat.

29

Chapter Six:

Guns Out

They were the first ones up. Already a different van had arrived in Warehouse 2. The quick response vehicle was disguised with flashing lights and decals reading Phoenix Ambulance Service, allowing for faster trips. Not that they had far to go—a rather nondescript hangar at the nearby Deer Valley Airport held Alpha's air-wing.

Ed walked out from behind the vehicle and approached them. "Agents, looks like I still get to go on a trip with you." He now had on a Kevlar vest and bore a couple of different firearms.

Chuck looked down at her watch. The burrito had done wonders to calm her stomach, but her nerves were still jumpy. She'd been out to pick up a fallen subject once before, but that trip hadn't been under duress. Her only other missions had been for more mundane tasks; switching out tracking chips, communicating with sasquatch families, or bringing subjects in for checkups.

She had mixed feelings about Josh and Marcy coming. The extra hands would be helpful, especially when dealing with a six-hundred-pound body. But those extra hands came at the expense of experience. She liked them both but couldn't help but feel a twinge of anxiety.

Ed entered the van first. Tillman climbed in next, turning as he did. "Here, I'll help you up." He held out a hand and she took it.

Marcy rounded the outstretched door of the van. "Hey, guys." She looked so uncomfortable that Chuck wanted to reach out and hug her. The recruit gave Ed, whom she'd probably never seen decked out for battle, a sideways glance. Josh stepped up next to Marcy and helped her as she joined the rest of them in the transport.

Marcy sat down next to Chuck, and she helped the recruit make some minor adjustments to her field gear.

"Everybody ready?" DeRosa called back as she climbed into the front of the vehicle. Tillman gave a thumbs up before pulling the doors closed and away they went.

"DeRosa chose you two personally," she whispered to Marcy and Josh, hoping to boost their confidence. The younger woman flashed a smile and sat up straighter. Josh smiled and then lowered his head. It looked like he might be praying.

Marcy, while not as physically strong as either Josh or Greg, excelled in the use of firearms. Chuck had been impressed by her knowledge and accuracy from day one. Once Marcy finished training she'd likely be assigned to one of the sites that frequently deployed tranquilizer guns to keep more unruly subjects under control.

Josh was a more every tool in the box style of agent. He had a good mix of strength, stamina, and dexterity. But even more importantly he had a very deep interest in protecting the cryptids the Family cared for. A chance encounter during his youth with a stray sasquatch had led him down the path to becoming an agent.

Tillman pulled a small earpiece out of one of his pockets and held it over his watch. Blue lights on each device began blinking simultaneously. Satisfied, he inserted the bud into his left ear. He turned his attention to the recruits. "I imagine you two want to know what it is we are doing."

Both nodded dutifully.

"A Mogollon died this morning. It's looking like it may have been poached by a Griffin, or group of Griffins. We're going to attempt to scare them off and bring the body back to base."

Josh cast a long look in Ed's direction. "Scare them off?"

Tillman cleared his throat. "We'll evaluate the situation more once the chopper gets us there. We won't face off with them unless it's completely necessary."

Chuck put her arm around Marcy and leaned out to talk to both recruits. "We wouldn't bring you out if we didn't think you could handle this." While not a lie, it still felt like one as the words left her mouth.

The vehicle turned sharply and then came to a halt. Tillman opened the door, revealing a well-lit airport hangar. A long, khaki-colored helicopter sat on the tarmac in front of the hangar, its single rotor already spinning slowly. As they were disembarking from the van, Chuck noticed hints of purple over the eastern mountains that signaled the approaching sunrise.

Ed gave the chopper a long look. "How long are we going to be in the air?"

Tillman shrugged. "Shouldn't be more than an hour."

Ed loosened one of the straps on his vest while turning in Chuck's direction. "Are the six of us going to be able to pick up a dead Bigfoot?"

"We should, though it's more like a relative," she replied.

"Mogs are basically yoked sasquatch," Tillman added. "About the same height but with a lot more muscles and a lot less brains. They're *way* more aggressive than their cousins."

"Get your helmets and get going!" DeRosa yelled over the whine of the chopper's engines.

One by one they grabbed their helmets from a rolling rack and boarded the chopper. DeRosa was the last to enter.

The pilot looked back at them, and DeRosa gave him a thumbs up. He returned the signal, and the chopper began heading towards the runway.

"Get comfortable, y'all. Got about forty-five minutes to the target." The pilot's southern twang penetrated the crackle of the headsets.

"Smalls says the signal still hasn't moved. Neither has the Jeep," Tillman relayed to the group. The helo lifted off the ground and began ascending rapidly.

DeRosa adjusted her mic. "And still no other signals?"

"Not yet. Our satellites are monitoring the immediate area."

Ed looked in Tillman's direction. "Other signals?"

"Yeah, the Griffins aren't exactly known for running solo." DeRosa pulled a magazine of 9mm rounds from her hip, checking the spring with her thumb.

Ed watched gingerly as DeRosa examined the bullets. "I thought the Griffins were pretty well washed up at this point."

"Inside the United States they are, for the most part. But they still have plenty of covert operatives around the world, some of which make their way stateside," Tillman spoke as though he were retelling a ghost story.

"Something like that." The tone of DeRosa's voice brought the conversation to an end. Chuck leaned over to rest her head on the window by her seat.

The lights shining from below them looked like Christmas lights now. Closing her eyes, she could see her dad's face in the darkness. The thought made her smile. Christmas had always been his favorite time of year. The holiday hadn't been the same after his death.

DeRosa and Tillman were talking back and forth with command. Their voices drifted into the background as Chuck kept her eyes closed. Between the time she'd spent yesterday with Greg, getting up extra early to listen to thirsty Jess, and now the whole surprise mission, her mind wanted to rest.

She must have dozed off because when she opened her eyes the ground was much closer and much more well-lit. Trees whizzed by below them, an almost endless sea of pines, stretching off into the distance. The bright white of the snowcapped mountains reflected the early dawn rays from the sun.

"Charlotte, glad you could rejoin us!" DeRosa yelled. The noise startled Ed, who appeared to have also been sleeping.

"How long was I out?"

"Long enough. We'll be over the target in five minutes." DeRosa elbowed Ed in the arm. He gave her a confused look, then rubbed his eyes.

Chuck's ears popped as the chopper descended rapidly. She looked at Marcy and Josh. Her recruits gave her thumbs up.

The pilot's voice came over the headsets. "I'm gonna do a fly by and get a thermal scan of the area. Regardless of what's down there, it looks like the closest landing site is a good quarter mile out."

She could feel the descent slow, watching as the tops of the trees started to sway with the wind created by the helicopter's blades.

The entire cabin pitched forward suddenly. Her stomach dropped as the chopper fell and then rose quickly. Marcy looked at her, and Chuck tried to put on her best reassuring smile.

Tillman held up a tablet for DeRosa to examine. The senior agent looked at the device for a long moment, then turned to look at Tillman. He shrugged.

DeRosa bent over to yell into the cockpit. "Are you sure that scanner is working?"

"Right as rain, agent."

DeRosa shook her head. "It's not showing any heat signatures."

"Then maybe there aren't any to see." The pilot responded, an edge rising in his voice.

DeRosa wore her frustration on her sleeve. "Command, we aren't picking up any heat signatures, please advise."

They all sat silent for a long minute. Finally, DeRosa nodded.

"Roger." She glanced back into the cockpit. "Mario, head for the landing zone."

The pilot gave her a thumbs up. "Sure thing, agent."

DeRosa looked directly at her. "Charlotte, as soon as we land, I want you and Marcy to accompany Tillman while he tracks down that Mog's signal."

Chuck nodded and gave Marcy a reassuring pat on the arm.

"Ed, Josh, you two are with me," DeRosa continued. "We're going to check out that Jeep." Everyone nodded their understanding. Dust and pine needles began to swirl outside the windows as the helicopter touched down.

They waited until the whole team had disembarked before splitting up. Chuck, Marcy, and Tillman made their way northwest, while the others headed due west. Tillman kept his hands securely on a tablet, but she and Marcy drew their firearms. The air felt cooler at this altitude, and she regretted not wearing her gloves.

"Is this what being an agent is like?" Marcy's voice could barely be heard over the fading sound of the engines.

"In my experience, yes. But I don't think you want to use me as your example," Chuck looked over her shoulder. "Actually, maybe this whole thing isn't a good example. We don't usually go in guns out." She scanned the area for the most likely ambush points.

"That's good I guess." Marcy responded. Chuck could see the younger woman was biting her lip. The recruit moved with a stature and care that didn't give away whatever nerves she might be feeling.

Chuck shivered involuntarily. The cold of the desert air had been made worse by a breeze blowing in from the north. They passed a cluster of dead trees, Tillman guiding them. He paused near a downed branch before continuing along a small hill.

"Moseby, how far are you from your target?" DeRosa's statement came from the tablet, and they all jumped. Chuck turned and gave her recruit a smile.

Tillman held the device over his head. "I'm showing a hundred yards or better."

"Copy. We have eyes on the Jeep. It looks like it's been here awhile. Keep your head on a swivel and ears open, people."

Chuck's small group looked at each other, then closed ranks. They moved along as quietly as possible given the heavy amount of debris on the forest floor.

Tillman's tablet made a series of beeps, and he paused, fixating on something ahead of them. Chuck peeked over his shoulder and spotted what might pass as an overgrown road. A movement at the corner of her vision caused her to twist her head back, but she couldn't find a source. Maybe it had been a bird.

Tillman looked back at her. "The signal is coming from just beyond that road."

Despite the cold, she could feel a bead of sweat rolling down the nape of her neck as she responded. "Lead on."

They moved cautiously towards, and then up the road's embankment, the tablet making a more aggressive series of beeps. Tillman paused again and let out a nervous laugh. "DeRosa's going to think we crawled to this body."

"She'll get over it. I—" Whatever Chuck had intended to say flew out of her mind like a bullet. She lifted her watch and swiped the display. As soon as she saw the green lines she spoke.

"Agent DeRosa, we have company!" It had only been there for a second, as though clearing a rise and then dropping back down, but she'd seen a pair of headlights.

DeRosa's voice came back, blessedly calm. "Who?"

"I don't know. All I saw were headlights. Whoever they are, they're coming this way."

"You three take cover, we're on our way."

"Understood."

Tillman fell back behind a large tree as Chuck and Marcy took up positions on either side of the barely there road. Looking at the overgrown weeds and fallen branches, one thing was clear. Whoever was in that car hadn't wandered out here by mistake.

Tillman silenced the beeping of his tablet as the sound of an engine first reached them. The vehicle seemed to be moving quickly based on the amount of noise it was making. Marcy made eye contact with her, and Chuck gestured in response, signaling for the recruit to stay hidden unless otherwise instructed. Marcy gave an affirmative nod as the sound of the engine roared. It would be driving right by them soon.

Chuck took in a deep breath as a loud screech sounded close by. The noise of tires dragging through loose gravel and underbrush followed. It took her a moment to process what she was hearing.

The vehicle had stopped. But why? Had they been spotted? The sound of a door opening gave her only a moment of warning before a male voice with an odd accent rang out.

"Whoever the hell's hiding behind those trees, yah might as well come on out! Slowly!"

Shit.

Chuck couldn't see Tillman, but she motioned for Marcy to stay. The recruit nodded and pressed herself against the tree.

"I'm coming out!"

After letting out a long breath, Chuck put out her left hand first, before stepping out fully onto the road. A black SUV sat parked maybe thirty feet away. The driver's side door was open. She could see an arm extended between the door and the vehicle. Their surprise visitor had a Colt .357 revolver pointed at her.

"Your friend there too!"

It felt odd that even with her dead to rights, the guy hadn't demanded that she drop her firearm, which she still clung to in her right hand. She could hear Marcy moving out into the open. The sound made her heart sink.

"How many more of yah are there?"

Chuck kept her voice calm as she lied back. "It's just us."

"Bullshit! Y'all aren't Wardens. That means there's more of yah!"

If he knew about Wardens then he likely knew about the Family. And if he knew about the Family, that probably made him a Griffin.

"How about you stop pointing that hand cannon at us and we can talk."

"Little lady, if I'd wanted to shoot yah, I'd've done it already."

Oh, good. A misogynistic *Griffin.*

"The rest of my team is about a mile further down the road. You want to give us a lift?"

He let out a laugh. "I think I'll pass." The arm holding the gun retreated behind the open door. After a long moment, the guy walked out into the open, gun still in hand but no longer pointed at them.

The man stood well over six feet tall and had greying hair. He wore black from head to toe. An old looking leather belt and holster completed the modern-day gunslinger motif.

Chuck glanced at Marcy, who still had her weapon in hand. At least they had this pig outnumbered.

"Listen missy, why don't yah call whoever it is y'all came up here with so the adults can talk, kay?" The statement dripped with contempt.

She stood in stunned silence, anger simmering inside her. Who the hell did this guy think he was?

As she started to respond a twig snapped off to her left. The brute pivoted raising his revolver. She turned to see Ed several feet off the road behind Marcy, pointing his own weapon in the man's direction.

Instinctively Chuck began to raise her own firearm, but as her eyes returned to the man she was shocked to see DeRosa immediately behind him, her pistol placed against the back of the Griffin's head.

"Drop it, asshole!"

The expression the guy made confused Chuck. He didn't appear surprised, angry, or even fearful. It was a look of recognition.

"Why, Sally DeRosa! As I live and breathe, is that you?" The man gently placed his weapon on the hood of the still running SUV. DeRosa's face contorted at the mention of her name.

The senior agent shifted ever so slightly to get a better look at the guy. "Well, shit." DeRosa kept her pistol trained on the man, shaking her head.

"Come now, is that anyway to greet an old friend?" The Griffin turned fully, looking right down the barrel of DeRosa's weapon.

"Go to hell, McFadden!" DeRosa nearly spit the words as she lowered her pistol.

The man stretched out his arms, as if expecting a hug. "You know you're glad to see me, Sally!"

Without warning DeRosa punched him in the gut, knocking the wind out of him.

Clutching his stomach, he wheezed. "I deserve that, I guess."

DeRosa kicked dirt at him for emphasis. She grabbed the revolver from off the vehicle's hood and crammed it into her belt.

The man, McFadden, stood and dusted off his pants. He didn't even appear to be phased by the attack. "Ain't yah gonna introduce me to your family here?"

Chapter Seven:

The Body

DeRosa stepped back and investigated the SUV. "Are you alone?"

McFadden reached out and slammed the door shut. "Just me, darling. You want to team up, you know, for old times' sake?"

"How about you eat shit, McFadden."

Chuck pulled her eyes away for a moment. Ed, Josh, and Tillman had all joined her and Marcy on the road. They each stood staring at the exchange between DeRosa and McFadden.

DeRosa looked in the direction of her group. "We already found the Jeep. Who're you out here backing up?"

McFadden likewise peered up the road. He seemed to be studying them. Then he cupped his hands over his face and said something to DeRosa that Chuck couldn't hear. The senior agent cast another glance their way and started speaking to McFadden in hushed tones.

Chuck looked at Tillman. His only response was to shrug. She holstered her weapon and motioned for Josh and Marcy to do the same. Ed seemed distracted by something out in the woods.

The secret conversation got a bit more intense, though no more understandable. After a pause, DeRosa pulled out McFadden's revolver, emptied the bullets onto the dirt road, and then handed the weapon back to him. He pivoted and gave the group an exaggerated nod and wink, then climbed into his still idling vehicle.

DeRosa motioned for them all to spread out to let the SUV pass, which they did.

As the vehicle rolled by the group, McFadden blared the horn. The whole group jumped. Marcy kicked the side panel hard. Josh and Tillman snickered.

Dust filtered through the morning sunlight in the wake of the SUV, which continued down the road as they watched it.

Josh looked towards Chuck. "Was that guy—"

"A member of the Griffins? Yes, he is," DeRosa answered as she joined them.

Ed holstered his weapon. "Um, what was that all about?"

DeRosa contemplated the answer for a moment. "*That* was Hank McFadden. He used to be a Warden. We caught him selling our tech to the Griffins. Nowadays he works for them. Calls himself an enforcer, whatever the hell that's supposed to be."

"What exactly was he doing out here?"

DeRosa grimaced. "Besides wasting oxygen? Evidently he's trying to track down a group of deserters, says they stole that Jeep a few days ago."

Marcy did nothing to hide her irritation. "You believed him?"

"Not really, recruit, but our mission isn't to pick fights with shitheads. Our mission is to retrieve that body and get the hell out of here."

"Did you work with him back when he was a Warden?" Chuck didn't know if DeRosa would answer the question, but they were clearly familiar with each other.

"Unfortunately." DeRosa turned towards Tillman. "Lead the way. That body has got to be close. I can smell it."

Tillman dutifully set out with the rest of the group in tow. Now that the encounter had ended, Chuck could smell the body too. Like a skunk mixed with rotting plants. They hadn't gone far when Tillman pulled up at the edge of a tight cluster of pines.

There, face down on the forest floor, lay the body of the Mog. Blood covered a pair of nearby trees, and a darkened pool had formed around its head. The funk of the beast mixed with the iron smell of the blood and viscera made the burrito, previously resting calmly in her stomach, come roaring up. Chuck forced it back down, but Marcy wasn't so lucky.

The recruit turned and vomited. She bent over and retched a second time. Chuck moved to stand next to the younger woman, offering her a drink of water.

Marcy looked ashamed. "Agent Barnes, I'm sor—"

"Don't be. That smell is something else."

DeRosa cast a glance at the stricken recruit. "Ed, Josh. I want a perimeter. With that much blood I'd say it's pretty safe to assume this thing didn't have a heart attack."

Ed led Josh towards the far side of the grove. Tillman had pulled out a satellite phone to contact command. DeRosa stepped back and patted Marcy on the shoulder. "You good, Marcy?"

"Yes ma'am."

"Good. Charlotte, how about you two check the area for any signs of struggle or even other blood splatter. There aren't many things out here that should be able to take on a Mog."

She and Marcy headed directly into the most densely packed group of trees, giving the actual body a wide berth. A feeling of uneasiness came over her as the tightly packed trees blocked out the early morning rays of sunshine, creating odd shadows and tiny shafts of light.

That feeling became more pronounced as they discovered the corpse of a deer that'd been torn apart. Organs, fur, and horns seemed to have been haphazardly dropped in a pile.

"Did the Mog do this?" Marcy's voice was little more than a whisper.

"It could have. Then again, it might have smelled another predator's kill and come to investigate. Or vice versa."

Looking around she couldn't see any obvious signs of fighting. Besides the deer corpse there were no blood stains. No broken tree limbs. No—

A glint at the base of a nearby tree caught her eye. She reached down and picked up the object, a pocketknife. And not some cheap, convenience store knife, but a nice one, imprinted with the name 'Stan.'

She flipped it over and blinked twice, making sure what she saw was real. It had been engraved with a circle, inside of which two winged creatures faced each other, claws reaching. The symbol of the Griffins.

Marcy looked at the knife. "Is that…?"

"Yeah, I'm guessing it must have belonged to one of the asshole's deserters. Come on, let's go show DeRosa."

They headed back, finding DeRosa on the Sat phone with Tillman near at hand, holding up his tablet and taking pictures. DeRosa waved them over and then held the phone away from her face. "Call

Ed and Josh and have them get back here. We're going to have to flip this body over so the CIT at Delta can have a look before we bag it up."

Chuck nodded, swiping her watch. "Ed, DeRosa wants everybody back here at the body."

"Roger."

The message delivered, she pulled her gloves out and put them on. Marcy did the same in preparation for touching the downed creature. The helicopter suddenly felt far away, and she looked in its direction as though she could catch a glimpse of it. Of course, she couldn't, and the thought of carrying the dead weight of the Mog all the way back made her legs hurt.

Ed and Josh arrived soon after, and DeRosa handed the phone to Tillman so she could join them in flipping the beast. As they did, she heard DeRosa and Ed both say, "Woah."

Looking towards the creature's head, Chuck could see what caused the reaction. The monster's face was frozen in a mask of fright. Eyes wide, jaw locked as though it had been grinding its teeth. But more shocking than its look was the fact the monster's throat had been completely ripped out. The ruddy brown fur at the edges of the tear were caked in blood. Red stains extended nearly to the beast's navel, made obvious by the fact that Mog's chests and bellies were mostly bare.

Ed rubbed the back of his neck. "What the hell happened to this guy?"

DeRosa shook her head. "I'll be damned if I know." She turned to Tillman. "Moseby, get photos and forward them to Dr. Keech at Delta. He's going to want to see this."

Chuck took a couple of steps towards the monster's head. Something seemed off about the area around its mouth. "Are his lips blue?"

Ed leaned over to get a closer look. "It looks like blue dust, or powder."

DeRosa directed Tillman to get a couple of shots of the powder as well.

Josh grunted as he lifted the creature's arm. "Look at its hand. Could it have done this to itself?"

He had a point. The creature's fingers were covered in viscera, with ragged flaps of skin and fur still stuck in the nails. Chuck glanced at the creature's face again. "Even if he did tear his own throat out, why's he making that face? Marcy and I found a deer carcass in the grove, but there were no signs of a struggle." The pocketknife suddenly returned to her mind. "Oh, and this." She held it out towards DeRosa.

"I'll be damned with Uncle Sam!" All of them jumped as McFadden yelled from behind the group. "Where'd you say you came across that, young lady?"

DeRosa rose slowly, turning to face him. "You sneak up on me again McFadden and I'll put a slug through you quicker than you can blink!"

McFadden smiled, an e-cig protruding casually from the edge of his mouth. He let out a great cloud of vapor. "You're just as pleasant as I remember ya, Sally. But, uh, your girly there's got something I reckon belongs to us. That is unless y'all are taking trophies these days."

"What are you really doing out here, McFadden?" DeRosa took a step towards him. He in turn side-stepped her and walked with long strides towards the Mog, another white puff escaping him as he did.

"Damn hell, Sally. Looks like y'all got quite a mess on your hands. I suppose you're gonna try and blame this on us somehow?"

Chuck had to shake her head as the smell of licorice filled her nostrils. She *hated* when people vaped around her. She could almost rationalize smoking more easily than she could sucking on the same dirty ass mouthpiece repeatedly.

DeRosa spit on the ground near McFadden's feet. "Yeah, I was sure thinking of blaming you. When exactly did your *deserters* come out here?"

"Oh, about a week ago. Only trouble is I didn't see much evidence of them leaving in another vehicle. And seeing as how they've left some gear behind, near a dead Mogollon no less, well, seems like a mighty odd coincidence." Blessedly he put the e-cig back in his pocket.

DeRosa rolled her eyes. "A coincidence, maybe. But this Mog died a few hours ago, not a week ago."

McFadden gave the creature another look. "A few hours ago, huh? Now that is odd. What the hell did that?"

"Not our concern right now. We're here to retrieve a body and bug out."

McFadden rubbed the stubble on his chin. "Hmm, that sure as shit don't look like the work of one of our boys. Tell you what, Sally. How's about you all give me that knife, and I'll get out of your hair."

The knife still in her hand, Chuck looked to DeRosa. The senior agent kept her glare trained on McFadden.

It was Tillman that broke the silence. "Agent DeRosa, Delta says they have what they need. We're cleared to transport the body."

DeRosa's eyes never left her Griffin counterpart. "Charlotte, give him the knife."

McFadden nodded and turned towards her. She held out the knife, which he took, flashing a crooked smile at her as he did. "Thank ya, little lady."

"Now get the hell out of our way so we can do our job."

McFadden gave a bow, then turned towards the group. "You sure y'all don't need a hand?"

Marcy raised her middle finger and scratched the side of her face. The rest stood with folded arms or no expression at all. With McFadden's back turned to her, Chuck couldn't help but smile at the response.

"Gotcha a real classy group here, Sally." He shoved the knife in his pocket then started walking back towards the road, brushing Chuck's shoulder as he did. "Then again, with a leader like you in charge..." He let the comment hang, though DeRosa didn't take the bait. She continued to stare at him as he headed for the embankment.

Finally, she looked back to her crew. "Spread that bag and let's get this over with."

Ed helped Josh roll out the oversized body bag. Chuck jotted down some coordinates on an orange tag, explaining to Marcy how to do it so that CIT could quickly process the body once they had received it.

Five minutes later they were again rolling the corpse. Once they had it bagged and tagged, they spread out and began the long walk back to the chopper.

Chuck wasn't all that shocked to see McFadden's SUV sitting on the road as they crossed it. She couldn't see him through the heavily tinted windows, but she could still somehow feel his eyes watching her. The thought made her more than a bit nauseous. She resolved to one day talk to DeRosa about him, but that could wait.

Despite the cool morning, Chuck had broken a sweat by the time they reached the chopper. DeRosa talked something over with the pilot as the rest of them loaded the Mog's body into the cargo bay.

As everyone hurried to prepare for takeoff, DeRosa pulled Chuck and Marcy off to the side. "I'm sorry about all that. You ladies did great back there." She patted Marcy's shoulder, which the recruit clearly appreciated. "This has been a strange day, made even stranger by what is undoubtedly one of the most worthless excuses for a man ever."

She looked back over her shoulder as if expecting him to be there. "And trust me when I say, a haymaker to the stomach isn't even a tenth of what that son of a bitch deserves."

Marcy frowned. "He really was a dick."

Chuck snorted unintentionally.

DeRosa looked at the recruit, who blushed. "Sorry Agent DeRosa"

The senior agent shook her head. "No need to apologize, he's a first-class dick."

Marcy giggled then motioned back towards the helo. Chuck and DeRosa turned and saw Tillman and Ed leaning out the bay door.

"Let's go, ladies!" Ed called over the increasing noise of the chopper.

The three of them walked back, going through the same routine with their helmets and taking their seats. Sweaty and tired, the group barely spoke ten words to each other on the trip back to Phoenix.

Chapter Eight:

Bewitching

Bewitched.

By what means, I cannot tell. Whether they found some mystic or even another of my deathless ilk, the how is not important. But its effects on my captivity are another matter entirely.

In addition to binding me, the enchantments seem to attract whatever small vermin roam about my years-long resting place. I hear them, scraping at the metal, crawling over it, time and time again.

I spent many hours wishing that one would find a way inside. The feeling of their tiny bones crunching beneath my teeth would bring me immense joy.

But all thought of such small prey flew out of my mind when I first heard a different noise. Something I had hoped for, but long ago stopped believing I would hear.

Footsteps. And a voice.

Those first human steps. That first human voice. They came and went. I languished for days, weeks perhaps before they came again. I battered at the walls, croaked out a smattering of words, but to no avail. Again, my savior abandoned me.

When the sounds returned this third time all I could bring myself to do was listen. Immediately I recognized a difference. Multiple voices. Many steps. That devil, hope, again began to blossom somewhere deep within my shell. My mind, my precious mind which had suffered the most, began to race.

Then I heard the incantation. Ancient words, the power of which these simpletons could not begin to comprehend in their wildest imaginations. But I knew the words. I recognized them. The oafs misspoke most of them, but that didn't matter. The bewitched metal began to respond. The ancient power that had sealed me in this iron coffin began to weaken.

As they chanted the final words, I reached up, meaning to burst forth in glory. But my prison yet held. A fog came over my mind, a brutal, suffocating cloud. Pain suddenly wracked my form. The same power that kept me sealed must also have been sustaining me.

A sudden pounding on the container further disoriented me. A flood of images assailed me as memories I'd long repressed suddenly sprang forth. I could taste dust on my tongue. I could feel my eyes burning as if salted. I could feel my carapace crack as tissues long dormant flexed and strained.

Harmless and helpless as a calf, they dragged me from the box. What a pathetic and broken creature I must have appeared to them. Blinding, unnatural lights assaulted my burning eyes. I tried to take in a breath and vomited a thick ooze in return.

"What the hell is he?"

"Why is he dressed like that?"

I heard the mockery in their voices. The scorn in their words.

"Should we give him some water or something?"

Shuddering, I felt my body healing itself. My immortal nature, long held in some odd stasis, finally began to awaken. Each breath brought strength.

"Can you understand us?"

Vicious mockery!

"Stan, this doesn't feel right."

Revenge!

"Hey, we let you out!"

Deceit!

The fires within my breast rekindled.

Rising, I took stock of the three fools who'd come to grant me my freedom. They wore strange clothes and smelled of chemicals and fear. My thirst for revenge overtook my better senses of judgement. I flew into an exquisite rage.

Claws long unused rent tender flesh. Their cries were a symphony to me, and I relished even the echoes as they died.

Chapter Nine:

Recruits

Smalls had been waiting for them at the airport. She and DeRosa appeared to have a rather terse conversation before taking off in a separate vehicle. The rest of them returned in a modified box truck with the body.

Halfway back, Chuck's cell phone buzzed. She pulled it out, finding a text from Tillman, who was sitting literally one seat away from her. She gave him a slow eye roll.

'Would you be down with taking the recruits to dinner tonight?'

After reading the message, she gave him a quick nod. She understood why he'd asked the question by text and not out loud, but still. Not long after, the truck stopped, and the back door popped open to reveal Doc and Rita.

Doc flashed them all a wide smile. "Welcome back! I hear you all brought us a little something."

"We sure did, amigo," Ed replied as he accepted Doc's outstretched hand. He jumped down from the back of the truck. Doc gave Chuck a little wink, and then followed Ed around the side of the vehicle. Rita gave a wave to Marcy and Josh who hopped out next. Chuck was about to follow them when Tillman tugged gently at her shoulder.

"You're not gonna leave me hanging, are you?" he asked with sincerity. Tillman could be almost *too* wholesome at times.

"I promise. Scout's honor or whatever. But wait for me to come over to your apartment, okay?"

"Sounds good. Say, around four?"

"Yeah, that'll give me time to finish my paperwork and hopefully get in a shower." She stepped out of the truck and into Warehouse 2.

"Don't forget you promised!" Tillman called after her.

She raised a hand and waved at him without turning around. After the elevator ride, she headed straight for the debriefing room.

Not far from the Command Center, a circular room painted a drab yellow held a scattering of computers. The field agent in charge of a given mission would deliver their report and body cam footage directly to a senior member of the site staff; any other agents were given the privilege of spending half an hour or better in this little slice of heaven.

She'd heard the debriefing rooms at newer sites were nice. Alpha's, however, was not. The air in the room never seemed to move and it was always uncomfortably hot. The computers ran on Windows 7. To top things off, the lingering smell of Chupacabra urine hung like a permanent incense.

Chuck had brought the recruit's cameras with her, seeing no reason to submit them to this monotony so early in their training. She plugged them all in and sat back, waiting for the footage to slowly upload.

Pulling out her phone, she decided to check her emails. There were two, one of which had been sent by some presidential campaign. Unsurprisingly, the candidate needed additional funds to keep his hopes of reelection alive. A quick swipe deleted the spam.

She opened the second one, which came from her brother Cody. He'd addressed it to 'The Bullies,' a name he'd affectionately given to her and their brother Cameron. *Apparently* they'd been mean to him growing up. Joking name aside, the message within the email included some great news. Cody and his wife had discovered they were having a baby girl! She had a niece on the way.

The thought gave her pause. Being an agent with an organization like the Family had lots of perks, interacting with cryptids being among the most exciting. But it came with a heavy tax on your personal and family life.

Belonging to an agency that ninety-nine percent of the world's population didn't know existed meant you couldn't call up your cousin, or your brother, or even your mom, and tell them about your day. Or explain to them, with any level of ease, why they couldn't come out and visit you whenever they wanted.

Her mother preached the importance of family as long as Chuck could remember, and yet here she was. Thousands of miles from her nearest relative, living a large portion of her life underground. The irony of being part of a group nominally referred to as the Family, while at the same time having to sever many of the links to one's actual relatives, was not lost on her.

Had things been different between her and her mom when she graduated high school, Chuck may never have ended up becoming an agent. But that was in the past now, and you couldn't change the past.

***

"This place had lots of positive reviews on Yelp." Tillman said as he held the door for the group later that day. He'd picked out a newly opened barbeque restaurant, and while it looked a bit like a dive bar, the place smelled fantastic.

Normally they would undertake this meal early in the morning. Now, with the sun preparing to set in the western sky, the recruits seemed much more awake. The chattering started on the ride over and continued as they waited to be seated.

"I haven't had good barbecue in forever!" Josh declared as the waiter began taking orders.

"I don't even care if it's good. The fact that it's not being served in the cafeteria is enough for me," Rita said.

Separated from the need to *blend in* on campus, the recruits had instead worn actual civilian clothes. Rita and Jess looked particularly put together, combining clothing and makeup that brought out their best features. Chuck glanced down at the yoga pants and t-shirt she'd chosen.

Not all that long ago she wouldn't have gone out into public looking like a soccer mom. There were half a dozen nice outfits sitting in her closet back at Alpha, yet she threw this combo on without a thought. Had living underground for the last couple of years done this to her? Or maybe the responsibilities of being a trainer caused the change?

Chuck looked around the table as the appetizers started arriving, thinking about how well Josh and Marcy had performed that morning. She pondered how all of them had grown since those first weeks in Alpha, herself included.

On the job training had been hard for her at first. Having

graduated from being a recruit only three months earlier, she was very aware of what the recruits needed to be doing. As a trainer, what she needed to be doing was another matter entirely.

DeRosa had been her life raft during those first couple of months. Early on, she'd picked up on what aspects of being an agent each of the recruits enjoyed most. Those that liked the physicality of doing work outs or hand to hand training versus those that enjoyed studying the habitats, biology, and traits of cryptids.

DeRosa told her very few recruits clearly enjoyed all aspects of training. Which meant as a trainer, you had to juggle what you focused on.

Chuck thought back to a conversation she'd had with DeRosa after a particularly hard day with the group. "Agent DeRosa, I don't think I'm getting through to them, you know?"

"And why do you think that?"

"Half the time they look bored, and the other half they spend bitching."

"You never bitched while you were a recruit?"

Chuck thought about it for a second, admitting to herself she'd bitched a little. "Not like they do!"

DeRosa raised her eyebrows. "What can you do to be more engaging?"

"I'm not sure how you make the mating rituals of a Mongolian Death Worm engaging."

That got a laugh out of DeRosa. "Fair enough. What about approaching it from a different angle? How much time do you spend with your group when you aren't training, other than media days?"

"I'm not really sure. It's not a lot though."

"Think back to when you first got to Alpha, how confusing the Family's rules and regs can be. You probably walked around on pins and needles, worried you were going to do something wrong."

"Pretty much."

DeRosa's tone softened as she continued. "These kids are feeling the same thing. Ten to twelve hours, every day, for two years straight. If you really want to get to know what makes them tick, then you'll have to get outside your own comfort zone."

As soon as she'd been assigned as a trainer, living and breathing her job had become the norm for Chuck. It made sense that she might need to step back a bit and meet the recruits more on their level.

DeRosa wound things up by giving her a pat on the back. "Here's the thing. Every person that makes it through to become a recruit is going to have quirks. This type of job practically demands that you be weird. Look for strengths in every one of them, however small or insignificant to their training you may think they are. Give them recognition for the good, and when you see things that you don't like, tell them about it. Just do it in private. And make sure you tell them *why* you don't like those things."

The whole interaction had made her feel like she didn't know what she was doing. But in the days and weeks that followed, there had been a change in her recruits, mostly for the good. Greg was an early exception, but the previous day's experience with Doc may have been a turning point. He only annoyed her a couple of times during dinner, a marked improvement.

There were days she still felt unqualified. But this had, all and all, been a good day, and considering how it started, Chuck felt like this was a significant win.

She enjoyed a decent bowl of banana pudding before they headed back to Alpha for the night. Most of the recruits had fallen asleep by the time they pulled into Warehouse 2.

She turned to Tillman as they were waiting for the recruits to get unloaded. "Hey, I'm going to stay topside for a bit. I'll see you tomorrow?"

He ran a hand through his hair then smiled. "Sounds good, thanks for coming along."

"Thanks for having the idea in the first place."

Tillman headed for the elevator as Chuck walked out the big bay doors. She glanced at her watch and determined she had enough time to walk off at least a portion of the meal she'd eaten.

Her phone rang less than a minute into her walk. Pulling the device from her pocket, she saw her mother's name, flashing on the screen.

Chapter Ten:

Agent Sally DeRosa

"How's the weather?"

"It's fine, Mom. I mean, it's Arizona. Mostly like home, but without the humidity." Chuck's mom asked her about the weather every time they talked on the phone. For a while it had been annoying. But she seemed to have crossed over that annoyance sometime around her two-year mark. Nowadays, she was glad to have something, *anything*, to talk with her mother about.

"I talked to your brother. He said you might get to visit this summer?"

She shook her head in the cool night air. Yes, she'd talked to Cameron about maybe coming out when she finished training the recruits. But it would be *next* summer. Cameron could be relied upon to pass along exactly the information he'd been given. Her mother, however, possessed selective hearing.

"Maybe next summer, yeah. I can't wait much longer than that to come see my new niece, can I?" Hopefully, Cody had already shared the news with their mother.

"You know, you always have a place to stay back here, no matter when you show up." This was one of her mother's favorite lines. Chuck suspected when she finally did return to her childhood home, her room would look exactly as she'd left it.

"I know, Mom. Once I get done with this intern cycle I'll have time. Honest Abe."

A tiny but perceptible knot popped up in her throat. The saying had been her dad's and came out as natural as breathing. A heavy silence was all she could hear from the other end of the connection for a long moment.

"Honest Abe, you bet." The hurt in her mom's voice cut at Chuck's heart.

Her mother had never fully recovered after the death of their father. Chuck's brothers steamrolled along; their grief shared with each other during whatever passing moments they had together. Cameron had taken it the hardest. He'd just been accepted to Florida State a week before their father was killed and he used his studies as a kind of therapy, coming home that first winter break with a rather new attitude. His new boyfriend might have also had something to do with it. Cameron's change, combined with Cody's engagement, helped Chuck rise out of her own funk.

But mom never seemed to have the same outlet for grief. She tried, by God, she'd tried. Mostly she tried to use Chuck as her *de facto* therapist, stunting Chuck's own ability to grieve. Trying to sort out her own feelings, while at the same time trying not to be angry with her mother. In the end, it had been too much. Moving clear across the country had given them both time to work some things out.

"I love you, Mom, but I should probably get going." Silence answered her, and for a moment, she thought that maybe they had lost the connection. But her mom's voice finally came back.

"I love you too, Charlotte. I'm—I miss you. I'll talk with you later, honey." And with that she ended the call.

Chuck tucked the phone in her pocket and wiped moisture from the edges of her eyes. Adjusting to the distance between herself and her family had taken time. And in her heart, she knew she should *want* to go back. But the thought of it made her stomach knot up. Distance had given them space to heal.

What if returning tore open fresh wounds?

***

As she stepped back into her apartment, Chuck decided to take a shower. Unfortunately for her, the water was barely lukewarm. She did her best to suffer through it, but less than five minutes later she stood in front of her mirror drying her hair.

She thought about checking out Netflix to see if anything new had been added, but then ruled it out. After the body retrieval, the reporting, and the dinner, she was having trouble keeping her eyes open. Falling into bed, Chuck curled into the blissful cool of her covers. It had been a hectic day. A productive, but hectic day.

A knock at the door startled her. She sat upright, momentarily thinking she'd imagined it. Again, it sounded. Slow, but firm and unmistakable. She reached for the lamp next to her bed and turned it on.

For a fleeting moment, Chuck envisioned the person knocking to be in her room already. They weren't, but she sat a moment longer. A voice, muffled by the door, finally got her moving. It sounded vaguely feminine, and her mind raced at what could be the matter with one of the recruits.

She grabbed a robe and slipped it on as she stepped to the door. A single, louder knock pierced her room as she reached for the knob. She turned it hurriedly, fully ready to either comfort or freak out on her late-night guest.

DeRosa stood there, still wearing her field gear. In one hand she held two glasses, and in the other bottles of whiskey and wine, both opened. "Evening, Charlotte. Feel like a nightcap?"

Chuck looked at her, wondering exactly how she'd knocked on the door. Then she noticed a pink circle on DeRosa's forehead.

"Good deal!" The senior agent pushed past her, apparently taking her silence for acceptance.

She spoke to the back of DeRosa's head. "Sure, come on in."

"Thanks!" Chuck's visitor strode across the living area, coming to a stop at the extended counter that acted as a table. DeRosa sat in one of two bar-height chairs while placing her bottles and glasses on the counter.

Chuck closed the door. "Um, give me a second." There was nothing but her underwear beneath her robe, so she grabbed some sweats and headed into the bathroom. At least dressed for the occasion, if not totally prepared for it, she headed back out.

DeRosa had already poured one of the wine glasses full. The other wine glass contained about an inch of whiskey. DeRosa held it up in Chuck's direction then drank it down in barely a swallow.

Chuck picked up her glass. "I'll bite. Are you doing okay?"

"Oh yeah, peachy! I mean, I'm sitting here in the apartment of a subordinate, got me a good little buzz going, and it's eleven at night. I'd say I'm one 'Oops, clumsy me' from being the opening act to a porno, but you know. All in all, great!"

Chuck wasn't a big drinker but figured she could play along. She gave the glass a look then took a sip. "You want to talk about it?"

"Hey, I'm sorry. I'll go if you want. I didn't really feel like drinking alone tonight is all."

"As long as this *isn't* the opening act of a porno, I'm okay with talking. I mean, it's not like I'm going to be able to get back to sleep anytime soon." She said this as jokingly as possible, though she truly would have preferred to be snuggled in bed.

"Bottoms up then!" DeRosa skipped the glass and toasted Chuck with the bottle of Jack Daniel's. She tipped it back, and the smell of the whiskey made it hard for Chuck to drink her own beverage. She shifted her chair back as compassionately as possible.

"Did Smalls chew your ass about this morning?" Chuck asked.

"Ha! You could say that. I was way out of line, but you can only eat so many shit sandwiches before you need to puke. Know what I mean?"

Chuck did understand DeRosa, the ineloquence of her comparison notwithstanding.

"I'm glad we brought along Marcy and Josh. They're going to be really good agents someday."

"I think so too," DeRosa held up her glass in a toast. "Here's to telling our boss to blow it out her bony ass!"

Chuck smiled, "Cheers!" She took another drink of her wine, realizing suddenly that her glass had somehow become nearly empty. As she sat it down DeRosa helpfully poured some more. The senior agent took another drink, her face suddenly getting serious.

"It's just, McFadden has me all twisted up. Dumb son of a bitch. When I saw his face today, I mean, God! I wanted to kick the shit out of him." DeRosa let out a strange noise that might have been a laugh.

Chuck stifled a yawn. "What did Smalls have to say about him?"

"You'd have thought I told her we stumbled on the damned Pope wandering around in the woods. We spent two hours on the line with a bunch of big shots at Delta. A root canal would've been more enjoyable to be honest."

Chuck pondered her next question. She wanted to know the story of DeRosa and McFadden's history, but she didn't really want to piss off the senior agent. "What's his deal anyway?"

"Hank McFadden, my dear girl, is a walking, talking, pile of monkey shit. He must have joined the Family a couple of years before I did." She paused, swishing around the whiskey. "He'd just become a Warden when I became a field agent, like not even six months out. That's when I met him. We were both stationed at Gama when Katrina hit Louisiana. A bunch of subjects were lost to us or forced out of their usual habitats, so Command dispatched several squads."

"McFadden said something about teaming up with you?"

"The team I had been assigned to, yeah. When the shit started hitting the fan somebody far up the food chain must have called in some favors. The next thing you know we have a bunch of Wardens mixed in with us. The whole ordeal was a shit show from day one. The Wardens didn't want to listen to us, and we didn't want to deal with their holier than thou bullshit."

Chuck put down her glass, her head finally registering that she was, in fact, drinking something alcoholic. DeRosa marched on.

"I mean, he had this kind of rugged handsomeness. We were both the newest members of our crews, so we kind of clicked, I guess. I had no idea what a total ass he would become. The missions they had us on—they weren't like missions we go on now. We were out for weeks and months at a time, staying in hotels, going out drinking after we had captured or contained something. Pretty soon, late night talks turned into… other things."

"Okay, hold up, I'm sorry. *McFadden*? I mean, the guy I met today was a total douche. Not to mention he sounded like an actor trying to fake an accent."

This made DeRosa laugh out loud. She put the bottle down for the first time since she'd been seated. The sight of DeRosa cracking up caused Chuck to laugh along with her.

"Oh my god! You noticed that too? I was so angry I couldn't tell if he was really talking like a backwater hick or if I was hallucinating!" This made Chuck laugh even harder. It was probably the wine but carrying on with DeRosa felt hilarious to her. They laughed together a moment longer before again toasting and taking another drink.

"I fell for him hard… You know what he did?"

Chuck shook her head.

"He proposed to me! Can you believe that shit? Proposed to me in Branson, Missouri of all places! And what did my dumb ass say? Yes, of course!"

Chuck had to steady herself a bit. She'd been carrying on one continuous giggle at this point, and her head was responding to the alcohol a little more. She watched as the animated DeRosa topped off her wine for the third time.

"You said yes? To that?" she spurted between giggles.

"I sure as hell did! And I probably would have gone through with it too. Luckily for me he dicked that all up when he got caught selling tech to the Griffins." DeRosa laughed hard at this.

Chuck took the pause to sip a bit more of her wine. "How did that even work?"

DeRosa's words slurred a bit as she continued. "I wish I could tell you. He had some connection, somewhere…"

She paused. Picking up the bottle to look at the quarter of liquid that was left, DeRosa evidently decided against another drink.

"Listen, besides getting caught up in satisfying whatever carnal needs I had at the time, I was doing a lot of drugs. None of the hard shit, but you combine enough pot, booze, and pills and you can get yourself plenty messed up. I had been on the road so long. I should have taken a break. Hell, we both needed to take a break.

"One night in some no name town, we concocted this plan to spend a week shacking up at this house he had in Louisiana. We both put in some bullshit paperwork about needing temporary emergency leave. Looking back at it, we should have been suspicious that they rubber stamped us both."

"I didn't even know we could get emergency leave. Is that still a thing?"

"I wish." She laughed and took a small sip from her bottle. "The whole deal was a set up. Delta must have figured out what he was doing and decided to set a trap. He, in turn, must have gotten tipped off by somebody. And what does he do? He sells out his brand-new fiancé. Told someone at Gama he suspected me of stealing a bunch of guns."

"Seriously?"

DeRosa gave an exaggerated nod. "They were waiting for me when I pulled into his driveway. Even had me cuffed up in the back of a transport before Delta figures out the whole operation got blown to shit. The worst part of all? That bastard got away. Disappeared for five years."

"What did you do?" Chuck asked, becoming more invested in the story the further along it got.

"I went back and burned his damn house to the ground for one." This brought a wistful smile to DeRosa's face.

"I mean when you found out what he'd been doing?"

"Oh, the Family didn't want to look weak. Having tech stolen by one of our own would've been too big a scandal. It certainly wasn't like he was the only one, on either side, that was playing double agent at that time. I came clean about doing drugs though. They made me go to rehab for six months. Got knocked down a couple of ranks and had to re-earn my field agent status."

"Well, damn."

"Yeah, I pawned the tiny little ring he gave me. That asshole had the nerve to call me after five years to tell me sorry. Like I wouldn't have heard he was playing for the other team by then." She shook her head and put the lid back on the whiskey bottle.

The alcohol in Chuck's system emboldened her, and she decided to delve a little deeper into her new friend Agent DeRosa.

"Is that why the Family has been screwing you over so much?"

"Screwing me over? Charlotte, if it weren't for you, I might actually believe that." She patted Chuck on the elbow. "Am I the current whipping boy of the year? Damn straight I am, but the pot I smoked thirteen years ago isn't the reason."

Chuck was already sure what the reason was, but she wanted to hear it from DeRosa.

The senior agent leaned forward.

"The reason I'm getting bent over right now is all thanks to Fitchburg."

Chapter Eleven:

The Fitchburg Incident

Chuck, like every other active member of the Family at the time, knew some version of the story. The incident made national headlines. Every Kangaroo in America had to work overtime to keep the truth covered up.

Four agents and two civilians died on a little farm outside Fitchburg, Massachusetts. The media eventually reported that a gas line had exploded, killing four construction workers. The civilians, a married couple who owned the property, had evidently been in the field, observing the work when the accident happened. The explosion even killed their small herd of goats.

One thing the media never reported on however was the sole survivor of the incident. Team Lead Agent Sally DeRosa. The Family didn't even release any information about a survivor internally. It wasn't until word leaked out of Delta that someone had walked away from the explosion that rumors began to swirl.

Chuck had just graduated from training when the stories began to trickle down. Some loose cannon agent acted recklessly and got her whole team killed. Even let a couple of civilians die. The name of Sally DeRosa was run through the mud. Repeatedly.

The incident remained a hot topic for about a month and then quietly disappeared from conversation as new gossip and rumors took its place. That was until July 15th. That day Chuck had walked out of Hines's office, having been officially assigned to Site Alpha. She'd made her way to the cafeteria, planning to share the news with her trainer.

She found him in the company of most of Alpha's agents. Except they hadn't been waiting excitedly to find out her assignment. Instead, they were all sitting, faces glued to their phones. She could tell they weren't happy. Sitting down next to her trainer, he promptly turned his phone so she could read it. The subject line of the email said it all. Agent Transfer: Sally DeRosa to Site Alpha.

The other agents started in again with the stories. They'd warned Chuck not to talk to DeRosa once she arrived. Told her, "Stick with us, kid, and you'll be fine." That had been around seven months ago. Those agents were gone, but she was still here. Her career path had changed in those months.

So had her perception of Sally DeRosa. Chuck realized early in their time together that DeRosa cared deeply about the subjects, and even more deeply for those she was put in charge of. The two of them were together nearly every day, and yet had never once talked about the incident.

***

DeRosa said the name, and then sat there, quiet. Her eyes were bloodshot, the only indication of the three-quarters of a bottle of whiskey she had running through her system. Finally, she blinked, as if remembering where she was. "You ever seen a Dover Demon?"

"Can't say I have," Chuck replied truthfully.

"But you've heard of them?"

Chuck gave a goofy nod. "They're Class Fours and uncommon. The book said they don't have hair, are translucent-skinned, about yea big," She spread her hands out to around four feet apart.

DeRosa stared at her for a moment, then let out a grunt. "Yep, that's them."

Chuck blinked. "Are they the ones with queens?"

DeRosa nodded approvingly. "Bonus points to Charlotte!" She raised her bottle. "The whole thing started because the Kangaroos got wind of cryptid activity to the west of Boston. The usual stuff. Livestock being attacked, people catching glimpses of weird 'dogs' in their headlights. A bunch of kids were having a bonfire one night and caught a blurry picture of this crazy hairless badger as they called it in their viral video."

DeRosa paused, exhaling slowly. "Delta deployed a scout crew. After about a week they report back that they'd found a Demon nest on this farm outside Fitchburg."

Chuck suppressed a burp. "They were rogue?"

DeRosa unscrewed the top to the whiskey. She looked at it for a minute then put the lid back without taking a drink.

"Yeah, they were rogue. It should have been a warning sign. Hell, where they were at should've been a warning sign. Demons usually live deep underground. These ones were a quarter mile from a damn farmhouse."

"Did the scouts know why they were acting weird?"

"I couldn't even tell you. I didn't hear about them until my team answered the code green. Clevenger gathered us up like we were going out on a picnic. Told us how easy this mission would be. Just a quick tag and bag!"

Chuck recognized the name Clevenger. "Oh! I met her once!"

DeRosa raised an eyebrow. "Real Amazon of a woman, like six foot six? Caked on tacky eyeliner?"

Chuck nodded, an action she quickly regretted. "Some people came here for an inspection during my training. She was with them."

DeRosa frowned, then sat staring at the wall for a moment. Her voice sounded strained as she continued the story. "We loaded up and headed out to the property. At night, of course, so as not to arouse too much suspicion. The scouts had mapped the whole place out. Entrances, tracks we could follow to get up to the nest. Patton joked we'd be back in time for her to catch the end of the Sox game."

Chuck looked at DeRosa, surprised to see a single tear had started rolling down the woman's cheek. DeRosa wiped it away. "The Demons were under this old workshop that sat in the middle of a field. We were all laughing and joking as we pulled up to the building. Then Welch taps me on the shoulder and points up towards the shop's roof. A Demon drone was sitting up there. Watching us. I didn't want anyone to get sprayed with acid, so I had Welch roll down a window and put a tranq dart in it."

"Acid?"

"Yeah, they can spit acid. The shit smells terrible, causes second degree burns if you get enough of it on you. Not as bad as those things they have down in Argentina, whatever they call them, but still bad. Anyway, I had Perry collect the thing, while Patton, Welch, and I headed for the nest. I told Fletcher to stay by the vehicle." DeRosa looked at her with haunted eyes. "I'm sorry. You probably don't want to hear all this shit."

Chuck shook her head vigorously. The action felt exaggerated, likely due to the alcohol. "No, please. I want to hear your version of what happened."

DeRosa flashed her a thin smile. "Thank you." She cleared her throat. "We found the queen in a burrow, underneath the shed. She had a small brood, only four workers. I helped Welch throw down some meat spiked with tranquilizers. Patton said she was going to run a sweep around the shed. Next thing I know she's calling for me."

"I walked around the shop and found Patton shining her light into a window. 'You better see this' she said. I peeked in and saw all these bags of fertilizer. Next Patton shined the light at the base of the wall. A pipe ran out from the shed and into the ground. 'Gas line. You don't think these things cut it do you?' I couldn't smell any gas and I told her probably not. We went back to the burrow. Things were running smooth, and the only job left was pulling the queen up."

DeRosa looked at Chuck suddenly. "Wasn't your dad in the military?"

The question was innocent enough. And though she seemed straight as an arrow, DeRosa must have been at least somewhat drunk, because she knew the answer to that question.

"A police officer," Chuck said softly.

"Oh, shit, that's right. I'm sorry, he got killed, didn't he?"

"He got shot serving some dickless loser a warrant, yeah."

"Shot, that's a bitch." DeRosa shook herself, not her head, but her whole body. "If he'd been in the military, he would've called what happened next a snafu." She let out a long sigh, then continued as if this little interlude never happened.

"Fletcher had gathered up two of the workers to take back to the vehicle when he says, 'Boss, there's another drone out in the field.' He points and sure as shit, one of the little bastards had pulled itself up onto an old scarecrow. I grabbed the tranq gun from where it was sitting and popped the sucker from fifty yards. I told the others to finish up, and I'd go get the last one myself. I ran out to where it fell, except it's not there. I looked down to pull a pair of night vision goggles off my belt, and I saw them."

DeRosa stopped. Her breathing had become anxious, like someone waking from a nightmare. "The farmers, they were lying on the ground. Their faces, Christ, their faces. I'll never forget those looks of sheer terror. I heard Patton say something over the radio. I looked up, and that's when I saw the eyes."

"Eyes?"

The senior agent blinked away another tear. "Something with red bug eyes was standing in that field. I only saw them for a second. And then I was flying. I could smell burning fabric and hair. I don't know how far I went in the air, but when I hit the ground I blacked out.

"When I came to, I saw this fountain of flame burning into the night sky. The hairs on my arms had burned off, and I could see steam coming from my uniform. I saw the eyes again—I swear to God they were in the fire. Then they were gone."

DeRosa paused a moment, as if seeing the eyes. When she spoke again, her voice was barely more than a whisper. "It took me a minute to realize where the fire was coming from."

"The shed?"

DeRosa wiped moisture from the corner of one of her eyes. "No... I mean, yes, but the shed had disintegrated. The team, the vehicle, the Demons, they were all gone. And the farmers, the damn field had caught fire all the way out to them. I could smell their bodies burning. But those eyes, I couldn't unsee those eyes. Like they'd burned into my brain even after just a second. My comms were fried. All I could do was sit there and watch. It kept burning, you know. That damn gas line kept the fire going."

Chuck scrunched up her face. There were details from DeRosa's telling of the story that she'd never heard. The goats being the Demons, the farmers already being dead, the red eyes. She could understand covering up the accident, but why would the Family not want to talk about an attack that happened to one of its own teams?

"I don't even remember the ride back to Delta. My back had been broken when I landed, and I spent five days in the infirmary. They had me on so many pain killers that the whole thing passed by in a kind of haze."

"But you told them what you saw right? The eyes, the dead farmers?"

"I told them everything I've told you. And then I told them again and again. They kept asking me the same questions, like maybe I'd remember things in a different way. But I can't ever forget what I saw. I'll go to my grave remembering that night."

"They didn't believe you? Didn't you guys have body cams?"

"We did—we all did. But mine and Patton's were the only ones they could get any footage from. And mine never picked up the farmers, or the eyes. Patton's camera had the footage they started the witch hunt over. You could hear it clear as day when she pointed out those bags of fertilizer. But you know the real bitch of it all? I think Patton saw the eyes. Or whatever they were attached to. I never did find out what she said right before the explosion, but I'm sure she saw those eyes."

Chuck's stomach had started to protest the influx of the sweet wine. She didn't want to interrupt DeRosa though.

"They put me in one of the holding units that normally hold Class Fives. Treated me like the lowest rung of the human totem pole. Had to keep me isolated until they could hold their little kangaroo court."

"Hold up, the Kangaroos hold a court?"

"Oh, sorry, old phrase, I guess. They could have taken me through the normal disciplinary channels, but the Board sure wanted to get their pound of flesh from somebody. And the only one left standing after the cleanup was me."

Chuck sat, transfixed by the story, and confused by the Family's actions. Why would they be out to destroy the reputation of one of their own?

"The strangest part of the whole charade is you don't even get to be present at your own hearing. The Family march in their witnesses, and you get notes the night after they've happened. Complete nonsense."

"That sounds really unfair. What exactly did they accuse you of?"

DeRosa laughed. "They accused me of being derelict in my duty for not stopping the whole thing when we spotted the gas line. One of the notes said I knew the shed might explode and that's why I ran off into the field. All of that, and their biggest problem, the thing that really pissed the Board off the most, was that I claimed we'd encountered a Class One."

"Wait, are you talking about the eyes?" Despite her buzz Chuck had kept up well to this point. But now it felt like something had slipped by her.

DeRosa nodded. "The eyes. Because I said I saw the red eyes." DeRosa's voice bore a hint of anger.

Realization began to grow within Chuck's alcohol slowed mind. The Family deemed the most powerful cryptids Class Ones. The Mothman, The Jersey Devil, and the Kraken down in Mariana Trench were some of the better known among them. They were unique cryptids that agents didn't usually deal with.

DeRosa seemed to be in a bit of a trance, as if she were speaking to someone besides Chuck. "It's widely accepted in the Family's hierarchy that Class Ones have eyes that glow. Usually, red. There are some exceptions, but if you tell a Warden or CIT that you encountered a subject with glowing eyes, they'll probably say you're full of shit. Alternatively, they'll tell you if it had been a real Class One, you'd be dead."

"Are we not on good terms with the Class Ones?"

"We are. At least, that's the line they give us. But if it's rogue and it's a Class One, then it must be out to kill us. That's the position the Board takes at least."

Chuck suddenly felt like a recruit, hearing about Class Ones for the first time. Agents didn't get a whole lot of training concerning these most powerful cryptids. One obvious reason was that the Wardens usually dealt with them. And for as little training as they received concerning Class Ones, they received even less regarding the Wardens.

"If they thought you were such a liar, why are you here?"

DeRosa raised the bottle. "I had a guardian angel."

"Come on. What really happened?"

DeRosa smiled, but not warmly. "Three days they carried on with that crap. And each night I'd get an almost unreadable transcript. Best I could tell the Warden that is arguing to punish you presents a bunch of evidence that you don't even get to see."

"But?" Chuck coaxed.

"But the doctor who was defending me finally started proving the evidence wrong. They were able to show the bodies were already out in the field. Hell, whoever they were even convinced the Board that the gas and fertilizer alone wouldn't have caused that level of destruction. They couldn't prove *what* exactly caused the explosion, but they could prove it *wasn't* due to any negligence on my part."

"You never found out who defended you?"

"Correctamundo. They strike all the names on the reports. I

know they were a doctor, but everyone in CIT has some combination of letters in front of their name, so that didn't really help. In the end—" DeRosa wiped more moisture from her eye. "In the end, they ran my name and my team's names right up the flagpole. The official report said that while no single action could be pointed to that would have caused the incident, one of us must have screwed something up. I'm guessing the Board slept with a clear conscience knowing they had taken a shit all over a group of good agents.

"As a bonus, they got the pound of flesh they wanted out of me. I should've been in line to get Chief Agent. 'Not anymore, Sally. We're sending you out to Alpha, Sally'." DeRosa wiped her eyes again, then winked at Chuck. "Hines called me and said he needed my help with this hotshot new agent that had recently graduated. Asked if I'd come and show her the ropes while she's training a recruit class."

"You're funny."

"The rest, as they say, is history. I doubt there's a single member on that Board that doesn't still consider me responsible. I'm like their own little O.J. Simpson. Guilty even when ruled innocent. Wait, that's not a good comparison." DeRosa let out a hiccup.

"Agent DeRosa, I'd heard of Fitchburg, heard a lot of bad things about you before you arrived. I realize it's only a small sample size, but I don't think you're a liar. I'm sure if you say you saw it, you saw it."

DeRosa smiled. "Don't go being too trusting there, sister. You'll end up with a McFadden!"

Chuck snorted a little, tried to cover her face, and then snorted again.

"And unless we're with the kids," DeRosa continued, "you can call me Sally."

"Oh, in that case you can call me Chuck!"

She froze.

Her dad had once revealed to her he thought of her as Chuck, even though he rarely called her that. The only times he ever used the name, it had been just the two of them.

She adopted the habit after his death, a kind of odd, personal way to remember him. She'd never revealed her dad's nickname to anyone before, ever. The words had fallen from her mouth, practically without effort.

"Chuck? I didn't realize you had a nickname."

Chuck blinked, feeling a sharp, self-directed anger blossoming within her chest. Hot tears welled up in her eyes, causing her anxiety to spike off the charts. The only other adults she'd ever cried in front of were her mom and brothers.

DeRosa reached out an arm. "Hey, it's okay… You don't have to call me Sally."

Chuck accepted her hug as embarrassment and frustration at the whole situation caused even more tears to flow. Slowly, minute by minute she walked it back while DeRosa held her gently. It wasn't a response that Chuck had expected from the senior agent. She didn't know how long she ugly cried, but finally the emotions burned themselves out.

She sat up. DeRosa looked at her with a mix of concern and bewilderment. Chuck closed her eyes, forcing down a second wave that threatened to break her all over again. DeRosa pulled some napkins from the counter and handed them to her.

"Thanks, god, I'm sorry."

DeRosa shook her head. "No need to be. I've been dragging you through all my life's bullshit. That's really not fair of me."

"It's not that. I actually kind of liked hearing about your shitty life." She attempted a smile, which DeRosa warmly returned. The embarrassment had eased, thanks largely to the look of genuine concern in Sally's eyes.

"I just—my dad, he called me Chuck. Like a little secret, that was just between us." She wiped her eyes, composing herself more fully. "I've never told anyone about that name." She took a deep breath. "I started using it when thinking of myself, kind of like I was keeping his memory alive in some small way. It probably sounds stupid, but I got mad that I said it to you."

"Hey, I'm good with Charlotte, Agent Barnes, whatever you like." DeRosa held up her hands as she spoke.

Chuck gave her nose a final wipe. "Sally, I would be honored if you thought of me as Chuck. It's probably past time to let someone else in on my secret. But, you know, not in front of the kids," she finished. Her heart felt like a weight had been lifted off it.

"Scout's honor." DeRosa crossed a finger over her chest.

They laughed and talked for a little longer. By the time Sally had packed up her glasses, and bottles, Chuck wasn't feeling much of the alcohol's effects anymore. As they walked towards the door, DeRosa turned around and gave her another hug.

"Thanks, I really needed that," she released Chuck, smiled, and walked out of the room. Chuck closed the door behind her.

"Me too."

Chapter Twelve:

Abuse of Power

Their blood stained the strange lights they wore, painting the walls a deep shade of crimson. I stood in the light, waiting as my form healed fully. The joy wrought within me at killing these mortals subsided quickly.

I turned to look upon my former prison and quickly regretted it. The glyphs and symbols carved upon the box lashed at me. Their power should have waned, and yet they wracked my mind with voices older than the stones, more forceful than any crashing wave.

How? I shriveled to the ground, placing my hands over my eyes so they wouldn't burst from their slots. Fresh anger welled up from within me.

"What have you done!"

The sound of my own voice simply returned to me in mockery. Mortals, even those as esteemed in the occult as the Rogers, were not meant to dabble in the ancient powers of the world. Without the perspective of a millennia of existence they inevitably overused or abused such powers.

My form, the immortal shell within which I strode upon earth, had healed. And yet, my mind still bubbled with poison and bile. All because of them.

The Rogers must have used too powerful an enchantment on the container. Combined with the ridiculously poor quality of the ritual performed by these fools and now... Now the voices persist.

Voices more ancient than even the stones of this cavern. Voices speaking with the shared memories of a thousand souls. Voices who crave violence, fear, and blood.

These same voices led me out of the cavern, out into a wooded land unfamiliar and foreign to me. I stood a moment, then leaped.

A relief normally reserved for lesser beings filled my heart. Air, so dry and tasteless that it insulted my lungs, couldn't keep me from running and jumping about. Emotions unexpectedly filled my heart to near bursting.

Feelings both strange and exhilarating overwhelmed me, until the voices returned. The rhythmic cadence of their language scolded me, taunted me, reminded me that only one thing held any importance now.

Revenge. Sweet, merciless, revenge.

I had fled the cave too swiftly, chased away from studying the remains of my victims by the strange runes. I knew, with time, I would find new mortals. Ones which I would spare, bringing them under my sway. Mortals who could teach me of this new land I found myself in.

But in that moment, voices or not, I needed to eat. My form, long unnourished, quivered at the possibility of fresh meat and bones to grind between my teeth. I detected the scent of my next victim, and a smile spread across my face.

Chapter Thirteen:

Rochester Organism Gathering Examining & Research Society

Each explosion felt like a knife stabbing into the back of her head.

"FIRE!"

A fresh wave of bangs and booms rattled through the firing range. Of course, she'd have the first hangover of her life on range day.

"FIRE!"

The range instructor, much like Walt, was an old school field agent that'd stepped back to do something more relaxing. She doubted he was being intentionally louder than normal this morning, but still.

"Good work there, Roberts! But focus more on the vital organs."

Most of the last hour had been spent with their normal armament of pistols. However, during the last fifteen minutes he'd switched the recruits over to using rifles. Marcy and Greg were currently doing the best.

"Keep the end of that weapon up, Lee! And quit trying to make every shot a head shot! Damn Call of Duty junkies!"

Jess had long been the least capable at using the weapons. The fact she was pegged as being a future Kangaroo meant her failings at shooting weren't really held against her.

"Sorry, sir."

The instructor walked up and down the line a couple more times, finally coming to a stop a few feet from Chuck. "Cease fire! Cease fire! You have three minutes to present weapons for inspection!" Thankfully, he had brought the volume down to a much more tolerable level.

Chuck waited near the entrance until all the recruits had gone through inspection and then returned their weapons to the armory.

Rita was the final one to wander over to the assembled group. She gave Chuck a sideways look. "You sure you feel okay, Agent Barnes?"

"I'll be fine, Rita, thanks. We're going to go grab an early lunch, DeRosa wants to meet with me at two, so you'll be attending labs without me today."

The recruits shrugged, clearly not all that worried about the small change in routine. Walking single file, they made their way to the cafeteria.

A smattering of administrative assistants and security team members sat, mostly in solitude, throughout the vast space. The constant drone of the thirty-year-old TV's that ran on loop inside the cafeteria reached Chuck's ear as she got in line at the sandwich station behind Marcy. *"Maraleen Rogers, our society's founder, envisioned a world where creatures of all shapes, sizes, and histories, could live together in harmony."* She'd reached the point that she could almost recite the entire five-minute video from memory.

Though not all that hungry, she grabbed a plain ham and Swiss and went to pick up a couple of water bottles as the narrator rolled on.

"The first meeting was held in Rochester, New York State, on March 12th, 1865, at Maraleen's home. All four of the Rogers siblings, and several cousins were in attendance..."

Thankfully, the talk at the table drowned out the indoctrination stream. The recruits were mostly lamenting their missed day of phone access.

"They better use some of my good selfies to fill the gaps." Rita told Jess, as though she had some say in what the Kangaroos did.

Josh tapped Chuck on the arm. "You ever been to any of the other sites, Agent Barnes?"

She glanced at the faded map of the lower forty-eight states painted on the cafeteria wall. Embarrassingly, it only showed the location of sites up to Epsilon. "No, not yet. Is there one you have your eye on?"

Josh finished chewing before he responded. "I grew up not far from Gama, it would be kind of cool to go there. I'm an Atlanta boy, through and through."

"They don't usually assign new agents to sites close to their homes, but who knows, you might get lucky."

Rita, having evidently heard the conversation, joined in. "I want to go anywhere but Delta. I love Boston, but I want to see the rest of the world while I'm young."

Greg nodded. "Europe would be cool."

Chuck took a sip of her water. "You'll get plenty of action if you go there. Europe's crawling with Griffins."

Jess frowned. "I thought they were mostly in China and Russia. That's where Pisa Pharmaceuticals is based."

"True, though they operate a lot of other businesses besides Pisa. Most of their special operations units train in and around eastern Europe, and they recruit those regions hard."

"If they're all like that McFadden asshole DeRosa beat up yesterday, I'm not too worried," Marcy said confidently. The others nodded their approval.

Chuck didn't want to kill their mood, so she smiled and stayed quiet. Here in America, the Griffins didn't pose much of a threat. But based on what she'd heard, overseas they were much more sophisticated. Foreign Griffin operatives often looked like James Bond villains, regularly carrying cryptid enhanced tech, much like the Family's own Wardens.

In the background, she heard the video continue along its monotonous loop. *"Maraleen named the fledgling group the Rochester Organism Gathering Examining and Research Society..."*

***

Fifteen minutes ahead of schedule she arrived back in the cafeteria, having taken a quick power nap. DeRosa was already there, and Chuck sat across from her. The senior agent's eyes were bloodshot, and her hair was messy, evidently she hadn't recovered yet from the previous night's drinking.

"Hey, Chuck, I see you made it through the morning."

"It was rough, but yeah, I'm still standing. How about you?"

DeRosa simply shook her head. She tore the lid off a cup of mixed fruit and started eating. "I would have slept in if I could've gotten my head out of the toilet. I think this is the first thing I've eaten all day," she said between chews.

"Ouch." Chuck quickly pushed the image of Sally throwing up from her head. "Did you just want to check on me, or is there an ulterior motive behind this meeting?"

"I don't know that I'd call it ulterior. Hines moved up next week's physical exams to tomorrow."

She had to think for a moment about why this would be particularly interesting news. "Wait, you mean Gavin is coming tomorrow?"

DeRosa nodded.

While this would normally be a reason to celebrate, the repercussions of what it meant dampened her excitement. She and DeRosa would need to go out tonight to pick up Gavin and his family, ensuring another late night.

"Hmm, well, that's cool. The recruits will certainly be excited. What time are we leaving?"

DeRosa cracked the top of her Diet Coke and washed down the remainder of her fruit cup. "No later than nine-thirty." She rubbed her head. "God that drive is going to suck."

Chuck gave DeRosa a moment of silence hoping it might help her friend's headache. As she did, she again picked up on the sterile female voice coming from the cafeteria's TV's. *"group the Rochester Organism Gathering Examining and Research Society and began training fellow members how to identify and care for the local cryptid population."*

"I guess we can meet at Warehouse 3, say nine?"

Without opening her eyes or removing her hand from her head, DeRosa nodded yes.

"I'll see you tonight then."

***

Chuck arrived at Warehouse 3 a couple minutes late. Less than half the size of the other warehouse buildings, it stood out because of its lack of windows and pitched roof. A semi-truck and trailer emblazoned with Rice Lake Home Goods logos sat idling in front of the loading dock. DeRosa stood nearby, flipping through a notebook.

"Feeling any better?"

Sally turned to her. "Yeah, mostly." She pointed at the truck. "Looks like they got us a brand-new rig."

"Nice. We about ready to head out?"

Flipping the notebook closed, Sally headed for the driver's side door. "Yeah, let's get this show on the road."

Chuck climbed in the passenger seat. The height of the big rigs always took a moment to get used to. Sally was right about the truck, it even smelled new.

"Damn, these new electric engines run smooth," DeRosa said as they pulled onto the interstate and into the flow of traffic. At some point in her youth, Sally had learned how to drive eighteen-wheelers. It made wellness runs more comfortable, as they didn't need to bring along a driver.

"Did you hear anything about that Mog we recovered yesterday?" Chuck asked.

Sally nodded. "A lot actually. Doc gave me the skinny when I went to get Gavin's intake papers. You know how its throat had been ripped out?"

"I mean, it would be pretty hard to forget."

"Doc found its throat, in the back of the thing's mouth."

Chuck grimaced. "It ripped out its own throat and then tried to eat it?"

"That's the way it looks." Sally thankfully kept her eyes glued to the road as they picked up speed leaving the outskirts of the city. "Mogs are known to lash out, and even self-harm, but Doc thinks it might have something to do with that blue stuff around its face."

Between the previous night's drinking and her subsequent hangover, Chuck had forgotten about the blue substance on the Mog's face. "Did Doc figure out what it was?"

"No, he asked me if I'd noticed any fungus or other oddly colored plant life in the area. The stuff reminded him of spores when he looked at it under a microscope."

She tried to recall details of the scene. "There wasn't anything like that in the grove when Marcy and I checked it out."

"Yeah, I told him I hadn't noticed anything. Then again, McFadden had me so pissed off, I'll admit I could've easily missed something. Either way, it sounds like Delta took a serious interest in that Mog's body. Doc said they've already shipped it back east."

Chuck wondered exactly what method of transportation you would use to ship a six-hundred-pound monster corpse. "Is it normal for them to take over an investigation like that?"

"For Delta there is no normal. We could find a three-headed Bear Lake monster and they may completely ignore it. The next week you find a Lizard Man that happens to only have four fingers, and they lose their shit."

Chuck shook her head. "Welp, I guess that makes it their problem now?"

Sally flashed her a quick smile. "Spoken like a jaded agent. I must be rubbing off on you Chuck."

She reclined her seat a bit, the rhythm of the road beneath them making her sleepy. "I can think of worse things." Sally laughed, and Chuck closed her eyes, hoping to get some sleep before they reached Gavin.

Chapter Fourteen:

Gavin

"Hey sister, wake up." Sally's voice cut through Chuck's slumber, jolting her awake.

She wiped a bit of drool from the side of her mouth, feeling the big rig shake as it left the paved road for one covered in loose dirt and gravel. The forest always felt ominous during these night pickups. The headlights split the darkness directly in front of them, but on either side, shadowy shapes lurked, passing silently by.

"Do I need to call Alpha and have them send Gavin a signal?" Chuck asked as they rolled deeper into the mountainous terrain.

"Nah, this baby is equipped with all kinds of good stuff. I already sent him the signal. They should be waiting for us when we get there."

"Well damn. Okay then."

Sally shifted in her seat. "The one thing it's missing is a pisser. I'm going to have to squat in the woods before we head back."

"Thanks for that information. Although now that you've mentioned it, I'm probably going to have to do the same." The bumpy road wasn't helping matters.

A green light flashed directly ahead of them, and Sally began to slow the truck down. They soon pulled into a small clearing, just big enough for the truck to turn around. The western states were riddled with logging roads, some of which the Family maintained to provide convenient pick up and drop off locations for subjects that needed to be examined in person from time to time.

As the truck swung around, five hairy, bipedal shapes came walking into the beam of the truck's headlights. Gavin was the head of a large family of sasquatch that included his mate Sheila, their biological daughters Daisy and May, and an adopted daughter, Sparkles.

DeRosa parked the truck while the Bigfoot family waited

patiently. Chuck had barely gotten her feet on the ground before Sparkles was there, enveloping her in a hug. Chuck returned it, the earthy, pungent odor of her friend causing her eyes to water a bit. Daisy and May weren't far behind, each of the sasquatch youth taking an opportunity to show Chuck some love.

Gavin and Sheila waited their turn. He smiled as they approached, his yellowing teeth standing out brightly in contrast to his burgundy-colored fur.

While all the bigfoot variants had a common language, Gavin displayed exceptional intelligence and had learned ASL. He signed 'Hello Friend' to Chuck, simultaneously clicking in the normal sasquatch dialect.

Doc once told Chuck there were even higher functioning sasquatch that worked with the Wardens. Considering the source, she wasn't entirely sure if she believed it, but in observing Gavin she felt it could be perfectly plausible.

He picked her up and as usual she marveled at how gentle his hulking form could be. Sheila was looking around and it occurred to Chuck that DeRosa hadn't come from around the truck yet. Evidently she really did need to pee.

"Where is Sally?" Gavin signed after he returned Chuck to the ground.

"She's stretching her legs." Chuck replied, knowing she would also need to stretch her own legs soon enough.

As if on cue, Sally came around the back side of the trailer causing the youth to run in her direction. No longer being smothered with hugs, Chuck realized how much colder the night was at this heightened elevation.

"Okay, okay ladies," Sally called as she too disappeared behind an onslaught of hugs. "Let's get you all loaded so we can get home."

"Has everything been good?" Chuck asked Gavin as he took Sheila's hand in his.

"Cold, but good." He paused a moment to hug his mate. "No Griffins." Gavin signed with a smile.

She gave him a thumbs up. As Class Twos, sasquatches were the most advanced cryptids that typical field agents would encounter. They were also the most endangered.

Lower classed cryptids were prevalent enough that the Family primarily dealt in population control. On occasion they would have to herd creatures into new territories to shield them from humans.

Sasquatches however faced several major challenges, the first being habitat or more precisely, the lack of good habitat. Secondly, they reproduced slowly. Gavin's clan was the biggest under Alpha's sway. Most were no more than a mated couple with maybe a single offspring. The final and most pressing challenge was that sasquatch were a prized catch for the Griffins.

"Up you go!" Sally said as she helped Sparkles into the trailer. The inside had been adorned with oversized seats that allowed the creatures room to sit comfortably. Each was equipped with an oversized seatbelt, and a small compartment of snacks for them to enjoy on the journey back to Alpha.

"I'll see you in the morning." Chuck signed to Gavin as he climbed in last. He flashed a big toothy grin at her then disappeared as Sally pulled down the trailer's door.

"Let's get back and catch some shut eye," Sally said as she placed a lock on the door.

"One sec, I still need to make a pit stop."

"Okay but watch out for poison ivy."

Chuck frowned. "It's too cold for poison ivy." She turned, intending to make a run for the tree line.

"You sure about that?" Sally asked as she headed for the front of the truck.

Chuck stood in thought a moment, then pulled down her pants and leaned against the truck, not willing to take any chances.

***

Not long after finishing breakfast, she and the recruits were standing in the medical wing, waiting on the elevator up to Warehouse 3. The surprise news that Gavin and his clan were on site had the group buzzing. The clan were a favorite with most of Alpha's staff.

They piled into the oversized compartment. The elevator creaked and groaned as it ascended. Once they reached the warehouse, they followed a short hallway leading to a small room. Here a nurse checked their IDs, then readied them for decontamination.

All checked in, they lined up at the entrance to the decontamination chamber. One by one they donned surgical masks and entered the room. A faint whiff of lilac and a hot breeze, and you were done. Beyond the decom chamber two members of security waited to finish the check-in process. All this was only required when the labs were in use; most of the time Warehouse 3 sat empty.

Chuck led her recruits out into the receiving floor. The tractor trailer from the previous night sat parked in the middle. The walls, floor, and ceiling were covered in a stark white anti-bacterial coating that made the whole place exceptionally bright. Both sides of the warehouse were lined with what resembled oversized patient rooms.

Gavin's family currently took up a room each. Staff wearing black aprons and matching surgical masks were busy tending to today's guests, giving haircuts, manicures, and pedicures. Chuck could see Doc and a nurse in the last room. They were gathering swabs and samples from each member of the sasquatch family.

Gavin sat in the closest room, and as the recruits approached, he waved his huge hand in greeting. Marcy and Jess both knew ASL and began carrying on quite a little conversation with him.

Rita, and therefore Greg, moved down to look in on Sheila. Chuck blew a kiss to Gavin who signed back "I love you" before she followed Josh down the line of rooms. They came to a stop in front of Daisy's room. The diminutive squatch lay spread out on a massage table with two big slices of cucumber over her eyes. Chuck and Josh waved to the staff, and then proceeded to May, whose room Doc had now entered.

The Family cross-trained many of the administrative employees to be glorified pet groomers, a side effect of Alpha's staffing shortages. While it looked like they were getting a spa treatment, this was a way to make sure the subjects were healthy. Each registered and tracked clan were brought in once or twice a year to check vitals, replace or repair tracking chips, and the like.

The glass in front of Sparkles's room slid away, and Chuck waved to get everyone's attention. They all gathered as Sparkles came out and sat down on an oversized bench a few feet out from her assigned room. They immediately showered her with hugs and affection, which the medium-sized bigfoot returned with aplomb. She made a clicking noise with her tongue, followed by short little grunts. Sparkles wasn't as high functioning as Gavin, and her words were sometimes hard to make out, but Chuck got the gist of it.

"Yes, you are pretty, Sparkles," she replied.

Sparkles enveloped Josh in a hug. Her hand darted down and grabbed the recruit's butt. Josh let out a laugh, as did Sparkles.

Greg made a few short clicks with his tongue, then pointed at himself. Speaking to a squatch was a combination of making noises and pointing your fingers in different directions. Greg had gotten particularly good with the language. The masks, however, presented a problem, often muffling the intricate sounds needed to bring clarity to words. Despite the barrier, Sparkles understood Greg was claiming to be jealous. With bravado she hugged him and grabbed his butt too.

Chuck pulled out her hair tie and took up a position behind Sparkles. She pulled back a bit of Sparkles's hair and tied it up. This ritual stretched back all the way to their first meeting. Sparkles loved the feel of the topknot and once the tie was secure, she stood to give Chuck a hug.

A moment later May's wall retracted. She was the youngest and smallest of Gavin's clan, standing barely as tall as Rita. She also had the most energy, immediately jumping up and down, asking for high fives from the recruits. The group separated out a bit to accommodate the new arrival. Back in the now sasquatch-less rooms, the staff were vacuuming up hair and sterilizing all the surfaces.

Daisy got to come out next. Besides Gavin, she might have been the most human-like of the clan. She loved to play with the women's jewelry, hair, and nails. If it had been decorated in any way, Daisy was curious about it. She had a special fondness for Rita, who showed off the dyed tips she'd added to her hair since the last time Daisy saw her.

When Sheila came out, she modeled the small flowers the groomers had used to decorate her head. Daisy begged her mother for one of the flowers and Sheila obliged.

Once Gavin had finally been let out, he made a beeline towards the group. He met Marcy first and gave her a hug.

"My man!" Sheila protested.

Marcy held up her hands in surrender. "Your man," she clicked back.

Gavin shrugged his shoulders at his mate before going over and giving her a hug, which delighted Rita and Jess. Chuck was glad all her recruits were comfortable with the subjects. Despite the care and protection of cryptids being one of its primary tenants, there were still many members of the Family who weren't all that keen being around them.

Doc came walking over with a nurse who had a rolling trunk dotted with biohazard markings in tow. "How's the nose, Charlotte?"

"Fine, Doc. Everyone looking healthy?"

"The usual bumps and bruises, but nothing out of the ordinary." He looked down at the trunk. "Of course, we'll have to run the labs, but I didn't see anything that would raise alarms."

"That's good to hear."

"Alice and I need to get going, if I'm going to get in eighteen holes before dinner." Doc patted Gavin on the arm and gave him a thumbs up as he walked by. Gavin returned the gesture, and the others waved as Doc and Alice headed out.

Doc had barely left when Smalls and another Kangaroo Agent came in. She looked different without a phone glued squarely to her face.

Stepping up to Chuck, Smalls looked at the recruits and subjects with an indifferent eye. "Good afternoon, Agent Barnes."

"Hello, Deputy Smalls." She motioned to Gavin and then clicked out 'line up' to the other members of the clan.

Smalls pulled out a tablet. "Thank you."

She stepped up and began scanning the chips each of the sasquatch had embedded in their arms. She started with Gavin, holding up the tablet and reading information, some of which she passed on to the other techie who would feed it into a separate tablet.

Smalls' usual frantic nature always seemed to be on hold around the cryptids. Granted, Chuck had only ever seen her with them in this setting, but it made her wonder how comfortable Smalls was with the other creatures in their care.

When Gavin's turn ended, he returned to Chuck's side. He clicked away with questions about some of the other squatch families. As a species, they were somewhat territorial. Gavin probably wouldn't go into another group's territory unless pressed to, but he liked to keep up with how the others were doing.

After Smalls finished with Sparkles, she pulled out another device, quickly swiping and tapping at its screen. After some discussion between her and the other Kangaroo, Smalls headed back towards Chuck and Gavin. The deputy, who couldn't understand the sasquatch's language, asked Chuck to translate for her.

"Let Subject 100510 know that we will need them to come back a bit sooner than normal. We downloaded some new software today, but based on these initial readings, I'm guessing we are going to need to upgrade their chips." As was customary, Smalls said all of this without looking at Chuck directly. Having said her piece, Smalls turned and headed towards the exit, her assistant following close behind.

Chuck turned to Gavin and explained the situation, making sure to look at Sheila as well. Gavin's mate clearly appreciated being involved in these types of conversations.

Chuck and her recruits spent the rest of their morning with the clan talking or playing little games, but the arrival of Hines and DeRosa eventually brought a conclusion to their visit. Parting hugs were exchanged, and all in all she left feeling that it had been a good day.

Based on the recruits' smiles at lunch, it seemed they felt the same.

Chapter Fifteen:

Media Day the Second

The good vibes from Gavin's visit continued to reverberate throughout the coming days. The recruits were functioning more independently now, completing tasks without being instructed to. Alpha's Lead CIT, Dr. Ty Cole, returned from his Hawaii assignment as planned, easing Doc's workload. Chuck had a long but pleasant conversation with her brothers on Sunday. To top it all off, at Monday's command meeting Hines announced the agents attending training in Canada would be completing their assignment a full month early.

"I know that doesn't help you all that much right now," Hines said to her and DeRosa. "But at least there's a light at the end of the tunnel."

He paused and cleared his throat before looking at Smalls, who sat stone faced. "On that note, Agents DeRosa and Barnes, you have both demonstrated remarkable willingness to act under pressure, while also doing the work of multiple agents. I have submitted commendations for both of you to Delta."

Chuck sat up, the statement catching her completely by surprise.

"Agent Barnes, the work you're doing with this recruit class has been top notch. You should be proud, and when you have finished this cycle, I feel it would be appropriate to make you a full-time training agent."

Everyone at the table but DeRosa clapped in congratulations.

"Um, thank you, Chief Agent."

It was all she could get out. As hard as Chuck worked and tried to make an impression on her superiors, recognition, especially high-level recognition, was not something she'd fully learned to accept yet. Something tugged at the back of her mind. A promotion to training agent would catapult her much further into being vested with the Family.

She'd chosen to be an agent, and she loved the work. However, at least some of that had been predicated on the thought she had plenty of time. Before… before she became a lifer, like Sally.

Hines then turned to Sally. "Agent DeRosa, I am requesting you be reinstated as a Team Lead Agent."

Chuck had been pleasantly surprised by Hine's compliments. Sally, on the other hand, looked upset. Her brow remained furrowed as the other members of the table repeated their clapping.

Hines stared at Sally for a moment as though he'd expected her to react. When she didn't, he continued. "Now, I know you and I haven't always seen eye to eye. But I would say that considering the circumstances, you consistently performed at a level that few other Agents could have—or for that matter—*would* have done."

Smalls gave a little half cough that must have been intentional. It made Chuck want to throw a pen at her. DeRosa finally spoke up.

"I mean, Chief, I'm honored that you'd even broach the subject with Delta. But, if I may speak freely…" Hines held out a hand, inviting her to continue. "Isn't this kind of a glad-handing gesture at best? You don't seriously think Delta is going to approve that, do you?"

"I appreciate your candor, Sally, but frankly this is a change in name only. You have been *leading* your team for three months now." Hines gestured to Chuck.

DeRosa looked angrier but kept her cool. "May we talk about this later, sir?"

Hines narrowed his eyes, giving Chuck the impression this hadn't been the reaction he expected. "Certainly, Agent."

The remainder of the meeting had an air of tension to it. Smalls reported on the various shenanigans the Kangaroos were up to, while Doctor Ty reported on the labs that had come back from Gavin and his group. By the time lunch rolled around, Chuck was thankful for the chance to stand up.

They'd barely left the briefing room when DeRosa let out her frustrations. "He's shipping me off! That prick hates having me here so much, he's willing to put his ass on the line just to get rid of me."

Chuck frowned. "I don't follow."

"He wants to put me back at Lead Agent status, which means the next time a Team Lead position comes open, Delta can ship me off to take charge of that team. Hines knows that. Oh, he damn well knows that."

"Wouldn't that be a great big middle finger to Delta though, if they admit you're good enough to lead a team?"

"Sure, until they choose to send me to Alaska or Nova Scotia or Ecuador. One of those go-between stations with a little ragtag group of forgotten agents, where Wardens stop occasionally to take a shit and that's about all."

"Wait, are forward stations really that bad?" As an agent you learned they existed, but the Family didn't tell you much about them. Chuck assumed they operated like miniature versions of the primary sites.

"It's basically five people all crammed together with a common area, a communications hub, and a garage for some old-ass form of transportation."

"I thought Hines seemed pretty sincere."

"Maybe. I'll see you later. I have some calls to make."

And with that DeRosa and Chuck split.

Chuck thought about the whole exchange during lunch. Sally had become more than a mentor; she'd become a friend. The prospect of no longer having her around didn't sit well with Chuck.

As she walked into the gym that afternoon, a thought occurred to her. It had been exactly one week since she'd sparred with Greg. From here on out, self-defense training would be full contact. She knew at some point he would want a rematch. Today wouldn't be the day though.

Chuck sat down to wrap her hands a moment before Rita came into the locker room and took a seat right next to her. Chuck gave the recruit a look. Rita was watching Josh, who was stuffing clothes into his locker. With a grunt, he closed it and headed for the exit.

Once Josh was out of sight, Rita turned to her, "Umm, Agent Barnes?"

"Yes, Rita."

"Can I ask you a kind of personal question?"

She had to work hard not to let her shoulders slouch. "You can, although I'm not making any promises as to an answer."

"Why did you become an agent?"

Chuck looked at the younger woman closely. Rita studied her just as intently.

"I guess it had something to do with wanting to get away from where I grew up. Seeing the world and all that." Rita really did appear to be paying close attention, so she continued. "My dad, he used to tell me stories about things he'd seen while doing late night duty as a cop. Lights in the sky, big shadowy forms at the edge of his headlights."

"Hold up, your dad saw subjects?"

"He certainly seemed to think he had. Before he died we used to spend Sunday nights watching specials about Bigfoot and the Mothman. You know those ones with the guy who has the big hair? Honestly, if someone had told me back in those days what my life would be like at twenty, I'd have called them a liar."

Rita scrunched up her face. "I wish I got along with my dad like that."

"Rita, what's this all about?"

She frowned. "Sorry, I just. Today, for some reason I suddenly felt bad about leaving my mom. I used to think she was being a bitch to me and my brother, especially after she remarried. But the more I see how put together everyone around here is, the more I'm starting to wonder if maybe I was the problem. That probably sounds stupid."

Chuck swallowed the lump in her throat, Rita's words ringing a familiar note as she thought about the relationship she had with her own mother. "That doesn't sound stupid to me." She placed an arm around Rita's shoulders. "I think we all have to do some self-reflection once we join up. When was the last time you sent your mom an email, or recorded a voicemail for the Kangaroos to send her?"

The recruit shrugged. "Christmas, I think."

"Tomorrow seems like as good a time as any to reach out and tell her you miss her, or you love her, or whatever. I'm sure your mom is proud of you."

Rita smiled at her. "Thanks, Agent Barnes. I'm glad you're my trainer."

"I'm glad I get to have you as a recruit. You're going to make a great CIT one day."

"God, now you're starting to *sound* like my mom."

"I think my accent would have to change drastically for that to be true." Chuck replied, prompting a smile from her recruit. They stood and headed into the gym.

Everyone brought their best during the afternoon's training. Chuck particularly enjoyed seeing Greg be A) helpful and B) responsive to criticism. By the time everyone had gone their rounds in the ring, there were a couple of fresh bruises but also plenty of smiles.

She walked over to Greg as the group gathered their gear. "You didn't overreach once today. Good job."

He gave her his trademark smirk. "If I don't get better you'll just kick my ass again in a couple weeks."

She couldn't argue with the logic. "You're right, but don't go too hard on the others. I want them to learn, not get frustrated."

"Sure thing, Agent." He looked over her shoulder. "You think maybe tomorrow we can stay out a bit extra? You know, cause we got cut short last week."

Chuck glanced back to see Rita staring at her.

"Probably not, you two got something planned?"

Greg quickly picked up his bag. "Oh, uh, who? No, no plans." He stammered as he moved towards the exit. Rita hurried to catch up to him.

***

At three-forty-five in the morning Chuck's alarm went off. She immediately headed into her own bathroom, rectifying the mistake she had made the previous week. Mothman and his ridiculous penis would have to wait for another time to stare her down.

After grabbing her clothes, she headed for the locker room. She liked being there first, and as usual the other women didn't disappoint. Jess ended up being the first one down, a change in form for the tech recruit.

"Damn, Agent Barnes, do you even go to bed?" Jess said groggily.

"I do in fact, Jess. Although I'm not used to seeing you down here first. To what do I owe this early arrival?" Chuck pepped up her response beyond how she truly felt, her attempt to annoy bearing fruit as Jess groaned and then slinked into a stall.

"Do you think it's too late for me to switch to being a Field Agent?" Beyond the fact that it was called out from behind a bathroom stall door, the question surprised her.

"I don't really know. Why would you want to do that?"

"I mean, I don't know. I like Agent Moseby alright"—the flushing of the toilet interrupted her—"but you guys. You get to go, like out. I mean *out,* out. I like hacking and shit but, it's just *soooo* damn boring around here. And most of the people I'd be working with are fat old guys. Not that being fat and old is a problem, but it really limits the dating pool. I mean, you know what I'm saying right?"

"That's a lot to process this early in the morning, Jess, but I'll tell you what. Maybe we can talk about it later today once we get on campus."

Jess walked up to the sink beside her. "Thanks. Don't tell the others yet, I'm still not sure what to do."

"You keep the dick jokes to a minimum today, and I'll consider it."

Jess flipped her hair over her shoulder. "No promises there."

Rita and Marcy entered then. They looked about as awake as Jess. Chuck turned her head to greet them when suddenly everything went dark.

"What the f—" An alarm blared, drowning out the rest of Jess's statement.

Strobing lights pierced the darkness, casting an eerie glow over the assembled women.

Chuck's watch started its own wailing. She looked down, knowing what she would see: *ALERT.*

Rita threw her hands up in the air. "You've got to be shitting me!"

"Sorry, ladies. Duty calls." Chuck did her best to gather up her stuff in the dark. She didn't know why the lights had gone out, but thankfully before she'd made it down the hall they came back on. The drone of the recruits complaining disappeared as she headed through the doors.

She went straight to her apartment, changing into her field

uniform. She wasn't surprised to find DeRosa waiting for her as she stepped towards the command center.

"You're up early," DeRosa joked as she approached.

"Yeah, the recruits were pissed."

"God, the days are all running together on me lately. Sucks to be you I guess."

The alarms fell silent as Chuck shrugged. "Some days more than others."

DeRosa swiped her card and the door opened. Unlike the previous week, the center was full of people. These were admins, clearly preparing for the briefing. Chuck wondered if this had anything to do with the Mogollon from the previous week.

They'd barely made it into their seats when the side door opened. Hines, Smalls, and Cole entered the room.

"Do you have an update, Ann?" Hines called. The energy in the room was unlike any Chuck had felt before. The whole operation felt almost staged, like the previous week's emergency had been handled rather *laissez faire*, but today someone was watching.

"Bringing it up in ten seconds, Chief," Smalls responded.

"DeRosa. Barnes. About thirty minutes ago we received an emergency signal from one of Clan Seven's members." Hines pointed to the large monitor directly across from where they sat.

Chuck gasped. "That's Gavin's group."

A wide shot of a mountainous area came into view on the monitor. "Around three twenty we started seeing irregular readings from Subject 100701, Sparkles. Elevated heart rate, a sharp dip in oxygen saturation and blood pressure. About three minutes later, both Subjects 100510 and 100487, Gavin and Sheila, suddenly started showing equally elevated heart rates. At three twenty-eight Subject Sparkle's readings suddenly ceased, we believe due to interference. Less than a minute later Subject Gavin sent in the emergency signal." Smalls relayed this entire stream of information without looking up and in a tone that would have made someone only listening to the spiel assume that a computer had delivered it.

"We have a visual from the stationary satellite," one of the admins said from behind her.

The still frame changed. The location appeared to be the same, but it was a bit closer, and more in focus. The video shook badly, but even through its chop you could see three spots that popped with the red and yellow hues warm objects make through an infrared lens.

Hines moved closer to the monitor. "Is that them?"

"We have visual of Gavin, Sheila, and at least one offspring. Sparkles is not represented in this image," the admin responded.

"Where is she?"

The image refocused and panned back a bit. Suddenly it froze, and a red line appeared on the screen, remarkably close to where the three sasquatches were huddled.

"We believe this is a crevasse." As if to prove the point, a daytime image appeared overlaying the nighttime image. A long but narrow fissure was clearly visible.

Hines stepped back. "Damn, are we assuming she's down that cliff then?"

"It is the most likely scenario, based on the disappearance of the subject's signal and the gathering of the fellow clan members," Smalls responded as mechanically as before.

Hines' voice held a tinge of doubt as he spoke. "Is she alive? Can we even help her at this point?"

For the first time, Smalls raised her head as she responded. "I'm not sure, Chief. We are trying now to focus on that transmitter's feed. But it may take some time to get a confirmation of vital signals."

"I don't think Gavin would have called for us if he didn't think we could save her," Chuck pleaded. Gavin knew how to solve problems, but in the dark, on difficult footing, he probably didn't want to risk harming more of his clan. She felt sure that he'd called them because he truly needed help.

As Chuck finished speaking, DeRosa reached over and squeezed her arm. "I think Agent Barnes is right. We need to get up there as quickly as possible."

"Sally, I know you can see how dangerous a rescue in that area is going to be. The sun won't even be up for a couple of hours." Hines ran his fingers through his hair. Chuck hadn't seen him this concerned before. She felt goosebumps rise on her arms as her own nerves went into high alert.

"Doppler Radar indicates a strong storm will be arriving in the area from the west by mid-morning," Smalls said as she swiped at her tablet. A smaller screen switched to a wide view, indicating clouds and snow moving towards the region.

"What about calling for the Wardens?" another admin suggested.

"We can get there before they would even launch a squad." DeRosa brought up the keyboard in front of her. "That site is twenty, thirty minutes max by chopper."

"I'll go," Cole said, turning to Hines.

"I'm sure Agent Moseby would be willing to accompany again. He should be able to establish a solid connection to the vital readings once he is on site," Smalls volunteered.

DeRosa spoke, calm and levelheaded, "Chief, if we are going to help Sparkles then we need to go. This is what we train and run drills for. Unless we plan on calling in the National Guard."

Hines scratched at the stubble on his face, then nodded. "If we're going to do this, we'll need at least one security team member." He nodded in the direction of one of the admins, who quickly left the room.

"Listen Sally, I'm trusting you to make the calls on this one. If we can facilitate the save, we do it. If we can't, well." He paused as the room absorbed his words.

Sally exhaled audibly. "Despite reports to the contrary, boss, I don't put my teams in danger. I'll make the call."

Hines nodded. "I'll submit the request to Delta. Those of you that are going need to get ready. You'll want to bring climbing gear. Ty, call ahead to Deer Valley so they can make sure the chopper has any medical supplies you may need." Hines rattled all this off while furiously typing in approval codes. "Let's get moving people!"

Everyone in the room moved at once. The fact this was Gavin's family clearly held weight with all present. Chuck hurried to her apartment and gathered her gear in record time, even remembering to grab a protein bar for the flight, then rushed to the elevator.

During the ride topside she couldn't stop thinking of the satellite images. Could a chopper even land in that area? What effect would the storm have on their efforts? How had Sparkles ended up falling into the crevasse in the first place?

As she stepped out of the elevator she saw that an emergency van already sat idling in the warehouse. Walt handed gear to a member of the security team who loaded it into the back of the transport. She recognized the security member's face but could not think of his name as she approached them.

"Good morning, Ms. Charlotte!" Walt beamed as he loaded climbing gear from a cart that had been pulled up to the back of the van. His rather cheery mood grated on her for a moment, but she pushed the feeling aside. Walt had one mood, even under pressure.

"Hey, Walt." She stepped up, hoping she didn't sound as dour as she felt.

"You brought gloves, right?" DeRosa's voice startled her. Somehow Sally had beaten her to the warehouse floor.

"Jesus, Sally, you scared the shit out of me."

DeRosa gave her a wink, then sat down on a compartment lid to close it enough to be latched.

Ding!

Tillman and Cole stepped out of the elevator. Chuck really liked the look of the Kangaroos' field gear, but CIT by far had the most badass of any of the uniforms she'd encountered while in the Family. The dolphin grey suit was something out of a sci-fi movie, complete with a utility belt. Red pockets and straps completed the look, hiding various medical instruments.

"Deer Valley says the helo will be ready in ten," Cole said, climbing into the vehicle.

"Then I'll have you there in eight!" Walt declared as he closed the doors.

Chapter Sixteen:

In the Dark

As promised, eight minutes later they were pulling up beside a remote rescue helicopter. It had a larger body than the one they'd used the previous week. The dual bay doors were open, and the rotors were spinning slowly.

They switched modes of transport as quickly as they could. Cole took an inventory of the equipment while the rest of the group put on warm outer layers. They each took a seat, grabbing the headphones resting above each station. Chuck sat between Tillman and their assigned security member. Cole climbed up last, closing the doors behind him.

This chopper had two pilots, and Chuck quickly recognized one of them as the pilot from the previous week, the southern drawl giving him away. Cole signaled the cockpit with a thumbs up, and almost immediately the big helo lifted off the ground.

During the flight she discovered the security member's name was Jordan Kahn, who grew up not far from where Chuck lived in Florida. The former marine had been with the Family for nearly ten years. The conversation provided a distraction from the task at hand, if only a brief one. Her watch had barely logged thirty minutes before the pilot's voice came over the headsets.

"We're approaching the LZ! I need to do a flyby for radar imaging!"

"I'll try and get a lock on Sparkles's chip," Tillman said as he pulled out a tablet and Velcroed it to his left arm.

"What if you can't get a signal?" Chuck asked.

Tillman shook his head and shrugged. Hopefully, it wouldn't come to that.

The helicopter suddenly dropped—far. Anything that hadn't been tied down flew around the cabin. Tillman grabbed Chuck's arm and she proceeded to break a nail digging her opposite hand into the helicopter's seat.

"Gonna be a bit bumpy, y'all," the headphones courteously advised them.

Chuck felt her cheeks flush as she realized her left hand was holding firmly onto Tillman's thigh. She let go and mouthed *sorry*.

Instantly Tillman grabbed her now free hand in his as the helicopter made another stomach-turning drop. Alarms sounded and for a moment, Chuck completely forgot about Sparkles's plight. She became aware of the screaming of the engines, as if they were working double time. A sudden sensation of weightlessness did nothing to help the situation.

The pilot's voice crackled back over the radio. "Just a bit more." She wished he would concentrate on not getting them killed.

The sensation of rising caused her muscles to relax. Tillman released her hand and gave her a wink. Chuck smiled, then tore off the nail she'd broken.

Tillman craned to look out the small window by his seat. "Hey, I think I got something back there!"

"Sparkles?" Chuck asked, adjusting her straps a bit.

"Yeah, I had all five readings for like a click, and then it went back to just the four. I'm sure it was still reading vitals though." Tillman's fingers were a whirl as he tried to adjust his settings.

The chopper slowed its speed and pitched to the right at a steep angle. They hovered for a moment or two before the pilot came back over the headset.

"Agent DeRosa, we are a no go for a landing platform! We're requesting direction from Alpha!" DeRosa clenched her lips as she heard the news.

"Can we do an air extraction?" Kahn asked.

DeRosa shook her head. "Not without Command approval."

"I got her. Vitals are bad, but her heart is still beating." Tillman's gaze was focused on the screen, the glow of which gave his face a shadowed and sinister look.

DeRosa nodded. "Make sure Command gets that!"

Tillman swiped away at the screen. "Already starting an uplink. Dr. Cole, I'm syncing the signal with your equipment."

Cole reached up and touched the frame of his glasses. "Cole to Command."

DeRosa held her hand up as if listening to something herself. She nodded. "Charlotte. If they can put me down on the cliff with Gavin and his family, can you handle dropping in with Cole?"

Her heart leapt into her throat all over again, but she nodded. How often did you get to rappel from a helicopter, into a ravine, to rescue a sasquatch? She decided it was best not to look for an answer.

"Agent DeRosa, we're getting a heat signature!"

As the pilot finished speaking, the floor of the cabin lit up showing the area through the chopper's FLIR. She could see the other sasquatches waving as if trying to signal the helo. A long dark slash showed the void of the fissure. A small box with the reading 43.58m/143ft along its top held a roughly bipedal shape. The yellow and orange hues were faint and blurry but there.

DeRosa looked at the image for a moment. "Shit! That's a long way down!"

Cole pulled his mic down. "We have plenty of cable. Mario, can you keep us in place long enough to lower the litter?"

"We can, but if you're doing this we need to get moving. The front of that storm will be over us soon," the pilot radioed back.

DeRosa unbuckled herself. "Okay! I'm going to go down and let Gavin and the others know what's happening. As soon as I'm on land, you two deploy! Moseby, you keep the lines open, and Kahn, you're on the winch!"

The helicopter pitched again as the plan swung into action.

Simply cranking the latch on the chopper's side door dropped the cabin temperature by fifty degrees. A full-on winter blast hit them as DeRosa slid the door to the side. The sound of the rotors and the wind was ruthless. DeRosa strapped herself almost immediately to a pair of cables as a winch arm extended from the helo's side.

Kahn stood now, latching himself onto an overhead loop. In the darkness Chuck could see the tops of trees reflecting the flashing lights of the helicopter. They were frighteningly close.

DeRosa called through the headsets that she was ready.

"You're all clear, Agent DeRosa," came Mario's reply.

DeRosa pressed the button on the side of her night vision goggles, then dropped into the darkness. She couldn't have gone more than about fifty feet before the cable stopped feeding. A moment later, Kahn was bringing up the empty hooks.

Chuck could hear Mario as he communicated with Command. "We've got boots on the ground."

The helicopter began to turn lazily. Images of the crevasse came to life on the floor of the cabin. And there, a bit off the center, lay Sparkles. She wasn't moving.

Chuck whispered to herself, "Hang in there, Sparkles."

Cole opened the other door, and the chopper pitched. In that moment she got her first glimpse of the light snow that was falling. Flakes whipped through the cabin, making sparkles in the lights. She took it as a sign.

"Let's get this litter set!" Cole called back to her. She got up and clipped her own line to a loop on the cabin's ceiling.

They popped handles up out of the floor and cranked simultaneously until the litter had extended from underneath the helo. The Bigfoot sized contraption had cables which they attached to the overhead winch. Cole threw a Velcro covered bag onto the litter, where it stuck fast.

They nodded to each other. As they were adjusting to change sides within the cabin, Tillman reached out and grabbed Chuck's arm.

His face had a look of genuine concern. "Be safe, kay?"

"Scout's honor. You just keep those communication lines up." Tillman smiled and went back to his tablet.

Chuck looked up just in time to see Cole stepping to the edge of the open bay door. Kahn affixed cables to the doctor and gave him a thumbs up. In a blink Cole was gone. More quickly than she would have thought, the hooks returned to view.

Kahn turned to her. "Okay, Agent Barnes, your turn!"

She stepped out. The wind was stunning. It practically challenged her to try and stand still. But with the sound of each carbine clipping, her resolve increased.

"Agent Barnes, you are clear to drop!"

Chuck flipped down her goggles and stepped into oblivion.

The rattling of the cables, the howl of the wind, the stinging of the snow crystals hammering her exposed cheeks. Her muscles tightened and every nerve ending in her body tingled. It felt as though she were falling freely, even attached to the cable. Chuck had never done any hard drugs, but if you could bottle this high, she would probably overdose.

And then it was—silent. As she passed the lip of the fissure, the wind, the snow, even the sound of the chopper seemed to disappear. Save for the rattle of the cables, she could have closed her eyes and been gone, absorbed by the darkness. Chuck looked down.

Closer than she would have thought, the bright outline of Cole stood out against the cold stone of the canyon. He was scanning Sparkles with a handheld device of some type. As her feet touched hard ground, Chuck pressed her contact button and the cable stopped feeding.

After quickly unclipping herself, she gave the button another push, sending the cables zipping up towards the flashing lights of the helicopter.

Chuck turned, taking a good look at the lay of the terrain, then flipped her goggles back up. She wanted to make sure Sparkles could recognize her.

"Oh God..." The words caught in her throat.

In the dim light of Cole's scanner, Chuck could see the damage. Sparkles's limbs were twisted and twitching. There was a bone sticking out through her right shoulder, and an ugly gash nearly bisected her forehead. A sudden, baleful sound broke the otherwise soft noise of Cole's footsteps and his beeping apparatus. Sparkles tried to turn her head.

"Agent Barnes, get her attention. Try and keep her from moving."

Chuck got down on her knees next to Sparkles's left side, clicking to her to get her attention.

Sparkles turned her head. There was so much blood on her face, Chuck winced involuntarily. The pitiful sasquatch gave another bray of pain. Chuck's eyes teared up at the sound, but she continued her clicks and coos.

"Pretty Sparkles." Chuck felt snot running from her nose and sniffed it back. Unable to continue the clicks, she spoke plainly to her injured friend. "You're doing great, sister. Hold on."

Sparkles finally seemed to recognize her and responded with barely audible clicks. "Pretty."

Chuck nodded, tears cutting cold lines down her cheeks.

"I need that litter now!" Cole yelled into the radio.

The response was more static than anything. "Co—back... nd—now."

"Agent Barnes, let her know we are going to get her out of here. Just keep her distracted!" Cole kept his voice calm, but the look on his face told Chuck how worried he was. She looked up and saw the helicopter coming back into view.

When she looked back to Sparkles, her heart broke. The glow of the sasquatch's eyes was dim and tear-filled.

"Come on, sister. Hang in there a little longer," she again spoke the words, not really knowing how to convey the feeling in sasquatch speak.

Sparkles's right hand twitched violently, and her eyes widened. Chuck felt the big creature's left arm start to move.

"No, Sparkles, don't move!"

The headphones crackled. "Litter... low—"

Sparkles brought her left arm up. Chuck grabbed it, but Sparkles fought her. The large hand got up right next to Sparkles's face, and then she retracted all but two fingers. It took Chuck a moment to realize she was pointing at her eyes.

Cole's voice came through clear as a bell. "Lower the front end more. It's uneven."

Chuck scrunched up her face. Sparkles pointed more emphatically, her eyes yelling at Chuck without a word being spoken.

"Eyes?" Chuck made the sign by pointing alternately at both of her own.

Sparkles gave two short clicks. "Yes."

"What about your eyes?" Chuck racked her brain to come up with an equivalent phrase. She raised her head, meaning to look up and check on the litter, but her gaze never made it that far. Chuck's bladder released involuntarily, and she felt warmth running down her thighs.

No more than twenty feet away, two bright red points were focused directly on her.

They blinked.

A dark shape, far darker than even the lightless void of the crevasse, took form behind the red glow of the eyes. Suddenly, it bounded backwards, deeper into the darkness of the canyon. The motion shocked her, but her body wouldn't respond as her mind screamed at her to draw her weapon.

The eyes disappeared, but she could still see that shape, like a spot where all light died. It hopped once, then again, ascending as it crisscrossed the canyon walls.

"AGENT BARNES! I NEED YOU TO FOCUS!" Cole's voice erupted in her ears. She turned to him.

"Get clear!" He waved his arm wildly at her to move out of the way.

She stood, shaky legs threatening to betray her as she stumbled slightly.

Cole looked at her with a mix of concern and frustration as he bent down. He hoisted up a box about the size of a microwave. With a shake, a set of four legs dropped out. He rested it near Sparkles's head. Chuck realized with horror that Sparkles had stopped moving, twitches and all.

"Start unlatching the restraints." Cole pointed at the fully lowered litter as he spoke. She did as instructed, quickly ripping several of the clasps apart. Message delivered, he looked down and pulled two wires from the top of the box.

Cole inserted the ends of the wires into Sparkles's ears. A flash ran down the length of the sasquatch's body, and an odd white glow emanated from several of the visible wounds. He ripped down one of the patches on his uniform and pulled out a syringe. A dimly glowing green liquid spurted out of the end. Cole applied a line to the forehead gash, as well as the broken shoulder bone.

Chuck finished unstrapping the last of the restraints. "Done!"

"We... not—long..." The message was garbled but clear. They couldn't hold that chopper in place much longer. As if to accentuate this, the litter jumped and shifted.

"Start lowering the personal hooks for retrieval," Cole said into his headphone. At the same time, he flipped up a handle on the side of the box. Dozens of wires erupted from the top, crawling over and under the limp form of Sparkles. She soon looked like a haphazard mummy.

With a gentleness only a machine could achieve, the wires lifted

Sparkles up. Its subject elevated, the box began walking the sasquatch's body towards the litter. Even with the gravity of the situation, Chuck couldn't help but be a bit mesmerized by the display.

"Winches deployed!" Thankfully, this message came down with nary a blip of static.

The box walked Sparkles onto the litter, then lowered itself into a depression a few inches above her head. Displays lit up across the top of the box, showing all kinds of numbers, too many for Chuck to decipher at a glance.

Cole pulled out a syringe and jabbed it into Sparkles's neck. Another white flash erupted from underneath the restraints. Chuck sprung to action, securing them.

"Litter secured!" she radioed up.

"Copy."

The cables that would take her and Cole back up hit the ground a few feet away. She flipped back down her goggles, looking up the canyon in the direction she'd seen the eyes. Nothing but rocks and darkness. She stepped to the lift cables as the litter began climbing slowly back towards the chopper.

"You go first. Sparkles needs you up there." Chuck offered a hook in Cole's direction.

"You good now?" Cole's earlier irritation had subsided.

"I'm with you. Just go!" she insisted.

He strapped in and hit the buzzer. "See you topside." His feet quickly disappeared out of her view.

Switching the goggles to the infrared spectrum, Chuck turned her gaze to the length of the fissure. Nothing, even after scanning for a full ten seconds. No hot spots, no evidence of a dark shape. Then she looked down, and her breath left her lungs.

Its heat was fading, but still very evident. Blood, too much blood. Pooled beneath where Sparkles had been lying.

Fresh tears stung the edges of Chuck's eyes as she looked up. The litter was halfway to the helo with Cole close behind. She pivoted, turning nearly a full three sixty. Nothing.

"Litter secured!" The radio caused her to nearly jump out of her skin.

A cold feeling, the kind you get when you think you're being watched, but a thousand times worse, sapped her strength. She wanted to look up but didn't dare. She knew that if she looked away, even for a moment, it would get her. If she didn't watch, those eyes would return.

Chuck stood perfectly still, guts twisted into a snarl of knots, the smell of urine and sweat filling her nostrils, but it was better than whatever that thing in the dark had in store for her. Instinctively, she reached for where her gun should have been. Except she'd removed it to don the winter gear.

The cables rattled on the canyon floor, mere inches from her feet. Chuck reached down, feeling for the hooks one at a time. Her eyes burned from being opened too long. But she couldn't blink, or even look away. She clipped the carbines on by muscle memory alone, one handed in case she needed to defend herself.

One, two, a third click and she reached her hand up and wrapped it around the button, pressing it. Immediately the cables became taught, pulling her upward. Chuck swiveled, and spun as she rose, but didn't blink. The ground fell away, the cables swayed, but still, she didn't blink.

Finally, the biting cold and spraying snow against her face forced her eyes to close, just as she crested the ridge. The wind and the engines of the chopper wailed. Spinning around, she caught a glimpse of DeRosa and Gavin, standing along the cliff edge. The shoulders of the sasquatch were slumped. DeRosa turned towards him, and Gavin took the agent up in a big hug, which DeRosa returned. The winch ground to a halt, and Chuck felt arms wrapping around her.

She screamed.

Chapter Seventeen:

Eyes

"Whoa there, Agent, I've got you!" Kahn tried to yell over the torrent of noise created by the wind, the rotors, and Chuck's scream.

She felt herself start to shake. Her head throbbed, and her stomach lurched. She fell on her knees, leaned out over the side of the chopper, and vomited.

Mario's voice, clear as a bell now, came over the headset. "The cross winds are increasing! We need to retrieve Agent DeRosa, pronto!"

"Lowering the cables now." Kahn leaned down towards Chuck. "Agent Barnes, you good?"

She spit some lingering bile then looked over her shoulder. "I'm fine. Help DeRosa!" Crawling away from the opening, her feet hit the litter, now resting in the middle of the cabin. Chuck stood and turned, her heart still beating hard within her chest.

Tillman was helping Cole tuck a large, foil-looking tarp over Sparkles. The doctor stood, coming face to face with Chuck. The frustration in his eyes made her wince.

"What the hell happened to you down there?"

The eyes. "I'm sorry—I—I just froze. I'm sorry." She wanted to tell him what she had seen, why she'd locked up. But had she really seen them? She remembered what DeRosa told her about nobody believing she'd seen a Class One.

Now high above the fissure and with the others around her, the fear was subsiding. The energy that came from being on a mission slowly filling the void. Chuck wondered if she'd seen something real, or if it had been her imagination.

Cole broke eye contact first. After rubbing his temple for a moment, he looked at her again. The frustration had been replaced with sympathy.

"Hey, listen, you did great. Neither of us could've expected what we were going to find down there." He looked towards the litter, a deep sadness gripping his face. "Her last memories are going to be of having a friend there with her."

Chuck frowned, looking down at Sparkles. Tillman had retaken his seat. In her peripheral vision, she saw DeRosa coming into view from below the chopper.

"What do you mean, her last memories?" She wanted the sentence to be louder, but Cole's words had jammed a lump into her throat.

"We're all in. Let's go!" Despite being mere feet from her, DeRosa's voice sounded far away. Cole turned back, his face close to Chuck's in the cramped confines of the chopper.

"She's not going to make it, Agent. Her injuries are catastrophic. That shot I gave her was to ensure she wasn't in agony when it happens."

DeRosa kneeled next to the litter, dabbing blood off Sparkles's face with a bandage. As Chuck looked at her, she saw the displays on the box. All of them were flashing red. She became vaguely aware of alarms going off as she turned back to Cole.

"Do something! You can't just stand here and let her die!"

"I did. We did all we could already."

"Bullshit! I've seen the shit you guys have! Rub some of that pink stuff on her!"

Cole didn't say anything, he just continued to look at her.

How could everyone else in the cabin be okay with letting Sparkles die? She gave Cole a shove. "Stop looking at me and do something!"

Firm hands gripped her and turned her where she stood. DeRosa's eyes pierced Chuck, her own grief bubbling up as she saw the heartache in the older woman's face. She pulled DeRosa in close for a hug but didn't cry. She couldn't. Her whole being was numb.

After a moment she stepped back. "Does Gavin know?"

Sally nodded confirmation. Chuck turned back to Cole, embarrassed by her actions.

"I'm sorry for that. I know you would do more if you could. Thanks for at least easing her pain."

A long, drawn-out beep marked the stopping of Sparkles's heart.

Chuck looked down at her friend. The expression on the young sasquatch's face wasn't pained; it was peaceful. Cole stepped around the litter, knelt, and turned off the box. He flipped the end of the foil blanket up over Sparkles's head.

Chuck sat down, defeated. Too many things were rattling around in her mind. What caused Sparkles to lose so much blood? How had she ended up falling into the ravine? And what was the other creature Chuck had seen?

DeRosa and Cole spent most of the flight back sending information ahead to Command.

"We'll know more once we get her autopsied," Cole said at one point.

"Agent Barnes and Dr. Cole did the best they could," DeRosa said at another.

Kahn had been sitting in silence for some time when he reached out and patted her on the shoulder. "Nobody should ever have to see a friend die like that. I lost buddies in the Corp. Guys I was really close to. She's lucky she had you there at the end."

Chuck turned to the former marine and nodded. "Thanks. She had such a big heart. It doesn't seem fair."

"Accidents are never fair. But we can't keep them all locked safely behind cages either. That would make us no better than the Griffins."

Chuck wasn't entirely sure that this *was* some freak accident. She looked at Kahn and smiled. "Yeah, I guess we can't."

The pilot's voice came through the headsets. "Starting landing procedures. Y'all get secured if you haven't already."

The sky above them was clear as they began disembarking from the helo ten minutes later. There were several vehicles at the airport. Hines, Smalls, Doc, and a few members of security were all standing not far from the point where the chopper came to a rest.

Hines and DeRosa almost immediately broke off and headed for a car. Neither appeared to speak to the other. Tillman and Smalls likewise headed back quickly.

Cole and Doc stood by as several of the security team removed Sparkles from the helicopter and transported her to one of the oversized medical vehicles.

Chuck walked up to the two CIT's. "May I ride back with her?"

Cole looked at the litter, then looked at Doc. The older man nodded. "Of course you may."

Once Sparkles was loaded, she and Doc climbed into the back, taking seats around the litter.

"Dr. Cole told me how well you did. Even seasoned doctors can lock up when called upon to perform triage for a friend or family member. You were there for Sparkles when she needed you. Think of those happy times when you think of her, not of what you had to see this morning."

Sure, except what she had seen that morning was going to forever be burned into her mind. Those eyes would be a permanent reminder of the broken form of her friend.

"She was a fighter right to the end. I wish we'd gotten there sooner." Chuck remembered Sparkles struggling to raise her hand. But that wasn't all she'd been doing. Her eyes! The eyes! Sparkles had seen them! Seeing those menacing eyes in the fissure had caused her to forget what the sasquatch had been doing. But now the memory came flooding back. Sparkles was trying to tell her about the eyes!

"Don't be too hard on yourself." Doc spoke, but she barely heard him. Sparkles had seen those eyes, and not at the same time Chuck had. No, she'd seen them *before* that. But had the mystery creature caused Sparkles's injuries, or did it simply happen upon the fallen sasquatch?

She needed to talk to DeRosa but couldn't until Hines had gotten his report. Not to mention, she would need to turn in a report of her own.

They were soon back at Alpha. The vehicle took them into Warehouse 3. Once parked, a team helped them take Sparkles down to the mortuary.

The security members left as the three of them stood for a moment more. At length Doc turned to her. "Thank you, Charlotte. We'll take it from here."

She reached up and pulled out her hair tie, setting it down on the covered form of Sparkles.

Cole patted Doc on the back. "Doc, I'm going to walk out Agent Barnes and go wash up. Can you handle things until I get back?"

Doc nodded. Chuck stood a moment longer and then walked out of the room with Cole.

"I can show myself out if you need to go clean up," she volunteered.

"Actually, I was hoping I could ask you something."

"Sure."

"How did you know about the pink stuff?"

She stopped and turned to look at him. "The pink stuff? Oh, right. One of the recruits got a bad laceration on his face, I guess it was last week. I saw Doc use this pink stuff with blue flecks on the cut."

Cole looked at her. When he spoke, his voice sounded accusatory. "*Doc* used some pink stuff did he? It smelled like a landfill, turned black, and flaked off?"

"Wait, Doc's not gonna get in trouble, is he? Whatever it is, it worked great! You couldn't even tell there'd been a cut afterward." She didn't want to get her friend in trouble. Cole had a reputation as a bit of a do-gooder around Alpha.

"I'll certainly have a talk with Doc, but unless he flat out punches the Chief, I doubt he'd get in trouble. Did he use the glove at least?"

"Yeah, a weirdly thick one actually. What's that stuff made of? Doc called it mermaid excrement."

Cole looked back toward the morgue and chuckled a little. "To be honest? I have no idea what it—or for that matter *most* of the stuff R&D cranks out—is made from. The pink stuff just happens to be more volatile. If it touches healthy unwounded skin, it burns it like acid."

He made a face like maybe he'd seen this happen before. "It's ten times worse if you put it on a cryptid. Even a wounded one. Their DNA is radically different from humans. Whatever that stuff is, it reacts violently with them. I don't think it was meant to be a first aid product. Seems more like a weapon the Wardens would use in my opinion."

Chuck nodded, appreciative of Cole's honesty. "I guess I figured if Doc had a miracle cure, you might have had one too."

"Trust me, if I'd had one, I would have used it. Fact is, most of what R&D comes up with goes to helping mankind, not cryptid-kind. It's where the Family makes most of its money. We have a few things, like that green stuff I used to close her wounds, but the scope is pretty limited."

His words surprised her. Chuck had never really questioned where the Family got its money from. The fact most of what they did benefited humans seemed odd, especially since they claimed protecting cryptids was their primary objective.

"Hey, don't go too hard on Doc. He was trying to help."

"I don't doubt that. Doc's a good guy, but he probably shouldn't be parading stuff like that around." Chuck frowned and Cole held up his hands. "I'll go easy on him. You have my word."

"Thanks."

"And thank you for going down there with me. You did great."

"I'm glad you were here for this one. I can't imagine Doc being rigged to one of those cables." This drew a chuckle from Cole, who waved goodbye to her as he turned and headed back to the morgue.

Chuck started the long walk back to her apartment. About halfway there, her self-consciousness kicked in as she realized how many conversations she'd been carrying on with vomit breath. She really hoped nobody had been offended.

That same self-consciousness tried to sort out if anyone would have noticed that she'd peed her pants. Thanks to the snow, everything was wet already, and the scent of sasquatch probably covered up the smell.

Once safely inside her apartment, Chuck removed the gear that couldn't or wouldn't be laundered and placed them all out on the breakfast bar. She glanced at her bodycam with contempt. There was no doubt in her mind the eyes wouldn't be on the footage. That thing could've been right in front of her and somehow it still wouldn't have been on the cam.

With her gear out of the way she began to strip off her clothes, throwing each article in a garbage bag. She had no desire to wear this clothing ever again.

She went into the bathroom and turned the shower on as hot as it would go, waiting until the glass had steamed over to step in. Uncomfortably hot water ran down her body in rivulets, the sensation comforting her soul. Pressing her hands against the tile, Chuck bent forward, and dry heaved. Her stomach, much like her emotions, simply had nothing else to give.

An undetermined amount of time later, she reached up, grabbed her body wash, and finally started to clean herself. The smell of coconut and vanilla was heavenly. She could feel her body recharging, and as she shampooed her hair, the sensation became even stronger.

Like a runner getting a second wind.

Chuck felt confident that what happened to Sparkles hadn't been an accident. Something or someone caused her friend to fall.

Her skin was wrinkly by the time she stepped out of the shower. Knowing she had to get her report in, Chuck got dressed, grabbed her cam, and headed for the round room of disappointment.

She sat down at one of the archaic stations and started her upload. Typing up the report, she ran through the memories of the morning again. The cold, the wind, and the look on Sparkles's face. She paused, needing to collect not only her thoughts, but her emotions. The sound of the door sliding open shifted her attention. Looking up, she saw Tillman approaching her slowly. He looked uncomfortable, but whether it was because of her or the room, she couldn't say.

She gave him her best fake smile. "Hey, you come down here to see how the common folk live?"

"No, I actually came to find you. Does this room always smell like a urinal?"

"It sure does. Why were you looking for me exactly?"

"It's just, in the chopper. I didn't really get to give you my condolences. The whole thing really sucked, and I wanted to, you know, make sure you were good."

Chuck's fake smile turned into a genuine one. "Thanks, Tillman, that really means a lot. And yeah, while sucked is the nicest word I can probably use to describe this morning, I'll be fine."

He grabbed a chair and sat down across from her. "You don't call me Tillman all that often. Are you sure you're okay?"

She thought about it a second. "I'm sure I've called you Tillman lots of times."

He sat back. "I feel like you usually call me Agent Moseby. Or, more accurately, *Agent* Moseby." He mimicked her inflection badly.

Chuck smiled, more to herself than Tillman. "I call you *Agent* Moseby when I think it will be endearing." His concern for her was sweet if a bit expected, and she was grateful he cared enough to seek her out.

"Well, would it be endearing if I offered to take you to lunch, you know somewhere other than the cafeteria?"

"That would in fact be quite endearing. Where are you thinking?"

"That Italian place next to the car dealership. Gegi's, I think?"

"Oh, I could go ham on some Stromboli right now!"

"It's a date then. Meet you up top in what, fifteen?"

"I'll be there."

"Sweet! I'll go check us out a car." He spun in the chair and headed for the exit.

Chuck typed a few final paragraphs and headed for the elevator, her mood a bit brighter at the prospect of getting to eat real world food. The fact she would be doing so one on one with Tillman didn't hurt either.

***

By the time she reached the warehouse, Tillman had already arrived with a car. They checked out at the gate, and soon enough were sitting in a comfortable booth, sipping on Italian soda.

"I feel bad for the recruits," Tillman said as they waited for their lunches to arrive. He had pretty much been talking about Alpha since they'd gotten in the car.

Chuck smirked. "Hey, let's not talk about work."

"Okay, um, what should we talk about then?"

"I don't know, just not work... what color is your toothbrush?"

Tillman looked completely baffled. "What?"

"What color is your toothbrush? I went to a dance in middle school, and this awkward kid came up to me and asked if I wanted to dance. I mean, it *was* a dance, and I didn't know any better, so I told him sure. Next thing I know we start dancing, and he asks me 'what color is your toothbrush?' He said his mom told him to say it as an icebreaker or something. So, what color is yours?" She never took her eyes off him. She wanted to see Tillman Moseby's honest feelings right now.

"Um, yellow, I think. I change mine pretty frequently."

"Well, there we go. Why do you change them out so often?" She took a long sip of her soda, giving him time to answer.

"Hell, I don't know. I guess it's because I saw this show once that said when you flush your toilet the water particles from it sometimes fly up and get on your toothbrush."

Chuck sprayed half the table as she choked on her soda. "Oh my God that is disgusting! You're kidding, right?"

"Scout's honor." Tillman held up three fingers on one hand while handing her a couple extra napkins with the other. It occurred to Chuck that he may have been an actual Boy Scout.

"No way! The second we get back I'm burning my toothbrush. Why did you have to tell me that?"

"Well, you asked."

"You've got me there." Their hands brushed as they tried to mop up the soda, and a silly, schoolgirl spark of infatuation ran through Chuck. She spent a lot of time working with Tillman, and yet didn't know much about him beyond his duties within the Family, and the fact that he liked anime. She sat back and studied him, feeling a sudden urge to learn more about her techie friend. "Why did you join the Family?"

Tillman scrunched up his face. "Are we playing twenty questions now?"

"That's only the second one. Come on, you joined so young. What made you want to commit to doing what we do?"

He looked out the nearby window. Chuck had never noticed how cute his ears were before today. "God, I don't... I mean. The challenge I guess. If you haven't ever been labeled a *child prodigy,* it's kind of hard to explain. Everyone expects this or that from you." He got quiet for a moment, then looked at the ceiling. "I guess when you're fifteen and there's all these expectations piled on you, someone offering to make you anonymous seems—appealing."

"Tillman, I had no idea."

He looked back at her, his eyes showing hints of moisture at their edges. "Kids at my school used to make fun of me pretty much all the time. I was either too smart, or won too many awards, or garnered too much attention. No matter what I did, or accomplished, someone always had a smartass comment. Five years removed from that world there's one thing I can tell you for sure. I don't regret my choice." He frowned, then looked back at the ceiling.

Chuck took another sip of soda, not sure how to respond. Thankfully, their food arrived at that moment. Her Stromboli smelled divine, and she tore into it, finishing her plate well before Tillman. The whole affair was a welcome relief, and driving back to Alpha, her life felt almost normal for the first time in a long time.

She'd told Rita the truth the previous day. Her dad liked to tell stories about creatures of myth and legend. He taught her about Bigfoot, Nessie, and the Mothman. But for her dad they were just fun stories to tell his kids. He didn't know it took a team of twenty dedicated Family members working twenty-four seven to protect the two Nessies that were still left.

And neither had Chuck. Joining the Family had given her amazing opportunities. Adventure, excitement, a great career, and a chance to stand face-to-face with fantastical creatures. Agents talked about what they did as if it were any other job, but it wasn't. It was a lifestyle, and consumed all your time, energy, and talent. You had to enjoy those fleeting moments when you stopped being an agent and you got to be a person.

She felt like she'd seen it in Tillman today as well. Beneath his awkward and sometimes goofy exterior, there was someone that wanted to get away from what his life had been. It occurred to her that she'd taken the same route, for nearly the same reason.

Tillman pulled up to the front of Warehouse 2 once they were back on site. "Here you go, I'll save you the trouble of having to walk from the back lot."

"Thanks, Tillman. I really needed that," she said as she exited the car.

Tillman gave her a wink. "Hey, we'll do it again. I had a really good time."

Chuck returned the wink and started heading for the elevator.

She hit the call button and stepped back. Standing in the large warehouse, alone with her thoughts, she began to replay the—dare she call it *date*—in her mind. The way his eyes lit up when he looked directly into hers. The way his smile looked somehow more prominent when they were alone. A feeling started to creep into her mind. A feeling she hadn't felt in a couple of years. She tried to suppress it, quiet it, but it persisted. A physical attraction—to Tillman.

"No."

The sound of her voice echoing in the warehouse surprised her. She'd meant to say the word to herself. But the need to bury the emotion had been strong and she'd spoken it out loud. Tillman was handsome and smart, but he also worked with her. Chuck had certainly slept with a co-worker in the past, but that had been in a whole different world.

In the Family, you didn't have co-workers, you had a couple of hundred roommates, and those roommates were more than willing to gossip. Nothing on site was secret, or sacred.

Chuck tried in vain to think of something besides Tillman, but her mind kept coming back to him, and the time they'd just spent together. She reached into her purse for a piece of gum, looking for any little distraction she could muster.

Ding!

"Shit! Oh, sorry, I forgot something," Chuck apologized to the pair of admins that came stepping out of the elevator. She'd forgotten her phone in the car. Maybe she could catch Tillman before he turned the keys back in.

Chuck rushed outside and headed towards the rear parking lot where the agency vehicles were kept. As she rounded the fence marking off the lot, she nearly crashed into Tillman who was coming around at the same time.

"Oh, hey, is ah, everything okay?" He asked, catching himself on the fence to keep from falling.

"Sorry, I left my phone in the car. I was hoping to catch you before you got too far."

"No worries." Tillman pulled out the keys and twirled around, heading back into the lot. Though not terribly proud of her actions, Chuck stared at his butt for most of the walk to the vehicle.

Fifteen feet away, Tillman hit the unlock button on the fob, causing the headlights to flash. Chuck looked over her shoulder at the bank of security cameras watching over the lot. They were the only eyes that could currently see the two of them.

Tillman opened the passenger door, then bent down. "Found it! Right here in the groove between the seat and the—" As he turned around, Chuck met him and pressed her lips against his. It took a bit of effort, considering the height difference, but was well worth it.

Warning signals went off throughout her mind, but she pushed them all aside. Screw the rumormongers. For nearly two and a half years her life had been regimented and her love life had been out of commission. The fact Tillman was kissing her back sent a flood of relief through her.

Their lips separated and Tillman leaned back, his eyes wide. They got wider still as he fell through the open door, into the passenger seat. His head hit the frame of the car as he did. "Ouch!"

"Oh my god! Tillman!" She reached out a hand, intending to pull him up. Instead, he placed her phone in her open palm, as she heard him begin to laugh. "I take it you're okay?"

He sat up awkwardly, rubbing the back of his head, but still laughing. "Wow do I feel like a dumbass right now." He looked up at her. "Now, I'm not complaining, I mean, seriously, but where exactly did that come from?"

Chuck bent her knees until she was looking more directly at him. "Sorry, I didn't mean to be quite so, forward." She brushed back a stray hair from her face. "That probably wasn't fair of me to come at you like that."

His ears were red, but whether from the fall or from embarrassment, she couldn't be sure. "No, please don't apologize, I'm already gonna make things weird enough for the both of us. It's just, I'm not going to lie... I've wanted to do that myself, I just thought you'd kick my ass or something." He looked down sheepishly. "I've never really... so where do we go from here?"

Chuck blushed herself, happy to hear Tillman's confession. "How about for now, we go get these keys turned in. Then we can figure out the next step from there." She offered him a hand again, and this time he accepted her help.

Tillman stood, still rubbing the back of his head with his free hand. "You can say no of course, but would it be okay if we, you know, kissed again? I mean before we go back to the requisition office?"

Chuck smiled, wondering what she'd gotten herself into with this charming, good looking, deliciously awkward man. Several minutes later, they finally left the lot, hand in hand.

Chapter Eighteen:

Little Bird

I am no mere animal.

I am no drooling beast of the night.

Broken or not, my mind is capable of reason.

There are many that walk in this world who in the distant, formative eras would once have been considered a relation to me. I advanced past most of these long ago. There are still some, others like me that possess abilities and powers. Some of us will never taste death, at least not by natural causes. Others may live extremely long lives, many generations of man falling away before time finally finishes them.

I succeeded in chasing down my first prey in ages, a lean but tasty deer. I took my time, savoring each succulent, savory bite. I'd made quite a glutton of myself when I detected the approach of another, the brute's scent giving it away.

Quickly climbing a nearby tree, I waited as the monster approached. Tall, hairy, and unreasoning, it wandered to the remains of my meal like a dog discovering a discarded scrap of meat. It didn't stop to ponder what had led the deer to its untimely demise, only whether it might find a morsel for itself.

I overcame this far distant cousin quickly, alighting atop his shoulders and looking directly into my victim's eyes as I applied my toxins. Once he'd been culled, I efforted to retrieve details as to where I found myself. My prisoner however proved completely unhelpful. He could not, even in his primitive language, relate to me any useful information about this land, other than simple markers.

The voices told me the truth of it. I could spend all day attempting to glean scraps and fragments of information from this creature and find little of worth for my efforts. There was only one memory, one image that mattered.

He revealed to me a lair. A lair inhabited by others of his line, though possessing of more intelligence. Others who were in contact with humans.

The passage of time had inevitably changed the world around me, but I felt certain of one thing. Assuming there were any members of the Rogers clan still about, there could be little doubt they would be in contact with others like myself and the brute standing before me.

The fog within my mind, the voices, made it hard to extract a proper path. Once I had done so, I commanded the buffoonish creature to tear out its own jugular and eat it. A wicked deed which brought a new thrill to my frenzied mind.

The voices caused my path to veer erratically over the ensuing days. I would find myself, staring into the night sky, or sitting high within a tree. Hours often passed away as I listened to them, their secrets, their machinations, each a wonderment to me.

Several days of travel finally brought me to my destination—a well-hidden, if cramped, cavern holding five of the bipedal brutes. Quite a large family, and much more intelligent looking than the previous subject I had encountered.

I wanted to take all five, but the voices forbade me. Wait, they said. Like the great predatory cats, wait until you can isolate one. It would be much easier to subdue a single foe, than wrestle with many.

And yet, this clan showed their intellect to me swiftly. They moved as a group, never venturing out of their cavern alone, always by two or three, or five.

Imagine the thrill I felt when one of the smaller members of the clan came shuffling out into the cold dark a couple of nights after my arrival. This one seemed intent to gaze upon the stars, and she walked several paces from the cavern mouth, head angled skyward.

Ages of practice allowed me to execute my attack exactly as I had days earlier, striking quickly, not allowing my prey to even make a proper call for help. Everything done to perfection, until my fevered mind touched hers.

This creature was addled, her mind a maze of thoughts and emotions. Prior to my time spent in the infernal prison this would have been of little matter. But now—now the voices erupted in a maelstrom of anger! The creature had seen the Rogers, that much became clear. But her understanding was rudimentary, and her mind did not sit idly as it should have when joined with mine. This young creature fought!

Rage overtook me, as it had within the cavern when I regained my strength. My victim let out a howl of terror and tried to turn away from me. I tore into her back with hardened claws. She struck out at me, attempting to push me back, and I grabbed her arm flinging her backwards.

My anger granted me uncanny power and my victim flew much further than I had intended. She disappeared from my view as I heard the rest of the clan bellowing.

I retreated swiftly, using the trees to help conceal my path. More brays echoed through the night air, though I doubt they ever truly pursued me.

Frustration gave the voices purchase deep within my being. My mind failed me again and I shook myself as if awakening from a stupor. A new sound now dominated the night: An angry mechanical screeching. I headed towards the sound, stunned at what I discovered.

There, flying in the sky, was a large carriage. Lights streamed from the contraption and its noise caused the voices within me to become muddled and distant.

A form then dropped from the carriage, attached to a rope of some sort. Carefully, I picked my way down into a nearby chasm, intent on getting a better view at whatever had been lowered. There I found a man dressed in bulky clothing attending to my night's victim. Looking up at the flying machine, I saw another gliding down, delicate as a little bird.

This second human joined the first. I crept closer, my curiosity getting the better of me. Another, larger form was lowering from the carriage, and I became further distracted as I watched it.

I still possessed a weak connection with the afflicted brute. Through her, I heard a woman speaking words of comfort and concern. I looked at her, and suddenly, she raised her head, looking directly at me.

She didn't recoil. Instead, the little bird stared at me.

AWAY! The voices screamed at me. This is not the place!

I bounded quickly back up the cliffs, unsure of what other surprises these humans had at their disposal. Even as I retreated I cursed the voices! My revenge had been stalled, but only for a time. I would wait, and I would learn, and in the end, flying or not, the Rogers would fall before me.

Chapter Nineteen:

Questions

"Hey, thanks for stopping by, you're sure you have time?" Chuck asked Sally early the following day.

"Yeah, I'm good."

"You need a drink? I don't have your usual, but I do have water."

DeRosa took the same seat she had the week before. "I'm fine, thanks. What did you want to talk about?"

"To get right to the point, I wanted to talk to you about the mission yesterday." She paused, struggling with exactly how she wanted to proceed. "When Cole and I were down in that fissure with Sparkles."

DeRosa nodded. Chuck swallowed, then sighed. "Sally, I saw something down there. Something that had red eyes."

Sally stared at her for a moment. The senior agent's face was difficult to read. "Chuck." DeRosa held her gaze a moment longer. "You're... You're serious, aren't you?"

"I am. It looked right at me. And then it hopped away."

"You couldn't see anything else?"

"It looked like it was made of darkness, like it radiated darkness somehow. But Jesus, I mean, Sally, those eyes. They looked human—but sinister. If I close my eyes right now, I see them."

Sally, frowned. "Well, damn. I'm guessing Cole didn't see anything?"

"He sure didn't say anything if he did."

"And your cam?"

"No way. I remembered what you said about red eyes, how people probably wouldn't believe me. I wanted to wait and talk to you first. But that's not the only thing. Sally, I think Sparkles saw the eyes too. I think whatever that thing was might have hurt her."

DeRosa let out a long breath, then rubbed her temples. "You

didn't put that in your report, right?"

"Hell no! But what do we do about it? I *know* I saw something down there, but I don't know *what* I saw down there."

"You said the eyes looked human?"

"Other than glowing red they looked human to me. I even saw them blink."

"Well then, your red eyes were different than the ones I saw."

Chuck sat back, grateful that Sally believed her. "So, what do we do now?"

"I think what we do now is wait for Sparkles's autopsy. Let's see what Cole and Doc find out before we get too far into this."

The thought of her friend's body being dissected sent a jolt through Chuck. "Sally, if that thing had anything to do with Sparkles's death, I want to take it down. Even if I have to do it myself."

DeRosa nodded. "Let's hope it doesn't come to that."

***

Chuck approached the recruits in the cafeteria, ready for an onslaught of questions about Sparkles, and they didn't disappoint.

"Do you guys know what happened?"

"Did she slip?"

"Are we gonna have a funeral?"

"Is it normal for this many cryptids to die in a week?"

"Leon heard from Nigel—who heard from the cafeteria lady with the mole, who heard from that weird janitor with the glass eye, who heard from one of the security guards—that you puked all over the helicopter. Is that true?"

This last one was Rita.

"Wait... No... What the hell?"

Rita snapped a finger and flipped her hair back. "I don't make the tea; I just spill it."

Chuck shook her head. "I think that's enough questions for now. Hurry up and eat so we can get to the range." They all grumbled, then continued to pick at their trays of food. The remainder of breakfast passed by in relative silence.

***

Once the recruits were set on the range, Chuck decided to get in some practice of her own. She'd always been a decent shot, but since graduating to agent status, she rarely took her gun out of its holster. Considering what she'd been through the day before, firing off a few rounds felt like a good idea.

After checking in her weapon with the range master, she grabbed a box of shells and headed for a lane. The pistol's familiar heft felt good in her hands. She'd fired off a couple of magazines when someone tapped her on the shoulders.

She turned around, surprised to find Leon from the Kangaroos standing there. He wore noise suppression headphones and held out a piece of paper. Chuck took it. His message delivered, Leon turned and headed for the exit to the range. She opened the note.

I need to talk to you at lunch. Cafeteria. Tillman

She crumpled the paper and slid it into her back pocket. What, were they in elementary school now? They'd spent an hour the previous day, talking about *them*. Tillman wanted to proceed cautiously, as he'd previously, in his words, *been in a pretty shitty relationship*. Chuck could live with that, but she didn't exactly know how to feel about him passing her handwritten messages.

Shaking her head, she turned and fired off three bullseyes in a row. After emptying a final magazine, Chuck walked away from the range, satisfied with her aim.

***

When she entered the cafeteria, she spotted Tillman sitting in a back corner. After grabbing her lunch, she went to sit with him. Chuck could practically *feel* the recruits watching her.

"Hey, you wanted to talk?"

Tillman smiled, and then looked around. Satisfied no one could hear him, he turned his attention to her. "I wanted to try and catch you before you heard it from someone else."

She bit into her sandwich, curious what all the secrecy was about. "Heard what?"

"It's about Sparkles's autopsy," he said, then weirdly paused as if for dramatic effect.

She raised her eyebrows. "Well?"

"There were gashes all over her back like someone stabbed her repeatedly. They said it looked like something attacked her before she fell off that cliff."

Chuck's nerves, still raw from the previous morning, immediately frayed, igniting a palpable fury within her.

"Delta has got everyone in command freaking out, sending reports, looking over satellite images."

She asked a question she already knew the answer to. "Do they have any idea what attacked her?"

Tillman rose from his seat and leaned over the table towards her. For a moment she had an odd fear he meant to kiss her. Instead, he put a hand to his cheek to keep his voice from carrying.

"I overheard Smalls talking to Hines. She said Delta thinks it might be a Revenant."

Chuck stopped mid-bite. The burning fury within her turned to a lump of cold lead in her gut. She put her sandwich down. "You're positive she said Revenant?"

"I'd bet a month's pay on it."

"Damn."

"I know, right?" Tillman looked down at the slice of pizza sitting in front of him. He picked off two or three individual pepperoni pieces, popped them in his mouth, then held out a hand as if wanting Chuck to wait for something. She used the moment to take a final small bite of her own sandwich.

Once he'd finished chewing Tillman resumed speaking. "What do you guys have going on Friday?"

"As in who? Me and the recruits?"

"Yeah."

"We're supposed to be doing a team building workshop with Smalls." She rolled her eyes. "It's the first one she's taught and I'm sure it will be cringey as hell."

Tillman nodded. "It all makes sense then. Smalls pitched me the idea of taking the recruits out on Friday, you know, for a make-up Media Day." He laughed. "She was acting sketchy about the whole thing."

"I'm up for it if you are. If this place goes into full alert it might be awhile before we get to." In truth, Chuck had mixed emotions about going out, but *not* having to do a class with Smalls was worth a day of not getting closer to Sparkles's killer.

Tillman looked down at his watch. "I've got to get going, but maybe we can, I don't know, see each other later?"

"I'd like that."

He winked, then hurried off.

Chuck sat looking at her tray, not wanting to eat, but knowing she'd just end up sick later if she didn't get some food. Peeling the top off her yogurt cup, she reflected on what Tillman had said.

A Revenant. She wanted to kick herself for not thinking of it sooner. DeRosa's story about Fitchburg had obviously made a bigger impression on her than she would've thought. The Family didn't talk about Revenants often, mostly because they rarely encountered them.

Humans might have nightmares about ghosts, unstoppable killers with axes, or creatures that slithered and stalked them through dark hallways. Cryptids, at least the cognizant ones, had nightmares about Revenants. In a world where creatures of myth and legend were as real as a corrupt politician, Revenants were a monster straight out of a horror movie. She'd heard her old trainer describe them as undead cryptids, and the limited training agents received concerning them focused almost exclusively on methods of escape, not actual engagement.

Nobody seemed to know where Revenants came from, or if they did, they didn't talk about it. But regardless of their origins, the monsters had several traits in common with Class Ones. They were powerful, deadly, and their eyes glowed red or orange, fitting in with what Chuck had seen the day before. Revenants were also nearly impossible to kill.

If Delta really did think there was a Revenant loose, then things were going to get interesting around here. She needed to talk to Sally again.

She fired off a quick text. *'Tillman told me Delta's thinking we have a Revenant on our hands. What are you hearing?'*

She picked up her tray, half of her food still untouched, and headed for the cafeteria's exit.

Chapter Twenty:

Goat Sucker

Chuck had never really been one to be bothered by nightmares, but that night her dreams were horrible. Shadowy figures with red, angry eyes chased her through the woods. Icy claws raked at her. She couldn't seem to outrun them. Every breath took more and more effort. A face—twisted, burned, and screaming—awakened her to a pillow soaked with sweat.

She sat up and reached for her lamp. As her fingers were alighting on the button Chuck froze. That feeling of someone being in her room returned. Squinting in the darkness proved completely useless.

The rational side of her brain finally woke up and she turned on the lamp, dispelling the shadows and her fears.

Chuck's phone vibrated on the nightstand causing her to jump. She picked it up, finding that DeRosa had texted her back. At three in the morning.

'sorry, been busy. moseby's right. i'll find you tomorrow afternoon.'

If Sally was still up, then something must be going on. Knowing she wouldn't be going back to sleep anytime soon, Chuck fired up Netflix and started watching the first non-horror movie she didn't recognize.

At some point she nodded off, awaking again when her alarm went off. She skipped breakfast, opting instead to take an early morning run. The cold was hell on her lungs, but a couple of hours later as she sat down to do evaluations, Chuck was glad she'd gotten her blood pumping early.

The evals were not the best she'd ever done. After reviewing them, she realized they, in fact, sucked. The events of the previous couple days made it hard to get enthused about sitting around and doing menial tasks. Glancing at her watch, Chuck jotted down a few more scribbles here and there until she felt the pages were at least passable.

She swung by Warehouse 1 and dropped off the evals before heading to the cafeteria. Walking past the recruit dorms, Chuck heard Tillman's voice coming from inside. Peeking her head in, she saw him sitting next to Jess on a bunk. They each had a tablet in hand, and Tillman made several swipes on Jess's tablet as he demonstrated one of its many features.

"You can group everybody's comms by hitting the link tab, then dragging their name into whichever group or groups you want them in."

Jess performed the action, then turned towards Tillman. "Under what circumstances would we have people in multiple groups?"

"The team lead may want to be part of multiple groups, in order to hear everyone while keeping overlap low within each group. The most typical reason is you'll frequently have a command group, so the lead and command can talk to each other without the rest of the team hearing them."

Jess nodded, just as Chuck cleared her throat purposefully. "Not to fuss, but you should probably get to lunch, Jess. You have labs this afternoon."

"Oh, hey Agent Barnes. Sorry, I guess we kind of lost track of time." Jess handed the tablet to Tillman. "Thanks Agent Moseby, you know, for the tips." Jess rose and headed for the exit, giving Chuck a fist bump as she passed her.

Tillman's eyes lit up as she approached. "Hey, how did evals go?"

"About as well as you'd expect when waking up at three-thirty in the morning. You wanna go grab some lunch offsite?"

His shoulders sunk slightly. "I'd really like to, but Smalls wants us to have a working lunch today, I'm guessing thanks to all the hubbub over this Revenant deal."

Chuck frowned. "Fair enough, maybe we can do lunch tomorrow, you know, on campus."

Tillman did seem to perk up a bit at this suggestion. "I'd be honored."

Chuck walked over and sat next to him. She still didn't know exactly what a *cautious relationship* was supposed to look like but passing glances and cafeteria lunches weren't exactly doing it for her. Tillman admirably read the room, leaning in for a kiss as her bottom touched down on the grossly uncomfortable mattress.

She pulled her lips away long enough to whisper in his ear. "Enjoy your working lunch."

"Um, I'm sure I could, you know, call in sick."

Chuck put a finger to his lips. "Nice try." With that she gave him a quick kiss on the cheek and stood. "Maybe I'll see you at dinner tonight." She turned and headed for the exit, quite pleased with herself.

***

After lunch Chuck met the recruits at the morgue. It occurred to her that Sparkles's body could still be resting inside one of the many bays set up along the far wall. She quickly pushed the thought out of her mind.

Today the group was learning about Chupacabra anatomy. Four cadavers were stacked on a rolling cart at the back of the room.

As a medical trainee, Rita clearly enjoyed opportunities like this more than the other recruits. She quickly volunteered to help Doc distribute the corpses, as the other recruits took their places behind a set of examination tables.

Doc was his usual excitable self as he started unwrapping the body he would be demonstrating with. "You all make sure you put some of that wax under your noses! These things can get pretty ripe, even in cold storage!"

Josh quickly donned a mask and goggles. "Whoa! Is this what these things smell like in the wild, Doc?"

Doc beamed as he placed a set of surgical tools on his table. "For the most part. They actually smell worse when they're mating!"

"God, how have we kept these things hidden this long? They smell like ass!" Greg held his head back as he attempted to help Rita with another of the creatures.

Chuck suppressed a smile. If this is what Greg thought ass smelled like, he should probably see a proctologist. It was a dumb and unnecessary thought, but she had a feeling dumb and unnecessary might be in short supply during the coming days.

Doc turned towards her and smiled. "It's not easy! You want to tell them about the Chupacabra's history, Charlotte?" Doc pulled down a large camera assembly that would project a close-up view of what he was doing so the recruits could follow along.

She wanted to go and seek out Sally, but she didn't see any harm in hanging around with Doc for a little bit. She stepped over to the body on Doc's table and took a closer look at it. The Chupacabras looked like scaly, medium sized dogs. Their snout was elongated like a Borzoi's, and they had two long frontal fangs that hung down almost even with the base of their bottom jaw.

Taking a professional stance, Chuck began. "As you can see, Chupacabras could be easily mistaken for dogs at a distance. In fact, rogue members of the species can be hard for even us to spot.

"Chupacabras are cannibalistic. It is not uncommon for males to fight over females and territory, with the victor often eating the loser. The smell is caused by high levels of ammonia in the creature's digestive system and significant concentrations of sulfur in its skin and scales. This helps protect them from biting insects but also tends to reveal their presence to potential prey."

Doc pulled out a laptop, bringing up an overlay of the cuts the recruits would be making.

Chuck continued. "We think this is part of the reason they are inclined to eat each other."

Josh raised a hand, and she pointed his way. "Don't they get blamed for eating chickens and goats?"

Rita perked up and quickly responded. "The name Chupacabra actually means 'goat sucker.'"

Chuck gave Rita a nod. "Chupacabras have been around for a long time, but they only really gained notoriety in the nineties when a woman claimed she'd seen one in Puerto Rico."

Jess raised her hand now. "But the monster that lady saw didn't look like these things."

She nodded again. "You're very right. The woman did encounter a cryptid, just not a Chupacabra. The creature was an undiscovered Class One, now named Olsiphrana. As a side note, Olsiphrana happened to be the first new Class One to have been discovered in several years."

Doc pulled his scalpel out, ready to proceed with the lesson. Giving the recruits a wave, Chuck turned to him. "I'll let you take it from here, Doc!"

She slid out of the morgue and started heading back towards the main concourse of Alpha. As soon as she left the medical wing she fired off a text to DeRosa.

'I'm going to the cafeteria if you have time to talk.'

Fate seemed to be on her side as she entered the dining area. Sally was already there, speaking with Smalls of all people. Chuck gave her a quick nod and walked a few rows away before sitting down. Ten minutes later DeRosa and Smalls stood up. Smalls headed for the exit and Sally headed her way.

"Hey. I was going to respond as soon as we were done talking."

Chuck nodded. "I don't know that I've ever seen Smalls in the dining hall before."

"I'm not totally sure she eats," Sally replied with a smirk.

"What exactly brought the good deputy down here?"

Sally answered her question with a question of her own. "When were you planning on telling me about you and Tillman?"

"Who ratted us out?"

Sally glanced back over her shoulder. "Who else? I think Smalls watches the video feeds more than my mom used to watch daytime soaps."

Chuck raised her eyebrows. "Are you going to be lecturing me about workplace romances?"

Sally laughed. "Me? Oh, hell no, I'm the last person who'd be qualified to do that. You two are adults, if you're happy, I'm happy for you."

"Bullshit. I can already see it in your eyes. I'm never going to hear the end of this."

"Damn straight. I guess you must've separated your faces long enough to have talked about the Revenant?"

Chuck nodded. "Tillman told me it was being discussed. Is that what Delta's going with then?"

"They sure as hell think that's what attacked her."

"Do *you* think it's a Revenant?"

Sally rested her chin on her hand. "I don't, although your encounter has as much to do with that as any of the evidence does. For once, however, I'm not alone in my suspicions. Hines doesn't agree with Delta. Very few do, in fact."

"Is that what you were talking about with Smalls?"

DeRosa shrugged. "Partly, yeah. Nobody in command is convinced it's a Revenant. Delta seems to have made up its mind, though, so who knows what they're going to have us do."

"I get why you would be skeptical, but what's with the others?"

"If you took both attacks and fused them together, then I think everyone but me would be on board with that being the cause. But individually, they're missing pieces. One of the big reasons that Revenants are such a danger to cryptids is that they eat them."

"Really? I've never heard that before."

"They don't eat *everything*, just some very particular parts. Something about certain cryptid organs gives them strength or helps preserve them or some shit. The Wardens have a bunch of info on it. That Mog had been messed up, but not eaten, at least not by anything else. That doesn't really jive with a Revenant attack."

"And whatever I saw hadn't been eating Sparkles."

"Exactly. Your encounter is the biggest indication. If that had been a Revenant, I doubt you and I would be talking right now."

Chuck leaned back as a cold streak went up her spine. "Should I tell Command about what I saw?" It seemed strange to her that Delta would be so bullish on something the very people serving in the area didn't agree with.

"My first thought would be hell no. I think under the circumstances it's not necessary. I doubt the game plan would change much, and if for some reason that wasn't a Class One you saw, well…" DeRosa shrugged.

"Yeah." The potential consequences were left unspoken between them.

They split then. Sally had yet another meeting, and Chuck needed to get back to her recruits. She arrived as Doc was making his final cut.

"When you finish cleaning up, stick around. I need to talk to everyone," Chuck announced.

Marcy peeled off a pair of medical gloves. "Can we go somewhere that doesn't stink?"

The room really *did* smell offensive. "Yeah, that's a good idea."

Once everything had been cleaned and put away, she led them

back to the gym, taking a seat on the ring apron. The recruits gathered in front of her.

"I'm sure you're all starving after playing with goat sucker guts all afternoon, so I'll keep this short. I would like you guys to get to bed early tonight."

The recruits looked at one another and then at her. She could see that they suspected what she was going to say next. "Tomorrow we are going to make-up for the Media Day we missed this week."

"Thank you, Agent Barnes!"

"Awesome!"

"Oh, thank God!"

Josh added his voice last. "The usual time then?"

Chuck nodded.

With that, the crew staggered off. She sat on the ring apron a little longer. The events of the last several days had worn her out, both mind and body. Chuck felt more tired, impatient, and more distant from her duties than ever before. Sparkles's death, her budding romance with Tillman, and the specter of whatever monster was out there hunting cryptids, all weighed heavily on her. Now the question became whether she could still be an effective teacher under these new circumstances?

She pondered the question until a group of employees entered the training center. Her solitude disrupted, Chuck popped off the apron and headed for the door.

Chapter Twenty-One:

Voices

Arizona, such a curious and nonsensical name. Not that I have a feeling for any other name that would adequately describe it other than inhospitable. *A barren waste of rocks and fruitless trees, barely fit to raise cattle. Why even humans would choose to make their homes here eludes me.*

The poor chap that has spent the last few hours bringing me up to speed, as one might say, has exhausted his usefulness. His christened name is Bradley Osborn, and once upon a time he was an electrician from a town called Kingman.

Trying to sort through more than forty years of memories has been rather taxing on me. The now-constant din of the voices does little to help the matter. On more than one occasion I have attempted to isolate one voice above the others, hoping to ease the maddening chorus. All such efforts have failed.

They did do their part in leading me to the soon-to-be departed Mr. Osborn however, and for that I should be grateful. Bradley has provided me all manner of wonderful discoveries! The humans have been quite busy it seems. Flying is only one of their myriad accomplishments. Extraordinary weapons of war have been invented. They have walked upon the surface of the moon. Wonders beyond any I had imagined them capable of.

Their short lifespans make them ambitious. Unfortunately, this also makes them dangerous.

My failed attack on the young sasquatch left me disoriented and confused for several days. In its broken state, my mind took far longer than it should have to sort out the small wisps of memory I got from the creature. Her understanding of the Rogers' dealings was rudimentary and piecemeal, but valuable nonetheless.

Combined with Bradley's more pedestrian expertise concerning modern society and its scientific wonders, I have begun to formulate a plan to draw the Rogers out once more. Because of this, I have done my new friend the favor of killing him myself.

He believes that taking his own life would damn his soul to hell, a hilarious notion, but one which Mr. Osborn felt strongly about. Against the urgings of the voices, I released his mind in time to witness me shred the soft flesh of his stomach, allowing his insides to spill upon the ground at his feet. His whimpering these last few minutes has been ecstasy to the voices.

This mercy has left me feeling odd, as though in some way his mind had influenced me, and not the other way around. There is simply no time to dwell on this, however.

I have but one focus, and that is to hunt. Like any good hunter, I must first procure my bait. The voices have brought me this far, and I must trust them to take me just a little further.

My revenge, so long desired, is close now.

Chapter Twenty-Two:

Media Day the Third

Chuck's alarm went off dutifully at four in the morning. Her sleep had again been restless, and she felt like a bus had run her over in the night. After her usual routine, she headed for the locker room. She was so tired and distracted she didn't even notice the lights were already on as she entered the little hallway. Still oblivious, she turned the corner.

"Good morning, Agent Barnes!" Jess's voice startled her, and Chuck reached out and grabbed at the wall to keep herself from slipping on the floor.

"Jess, you're very…"

"Early? Yeah, I know. The last couple of days have been kind of a mess. I just wanted to see if you had thought about me, you know, changing teams?"

Having gathered her wits, Chuck crossed the room to stand in front of her usual mirror. She didn't know how long this conversation was going to take, but based on Jess's being here this early, she guessed the recruit hadn't talked about it with the other women.

"This *has* been a mess of a week," Chuck agreed. "I wish I could say that I had given your request a bunch of thought, but I haven't. I'm sorry."

"I get it. I did kind of ambush you the other day."

Chuck wasn't looking at her, but she could hear disappointment in the younger woman's voice. She turned and looked the recruit in the eye. "Tell you what. Let's make some time to talk about it today."

Jess's countenance shifted almost instantly. "Are you sure?"

"Scout's honor." Chuck turned back to her mirror. "But this isn't a normal request. I don't want you to start getting your hopes up crazy high."

"Sweet! Thanks, Agent Barnes!"

"You need to keep it on the down low. I don't want Agent Moseby to hear about this secondhand before we've had a chance to talk."

"I don't think I'm the one that needs to worry about spilling the beans to Agent Moseby." Jess said sassily.

Chuck looked at the recruit, who smirked at her. Well, that cat was out of the bag.

She turned back to her mirror. The prospects for a relatively normal day off site were pretty much erased. All she could do now was grin and bear it.

At the edge of her vision, she saw Jess turn towards her as though she wanted to say something, but then turned back nearly as quickly.

Jess could be a handful, but she certainly seemed to be serious about making a change. Chuck didn't know what kind of protocols were in place to address a situation like this but sitting down and giving Jess a few minutes to explain her desire in more detail wouldn't hurt anything.

"What the hell, Jess? You trying to show us up?" Rita snapped as she entered the locker room, Marcy close behind.

"Bitch, get your ass to bed on time instead of flicking your bean to Chris Hemsworth fanfics, and you could be up early too!"

Marcy laughed. "Somebody hasn't had their coffee yet."

Rita flipped Jess off, then took her middle finger and rubbed it up and down on her crotch. Chuck smiled as Jess flipped back double middle fingers of her own.

The lights inside the room flickered suddenly and the recruits gasped.

Rita looked like she was about to have a full-on panic attack. "Agent Barnes, so help me God if that watch goes off!"

Chuck turned to the younger women. "That wasn't an alert. I need you ladies to bring the mood level down a bit."

A loud fart sounded through the locker room.

Marcy gagged. "God, Rita! Take that nasty ass of yours somewhere else!"

Rita smiled. "Just bringing the mood down."

"You can say that again," Jess replied.

Rita stepped up to her mirror. "Besides, I don't *flick my bean* to Chris Hemsworth, I have more discerning tastes than that."

"I wouldn't exactly call Greg an upgrade over Thor." Marcy deadpanned.

"Yeah, well, I haven't had to worry about my box getting dusty since we've been here, which is a lot more than either of you can say." Rita fired back.

Marcy chuckled. "You don't know what Jess and I are doing while you polish Greg's knob."

Jess coughed, spitting toothpaste onto the mirror in front of her as she grabbed ahold of the sink.

Rita, clearly wanting the last word, continued. "Bullshit! Don't be lying just because you don't have someone to help you get off... Isn't that right Agent Barnes?"

All three of the recruits giggled at that. Chuck gave them the best version of a mom glare she could muster. "Okay, okay, get it out of your systems."

Jess didn't even wait to finish brushing her teeth before opening the floodgates. "Is he a good kisser? How long has he been chasing you, or did *you* chase him? Are you guys going to have to share an apartment?"

Chuck rolled her eyes, then turned back to her mirror, allowing the waves of questions to crash over her without response. At length, the younger women returned to the topic of Chris Hemsworth, expanding it to other Avengers and who would be the best in bed.

After a fair bit of back and forth, Jess turned to Chuck. "Your turn Agent Barnes... Thor, Cap, or Bucky?"

Chuck smiled. "Wanda."

Rita and Jess laughed as Marcy applauded. Chuck finished tightening her ponytail, turned, and gave the recruits a wink.

Josh and Greg entered as the women were finishing up with their makeup and hair. The whole group seemed in surprisingly good spirits overall.

As she watched Jess interacting with the others, Chuck could understand why the younger woman might want to spend more time out and about. Jess really did get along well with the rest of the recruits. She may be a little rough around the edges, sometimes too rough, but at least there was chemistry there.

Ding!

Stepping into Warehouse 2, Chuck saw Ed leaning against the large passenger van. As the group approached, Walt came out from behind the vehicle and gave them a wave.

"Hey, Agent Barnes!" Ed greeted her. "Are we expecting any emergencies this morning?"

She patted her hands in the air. "Shh, don't jinx it!"

"Oh, my bad. Hey, I was sorry to hear about your sasquatch friend."

Chuck's stomach twisted but she gave Ed a half smile and a monotone, "Thanks."

Tillman arrived not long after. The ladies at least possessed the decorum to not assault him with questions, but they whispered amongst themselves as he passed out their devices. Everybody checked in one by one with Ed, until only Chuck and Tillman remained.

"They all know," she told him as Ed scanned her ID.

"Yeah, it was kind of inevitable," he responded as a goofy grin spread across his face.

Chuck climbed into the van. As she sat down, a long angry screech bellowed from her watch. The van shook from the chaos of the recruit's response.

"Come on!"

"Not this shit again!"

Chuck looked at the watch. A big green smiley face looked back at her from the screen. It took a moment to realize that Tillman was laughing. She looked back at the group, some of whom had now noticed the picture on the watch. The van went dead quiet, except for the chuckles of Tillman, who was clearly pleased with himself.

She reached back a hand and hit Tillman in the shoulder hard. "You dick!"

Her action garnered applause from the recruits. Jess, who sat directly behind Tillman, got in a jab of her own.

Tillman winced at the pair of blows. He started laughing harder as he pushed a button on his own watch that caused Chuck's to stop making the noise.

He rubbed his shoulder. "I couldn't resist!" He looked around, noticing he was the only one that seemed to have enjoyed the prank.

"Now that I've got your attention, listen up. You should all try and enjoy this day to the fullest, as I'm not sure when the next time we'll get to go off site will be."

That certainly did get their attention.

"You mean because of Sparkles?" Marcy asked.

Tillman nodded. "Among other things. The bottom line is that command will give priority to taking care of subjects over making sure you all get a day away from the complex each week."

The conversation ended there as Tillman turned back around and settled into his routine of prepping the various devices he would employ that day. Behind them, the nervous chatter of the recruits could be heard over the sounds of the road. Chuck wondered for a moment if the whole exchange was something Smalls had instructed Tillman to do, or if he did it on his own to redirect the recruit's attention. The tone felt decidedly *un*Tillman like.

Chuck closed her eyes, seeing red dots staring back at her. They were still there as she nodded off.

Chapter Twenty-Three:

On Campus

Tillman nudged Chuck awake as they pulled into the IHOP parking lot. Blinking away her grogginess, she was the last person to exit the van. She and Tillman followed the others into the restaurant. Their group easily took up half of one of the dining rooms.

Rounds of coffee, juice, and water were delivered. Most of them ordered roughly the same thing each week, out of habit as much as anything. Greg and Josh always ordered Denver omelets. Marcy and Rita would get stuffed French toast, though the stuffing changed week to week.

Jess and Tillman made a weekly spectacle of trying to see who could order the biggest breakfast. They'd usually get eggs, bacon, hash browns, some sausage for good measure, and a stack of pancakes. Basically, whichever one of them ordered first, the other would order in kind. Chuck had tried joining in with them once and spent the entire day regretting it.

Today she went with a very sensible toasted English muffin, egg whites, and turkey sausage links. Walt, who had sat down next to her, ordered his usual bowl of oatmeal with extra brown sugar.

The return to routine clearly lifted everybody's mood. Tillman's prank and lecture were quickly forgotten as they dug into their breakfasts. Chuck was even tempted to steal a slice of bacon from Tillman's plate. The crisp slices were enticing, but in the end she held off, deciding to play it safe and not give the recruits any additional reason to talk.

The whole rec/media/get-off-site day idea had evolved over the years. Nominally it was intended as a day to let the recruits interact with the real world—at least somewhat. As social media platforms and their popularity had grown over the years, the approach to the day changed.

Instead of just having to monitor communications with family or maybe one or two close friends, a multitude of people within a recruit's digital footprint had to be monitored. The screening process tended to eliminate candidates that had *too* much of a social media presence, but none of them were truly recluses either.

Chuck remembered her brother joking about the smart kids being unpopular when he was in school. It was a bias that she herself held until about eighth grade. By then, she had a close-knit group of friends, and they were all quite intelligent, at least by their own standards.

Even after she'd moved up to high school and pretty much changed out her entire friend group, the new squad were smart as well. They didn't always act it, but basically all her five or six closest friends had graduated with honors, at or near the top of their class.

Her recruits were all smart and seemed to have a healthy number of friends. Though now that they were several months into their training, most had finally begun to put a bit of distance between themselves and their former lives.

As the recruits spread about the ASU campus, Tillman would settle down at his favorite Starbucks and start the process of tracking and collecting data from each of them. The laptop he used had mainframe levels of processing speed. Even then, it required a boost from another device hidden inside his rolling case. It created a special little hub that all the devices the recruits used connected to.

Beyond keeping track of the recruits, Tillman's gear also spied on devices that might get within a few feet of a recruit. This feature was a secret that helped to ensure a particularly sneaky recruit couldn't switch out phones or otherwise use a different device. Tillman made sure things ran smoothly on campus while a few Kangaroos back at Alpha did most of the monitoring. While the whole operation was fascinating, it kept Tillman distracted enough that he wasn't all that much fun to be around.

Chuck usually headed for the library or sometimes used the day to get in a bit of sunbathing and relaxing. If she were needed, she would be called upon, but typically she just had the day to herself. Today, however, she had a conversation to carry out with a certain tech recruit. To keep the conversation a secret for the time being, she asked Tillman if he could put a temporary hold on monitoring Jess's phone.

"Jess and I need to have a talk. Woman to woman."

Tillman scrunched up his face. "Um, okay, sure. I can kill the connection. You'll let me know as soon as you two are done?"

"Scout's Honor," she replied, resisting an urge to kiss him right there in front of God and everybody.

Though cool, the temperature was still pleasant and most of them chose to walk to the campus, rather than load up the van. Chuck and Jess headed for Palo Verde Beach, a cozy area not far from the football stadium. There were several tables with umbrellas to keep the sun in check. They chose one and sat down.

Jess clearly couldn't hold in her excitement any longer as she began speaking almost immediately. "I really appreciate this, Agent Barnes. You could've told me to piss off."

"You're welcome. Just to reiterate, though, I don't know if this will go anywhere."

"Oh, I totally get it. And I promise I won't get mad if it can't happen." As she watched Jess, Chuck realized how much the younger woman used her hands while talking.

"Fair enough. So, besides not wanting to work with *old men*, what are the other reasons you want to be a field agent instead of a Kangaroo?"

"Well, yeah, that is one of the reasons. But I don't know. Like, I know I'm kick ass at programming and writing code and shit, but… well I've been doing that since I was like nine. Wait, damnit, should I not cuss?"

"You're fine. I'm not recording this, promise. Did you really start writing code when you were nine?"

"I mean, I'm no Agent Moseby, but yeah, I started working with computers pretty young. I made a game of it. How far could I push the envelope? I would rewrite code in existing games to make them harder, or easier. My mom and dad were cool, but they also had to work a lot of hours to afford living in DC. My sister and I spent most of our time on the weekends or in the summer in front of screens."

Chuck nodded. "You're self-taught?"

Jess threw her hands up. "Yeah, but here's the thing. There's only so far you can go teaching yourself and I had to improvise a bit."

"Improvise?"

"You're sure Agent Moseby isn't listening to us?"

"I can't promise he isn't, but I'm mostly confident."

Jess puffed up her posture. "My sixth-grade year, I started hacking into my school district's mainframe and awarding myself scholarships and awards that would get me into summer programs. A particular one caught my eye."

Holding up a hand, Chuck interrupted. "Let me guess, Rochester Advanced Development."

Jess nodded her head. "RAD camp, accepting children ages twelve to seventeen. Focusing on mental, physical, and emotional wellbeing." She laughed.

Chuck knew many of those recruited into the Family, including herself, had attended RAD. She also knew the camps were mostly glorified testing grounds, rooting out the best candidates. "And the rest, as they say, is history?"

A strange expression passed across Jess's face, like she'd seen something deeply disturbing, but she recovered quickly. "Not exactly. The summer between my eighth grade and freshmen years I attended the RAD camp, and while I was there I hacked into the Family's mainframe."

Chuck was surprised and a little skeptical. "Wait, as in, hacked into one of the sites?"

Jess continued, an air of confidence building around her. "I hacked into *the* mainframe. The one at Delta. During one of the classes that year they put us in front of a laptop to *test our coding knowledge*. RAD was so much different from the other camps I had attended, like TIP, I figured something must be up with it. Instead of doing the test, I started digging through the router all the laptops were pinging. Pretty soon, I'm looking at all this weird shit about cryptids and agents, and I was like, oh my god!"

Impressed, all Chuck could do was blink and continue listening to the story.

Jess's hands were a whirlwind as she continued. "For like, the next couple of years I would go to RAD and try to hack more and more systems. I think they caught on, because by my senior year, it was hard to get through.

"But you *did* get through?"

Jess grinned. "Oh, totally. I really thought all the creature stuff was cool, but the tech they were using was way beyond anything I'd ever encountered, commercially anyway. I couldn't wait to join the Family, and because I knew my way around the systems, that's what I signed up for. But now—now that I've seen what the field agents really do, I wish I would've gone for working off site."

"And you think you could handle what we do?"

"Hell yeah! I mean, I'll have to really step things up with my fight training and firearms, but we both know how good you are, and I'm a quick learner!"

Chuck wasn't entirely sold on Jess converting but seeing how serious she was gave her the impression the younger woman would put forth maximum effort if given the opportunity. "Now listen Jess. I can't swear anything at this point, *but* I will talk to DeRosa and Tillman. Fair enough?"

Jess nearly jumped over the table to give her a hug. "Thank you, Agent Barnes! I'll make you proud!"

"Like I said, no promises."

Still grinning ear to ear, Jess nodded. "Understood."

"Okay, you should get going, I'll let Agent Moseby know he can turn your stuff back on. Although, based on what you've told me, I'm not all that confident you can't just change your tech on the fly."

"Damn straight! Thanks again." With that, Jess stood, heading deeper into campus.

Chuck wasn't sure how she planned to broach the subject with Sally and Tillman, but she wanted to do it sooner rather than later. She pulled out her own phone, turned it on, and dialed Tillman.

"Hey Charlotte."

Though she thought of him as Tillman regularly, she was having trouble adjusting to him using her first name so freely. "Hey. Jess and I are done if you want to turn her phone back on."

"Great, I'll get her back online. Everything good?"

"Things are quite good in fact." At that moment, someone sat down at an adjacent table. She probably wouldn't have paid them any attention, except for the sudden smell of licorice that filled her nostrils, something familiar and unsettling. "We still on for lunch?"

"Sure thing, though our options are a bit limited beyond coffee and biscotti."

A cloud of white vapor billowed out from in front of the nearby figure. "We'll make do. Listen, I've got to go. I'll see you around noon." She ended the call without waiting for an answer.

Leaning a bit closer to the hunched over figure, Chuck cleared her throat. "Hey, you mind taking that somewhere else?"

"Oh, I think you'll be wanting me to stick around, missy."

A jolt went through her body like the onset of a violent illness.

Hank McFadden turned on his seat to face her.

Chapter Twenty-Four:

McFadden

Chuck really wished she had her sidearm at that moment. Or knew where Ed was. She wished she were anywhere but where she was.

McFadden put on the stupid looking smile she'd seen when they first met. He seemed to sense her discomfort. "Now, now. No need to get all coiled up like a rattler waiting to strike." His accent was as stomach-turning as she remembered.

Seeing him completely turned around, she couldn't believe she hadn't realized it was him by looking at his back. He was dressed like someone's dad who wanted to sneak into a frat, right down to his pair of crocs.

McFadden, disgusting and old as he was, moved with a quickness that shocked her. He slid into the chair across from her before she could even react to what he was doing. "I hope I didn't scare away your little girly friend."

Chuck suddenly remembered the strange look that had flashed across Jess's face. Had McFadden caused it? "Not an inch closer asshole."

He licked his lips. "Listen, you kids are harder to track down than a tick on a grizzly bear's nuts. What do ya do inside that compound of yours all day?" He held up a hand as if to stop a response, even though one would not have been forthcoming. "Don't answer that, I don't want to hear about all yer perversions." He placed an envelope on the table. It was the kind with one of those clasps you tie with a string.

She looked to her left and right, determining the best path of escape. "You followed us here?"

"Well, I had to piss in a Gatorade bottle for a couple days, but I finally caught a glimpse of your pretty little face riding out of the front gate this morning. Now… Agent Barnes, right? How about cha listen for a minute. There's a message I want you to deliver to Sally DeRosa."

The mention of Sally's name didn't change Chuck's feelings in the least. "You followed us. That means you know I'm not alone. I can have backup here in a heartbeat."

McFadden shrugged. "And make some big scene? Yeah, I guess ya could do that." He scratched the haphazardly growing stubble on his neck. "You could do that. But listen, if DeRosa is yer friend, and I think she is, then you should really have a look at what I have in this envelope. I think she, and by extension you, may be in danger."

Something about his tone kept Chuck rooted to her seat, but she wasn't going to let her guard down that easy. "Threatening me isn't exactly earning you any points."

McFadden raised both of his hands. "Honey, I don't want to be here anymore than you do. If the bosses find out I'm doing this, my ass is grass. Now, I'll bet Sally's told ya a ream of shit about me that a thousand Charmin factories couldn't clean up. But regardless of how she feels, I've got no desire to see her dead—or worse."

Chuck wondered what he thought was worse than being dead. Against her better judgement, she reached down and picked up the packet, slowly unwinding the string. McFadden leaned in. His breath smelled of sour licorice. She shook the envelope a bit and several pictures fell out.

The top one she recognized, if only from seeing it on the satellite image. It showed the Griffin Jeep from the morning she'd met McFadden. Lifting the pile, she discovered the next picture showed a cave entrance with logs and dirt framing it. It looked manmade, as if someone had dug or blasted their way through.

Chuck nearly dropped the whole pack as she turned to the next photo. Bodies, or what were left of them, lay scattered about the inside of a cavern, likely the same one whose entrance appeared in the previous picture. The scene was absolute carnage. The bodies had been mangled to the point she couldn't tell much about the dead, including their number. She looked up at McFadden. He simply nodded.

She turned to the next picture, and for a moment couldn't tell if she was looking at it right side up. The photo was dark, but it showed what looked like a shipping container, the kind she sometimes saw at the docks in Tampa, but smaller. The picture made her uncomfortable, and yet the longer she examined it, the less she could explain the feeling. In the shadowy image she could just make out what looked like writing along the container's edges.

"What is all this?"

"How about cha look at that last photo, then maybe you can tell me." McFadden's voice was calm and level, but his eyes were darting back and forth as if watching for something.

Chuck slowly turned to the final picture, which showed a different side of the container, this one with an opening. Two things jumped out at her immediately as she examined the more well-lit shot. Directly above the opening, among a string of odd glyphs, sat a symbol she knew very well: the Rogers' Family crest.

The second caused her arms to break out in goosebumps. The interior of the container was white, except for several long blue smears.

"*It looks like blue dust, or powder,*" Ed had said about the substance on the Mog's face.

She looked up at McFadden. "Wait, who are these people?"

"*These* people, my dear, are the three hombres I was out looking for the day we fortuitously met. The big bosses thought they were defectors. Even suspected them of running off to join up with yer little outfit. Imagine my surprise when I found a whole mess of Rogers cronies as I was closing in on their abandoned Jeep."

Chuck shook her head, not quite sure what he wanted her to say. "You think *we* killed them?"

He gave her a used car salesman smile. "Am I the first Griffin you've ever knowingly met face to face Miss Barnes?"

His look had a maniacal quality to it, and she didn't like his use of the term *knowingly*. "Yes, actually."

McFadden's smile widened until he laughed, a short little sound that made Chuck bristle. "Agent Barnes, Sally no doubt told ya that I used to play for your team. I know the deal, and I know the stories. Every half-truth is at least that—half a truth. What the Family calls protection, we call suppression. What we consider culling the herd, the Family calls poaching. You can find some real assholes working for both our groups. The bottom line is that neither side wants an all-out war."

"Who said anything about a war?"

He reached into one of his pockets and pulled out a small sandwich bag. He opened it carefully and removed a folded piece of paper with brown splotches all over it.

"I found this in that cave. One of them had been carrying it when they got attacked." He unfolded it, and as he did, Chuck realized the brown splotches were dried blood. Once fully expanded, he slid it across the table.

Through the brown stains she could see a drawing of the container, with various symbols and markers peppered around it. She'd only given it a momentary look before McFadden flipped it over. The opposite page had been covered in more symbols.

He grunted. "It's a code of some kind. But check that bottom symbol, right in the middle."

It only took her a moment to find the symbol he was talking about. Another representation of the Rogers Family Crest.

"Now between this and those runes on the container... well Miss Barnes, something smelled fishier than a boardwalk whorehouse."

"And you want Sally to see all this... why?"

"Y'all ever figure out what happened to that Mogollon of yours?"

"It had caused all the damage to itself." Chuck tried to sound resolute, confident but the look on McFadden's face revealed that he didn't believe a word of it.

"Someone tipped these guys off about this container being buried clear out in the middle of nowhere. But not just any container, a container that had been enchanted by the Family god knows how long ago. And when they opened that container, well." He gestured to the pictures.

Chuck blinked and saw the red, glowing eyes. Sparkles, the Mog, these Griffins. Were they really all connected? And what did he mean about the container being *enchanted*?

She frowned as McFadden soldiered on. "We got four bodies—"*Five*"—and an ancient, empty box. Now, I'm no Perry Mason, but I'll wager whatever got my men, got your monster."

The image of the darkened shape in the canyon flashed in her mind again.

McFadden tapped the paper. "This note, I'm betting someone on yer team sent it."

"And why would that be?"

"Because whoever it was picked these three dipshits to do the job. Dumb bastards had no business being in that cave. Hell, I'm not sure *I* had any business being in that cave. Whatever was in that box, it left behind one hell of a funk. And now it's running loose somewhere up in the mountains. I told ya, differences or not, DeRosa has my respect. I figured she'd want to know what she might be up against."

He refolded the paper, placing it back in the baggie.

"Soooo, I've got to bug out. You do whatever the hell ya want to with this. But if you're smart, and I've never known Sally to associate with dummies, you'll show that to her. Tell her she doesn't even owe me one. I'm washing my hands of it."

McFadden stood and immediately pulled out his Juul. Thankfully, the wind kept anything from blowing in Chuck's direction as he strode off.

She quickly stuffed the pictures and the paper back into the envelope so nobody would see them. Why had the Family buried the container? What manner of cryptid required an enchantment to keep it imprisoned? And why would someone from the Family recruit Griffins to dig it up?

Suddenly, Chuck had a feeling that she should call her mom. Pulling the phone from her pocket, she hit the contact button, scrolling down to her mother's number. After pushing the button, she brought the phone up to her ear, listening to several tones before the line picked up on the other end.

"This is Lisa Barnes. I'm afraid I've missed your call. Please leave your name and number, and I'll get back to you as soon as I can."

She'd almost started speaking but stopped upon hearing the message. It felt odd that her mom didn't answer, until she realized it was Friday. Her mom might be at work or a doctor's appointment. Chuck didn't leave a message; her mom would see she'd called and probably call back.

Placing a hand on her head, Chuck closed her eyes. McFadden really had gotten the drop on her. Life was much simpler when all she had to worry about was training a few horny kids how to be agents.

Unable to reach her mom, she decided to head towards the library. They had a small section on local folklore she could check out. It certainly wouldn't be the types of records the Family possessed, but it would help her pass the time.

Her mind wandered as she walked the familiar paths towards the library, mulling over her feelings of uncertainty. She thought about calling DeRosa right then and there, but ultimately decided against it. Sally probably couldn't do anything for her now anyway.

***

Tillman sat with his back to the wall at the far end of the small customer area within the coffee shop. Chuck had to maneuver her way around a couple of well-tanned, fake blondes to get to him. Her visit to the library had calmed her somewhat and having Tillman close by further brightened her mood. "Hey, everything running smooth?"

"All quiet so far." He looked up from his laptop and suddenly stopped typing. "Are you feeling okay? You look like you've seen a ghost."

For a split second she thought about telling Tillman everything that had occurred, the eyes, McFadden, the pictures of the Griffins. But what would that accomplish? What benefit would come from Tillman being in on her and Sally's secrets? She held up the envelope. "Um, I kind of went down a rabbit hole at the library, serial killers and stuff."

Tillman glanced at the folder, frowned, then went back to typing. "Gotcha. Is the food here going to be satisfactory, or do we need to head over to the food court?"

Chuck glanced over her shoulder. The shop itself was quite small. Most of the patrons were paying next to no attention to those around them as they waited for their name to be called. The thought of cozying up to Tillman here appealed to her, as any other food venue was likely to be less private.

"Here's good. What's your usual?"

He looked up again. "Ham and Swiss croissant, and an almond milk horchata."

"Almond milk horchata?" She asked, a bit skeptical.

"Oh yeah, don't knock it till you've tried it."

Chuck grinned. "I'll take your word for it. Be back in a minute." Tillman blew her a kiss, which struck her as an incredibly sweet gesture.

Taking her place in line, she looked back at Tillman, who sat oblivious to the world, and smiled.

***

"Friday is a strange day to be on campus," Rita said to no one in particular. Her and Greg had already been waiting at the van when Chuck and Tillman walked up together. "Everybody's in such a hurry to finish the week so they can start partying."

Chuck shielded her eyes from the setting sun. "It was interesting, that's for sure."

Walt looked up from playing Solitaire on his phone and quipped, "Well, beats a day at the office, eh?"

She nodded. "That it does, Walt. That it does."

Josh, Marcy, and Jess approached, joining Rita and Greg. The group began discussing the ins and outs of the day, with Rita casually bragging about how many likes and comments her various posts had received. With everyone now back, they returned to their seats in the van. Soon the vehicle was heading back to Alpha.

The encounter with McFadden kept Chuck on edge most of the afternoon, and her head had begun to hurt. She turned towards Tillman who was downloading information from the recruits' phones.

"Hey, mind if I rest my head on your shoulder? I'm not feeling all that hot."

He looked at her and smirked. "You're not *looking* so hot actually. Are you sure all you need is a shoulder?"

She raised her eyebrows. "A shoulder should be sufficient, and maybe a hand if you've got one free."

Tillman took her hand in his as she rested her head on his shoulder. Chuck didn't know exactly how much longer Tillman wanted to *take it slow*, but sitting next to him, hand in hand, she felt comfortable.

Comfortable enough to have nodded off, the van hitting a bump startled her awake. Tillman was still holding her hand, but he also looked to have just been awoken. She checked behind her, finding all the recruits similarly waking up.

Within five minutes they were pulling up to Alpha's gate. There seemed to be more traffic than usual, and they sat in a line of cars for some time before finally being allowed to pass through. Chuck turned to Tillman, who simply shrugged.

She leaned forward. "Walt, what's going on?"

Walt shrugged. "I'm not sure, Ms. Charlotte. The gate personnel asked us to disembark at Warehouse 1."

Ed got out and grabbed his clipboard. As he was opening the side door, she saw a transport van pull out of Warehouse 2. She got out, wondering what was going on in their normal offloading area.

She turned to Tillman as he got out. "You mind seeing them down? I want to go check on things."

"Sure, let me know what you find out, huh?"

"Will do." With that, Chuck headed one building over. Entering through the big bay doors, she was surprised by what she saw.

Two vans were parked in the warehouse, and another one was pulling in. There were at least two dozen people milling about. Some were moving boxes or bags, some held clipboards, and some were standing around. Chuck recognized many of them, but others she'd never seen before. After a few moments she spotted Sally, who was standing off to the side, talking with Kahn from the security team.

Chuck moved quickly to stand next to the senior agent. Kahn looked over at her and then politely excused himself.

"Hey, you guys just get back?" Sally asked without looking at her.

"Yeah, what the hell is going on?"

"*This* is an emergency response team. Delta empties out one or two of those hole-in-the-wall, pissant sites I was telling you about, merge them into one unit and put them under the command of a couple of Wardens. I'm told it takes a major event for the Family to round up ten jolly assholes and dump them on a site. It appears we have a major event on our hands."

"I might know something about that *major* event," Chuck said.

Just then a black car with deeply tinted windows pulled into the warehouse and parked behind the final van in the line. DeRosa didn't turn to her. She simply nodded in the direction of the car. "Here come the ringleaders of this three-ring shitfest."

A man and a woman, both wearing long black trench coats, white shirts, and black ties got out of the back of the car. It was dark outside by now, but both were wearing sunglasses.

Wardens.

Chuck had only seen a couple of them in her time with the Family, but they all looked pretty much the same. Smalls approached the pair and appeared to have a conversation, although if the Wardens spoke, Chuck couldn't tell. Their lips never moved. Before long, the three of them headed off towards the elevator.

Sally suddenly turned to her. "What do you mean you might know something?"

Chuck held up the envelope. "Guess who I got a visit from today?"

DeRosa looked at the envelope, then back at the commotion of the warehouse.

"Let me guess… Hank McFadden."

Chapter Twenty-Five:

The Wardens

She gave DeRosa her best *I'm impressed* face. "How'd you know?"

"The envelope. Son of a bitch loves those things. He never passes up a chance to try and play spy." She paused and then turned away from the warehouse, which had begun to calm down. "What did the self-righteous prick bring you?"

"A bunch of photos and a wild story about some members of the Griffins getting killed."

"Why the hell would he want to give you those?"

"To bring to you. But that's not all, I think some of the stuff in here has to do with whatever it was I saw while trying to rescue Sparkles."

Sally looked like she was chewing the inside of her lip. "Come on, we don't want to do this here." She turned around and started heading towards the bay doors. They exited the warehouse into the cool night air and walked towards the car lot at the back of Alpha.

DeRosa veered towards Warehouse 3 before finally coming to a stop behind some stacks of pallets. A spotlight stationed on one of the corners nearby provided broken illumination.

She held out her hand. "Let's see what McFadden gave you."

Chuck handed over the envelope, before looking over her shoulder. Why was DeRosa so worried about secrecy?

DeRosa opened the envelope and pulled out the photos and the paper. Chuck stood in the cold, giving Sally time to mill over it all. The light did not touch the senior agent's face, making it hard to get a read on what she was thinking.

"What did he say when he approached you?" DeRosa asked without looking up.

"Nothing. He sat down near me and started vaping. I didn't realize who he was and asked him to quit. He turned around and…" She pointed at the envelope.

"And why did he say he was giving you these?"

"He wanted me to bring them to you. The way he tells it, his *big bosses* would never have sent these men to open that box. Said they didn't have any business being there. Seemed to think somebody within the Family sent them that paper so they'd let whatever was in there out."

"And now he wants us to clean up the mess?"

"Maybe, but Sally, the blue in the box and the blue stuff on the Mog. The fact they evidently didn't happen all that far apart. It's the reason I even brought any of this to you. McFadden said something about neither of our sides wanting to start a war, and that he felt like you should know what you're up against."

"That's rich. I don't suppose my savior had any ideas about what actually might have done all of this?"

Chuck could only shrug. "I really think he got spooked by that box, he even mentioned it had been enchanted by the Family. Have you ever run into anything like this before?"

DeRosa stood for a few moments before stuffing the pictures back into the envelope. "At Delta you hear some pretty weird stories. Cryptids that aren't in any book. Relics that have been touched by angels, or devils, or god knows what. It's a good bet this box is way above our paygrade." Sally paused, then smiled devilishly. "You good, or should I call your boy toy and have him warm you up?"

Chuck glared back. "I'm fine... but what's with the cloak and dagger?"

"With all the new additions, I didn't feel like inside would be very private." Chuck nodded in acknowledgement. "A lot of shit has hit the fan since yesterday morning."

Sally handed the envelope back to Chuck. DeRosa looked up at the light. "Smalls and Hines were having some success convincing Delta this might not have been a Revenant. Then the Kangaroos started picking up some out of the ordinary Griffin transmissions. Seems they have a group arriving tomorrow, kind of like the one we just mobilized. Apparently that was enough to convince the Board they needed to take emergency measures."

"If the Griffins are doing that, then why did McFadden give me all of this?"

"That's a question that leads to more questions. Maybe he really is trying to watch out for me. Or maybe this is all bullshit, and he's trying to get us killed. I'll be damned if I know."

"He did say something about there being assholes on both sides. Maybe he really is trying to prevent a war."

DeRosa rubbed her head for a moment, her frosty breath bright within the glow of the spotlight. "Delta—well more specifically the Board—have always operated more on logic than common sense. You combine a couple mysterious deaths with an incoming Griffin team and it's easy to see why they want to protect their assets." Sally coughed. "Being the cool, calm, and collected group they are, Delta's response is to fight fire with fire."

"Where does that leave us then?"

"I don't really know, but I'd clear my Saturday calendar if I were you. I'm sure first thing in the morning they'll summon us to discuss whatever grand plan they've come up with." Sally looked skyward again and let out a sigh. "Have you ever met a Warden?"

Chuck shook her head. "I've seen maybe two of them, but always from a distance."

"This should be quite the educational experience for you then."

"What do you mean?"

DeRosa shifted, looking nervous. "Wardens outrank agents, even Chief Agents like Hines. When they call in an emergency response team, the senior Warden in charge of the team becomes the *de facto* boss of the whole site."

"Great." Chuck didn't like the tone of Sally's voice. Looking at her watch, she realized they'd been outside for nearly half an hour.

DeRosa glanced at her watch as well. "Yeah, we should probably head back."

They began to head back towards Warehouse 2. As they walked, she prodded DeRosa for more information. "Did you recognize those Wardens?"

"No. But they all look the same anyway. Dumbasses. About the only way you can tell them apart is by their hair or how tall they are. You do know they're where all the 'men in black' mythology comes from, right?"

"I figured they either started it or copied it. Didn't we have

Wardens before the nineteen-forties?"

"Yeah, they started the Warden program at the end of World War One. Took a bunch of gung-ho vets and made them into a strike force to protect or fight Class Ones. Wars tend to bring a lot of the powerful cryptids out of hiding."

"Any idea how many of them there are?"

"No, but they die way more frequently than agents. Delta probably doesn't want statistics like that floating around. I know most of the sites outside the US have two or three stationed there at any given time."

"They ever ask you to become one?"

"Once, yeah, maybe ten years ago. You get to play with all kinds of crazy shit, but they tell anyone who might know you on the outside world that you're dead." Sally chuckled. "Send your family a can of ashes, the whole nine yards. Some of the old guard in the Family will tell you these batshit stories about how Wardens get forced to have plastic surgery. I don't believe it, but..." She shrugged.

Chuck rubbed her hands for warmth. "I'll remember that if they ever ask me to join."

When they finally turned back into Warehouse 2, there wasn't a soul around.

Ding!

"What should I do with these?" she asked, holding up the envelope.

"I don't know. Put them somewhere safe for now though. We might need them later."

"You don't think we should tell the Wardens?"

"Like I said, we might need them later. I'd rather find out what the Family knows first before I start parading around potentially suspect intel."

They split as they reached Chuck's apartment. Once inside she removed the photos from the envelope and hid them in a cereal box in the back of one of her cabinets. It was the same hiding spot she used for her old social security card.

The irony of keeping secrets within a secret society wasn't lost on her. The more she thought about the pictures though, the more her mind wanted to jump down the crazy conspiracy theory hole. Maybe those Griffins were looking for something that even the Family didn't want found. What if all this was just some big cover up to excuse the killing of a few enemies?

Chuck set her alarm for six, trusting in DeRosa's prediction and wanting to get some self-care in before having to go to any meetings. It was the right call. At seven, an alert appeared on her watch declaring she needed to be in Briefing Room A by eight-thirty. After grabbing some breakfast and checking with the recruits she headed for the meeting.

Chuck got to the briefing about fifteen minutes early. These rooms were more like traditional auditoriums and could seat large groups. Only the seats in the middle section of the room were up. The two sections on the right and the left of the room were effectively closed off. Several members of the support staff were already seated. She headed for a row towards the back of the room and noticed Cole and Doc sitting in the middle. They both waved at her. She suspected Doc wasn't happy about being here on a Saturday when there was some perfectly good golf that he could've otherwise been playing.

More staff filed in, and Tillman entered with a crowd of Kangaroos. He gave her a look and a wave but didn't approach. About a minute later Sally entered, and after spotting Chuck, headed in her direction. The senior agent had a cup of coffee in one hand and a bagel in the other.

"Morning, Sally."

Keeping her coffee steady, DeRosa maneuvered through the seats. "Morning. I hope you wore boots. I have a feeling it's about to get really deep in here."

Chuck smiled.

After a short wait, Site Alpha's Command group entered the room. Hines and Smalls sat in the very middle of the front row. They were surrounded by their admins and the security leads, who took up the second row of seats.

At what she assumed was the stroke of eight-thirty, a set of double doors at the very front of the briefing room opened, and eight agents entered. They split off four to a side. Following them, the two Wardens also entered. The entire scene felt very surreal.

The Wardens were still dressed in their ties and trench coat getup, with the exception of their sunglasses. The woman had deeply red hair and Chuck guessed she was in her mid-twenties. The man didn't look much older, with short dark hair and a hint of a beard. Both were certainly younger than other Wardens Chuck had encountered in the past.

The male Warden spoke first. "Good morning, Site Alpha. I'm Warden Harold Flynn, and this is my partner, Ruby Voss. We are joined by agent teams from Forward Station Fairbanks and Forward Station Lincoln." His voice had a low register to it that sounded forced.

As the agents at the front nodded, Chuck could see what Sally had meant about ragtag. Some of them wore crisp uniforms, were well-groomed, and looked to be in good shape. But a couple looked less well put together, with patched uniforms and beer guts.

One of the agents looked like he could easily have been her grandfather. She'd seen plenty of older boomers who could hold their own in a fight, but this guy looked like he got pulled out of being in solitary confinement for six years.

Flynn continued. "I'm sure most of you are aware of why we're here. For those that aren't, my partner will provide a very brief summation."

Voss stepped forward. "Several events, involving both subjects and non-subjects, have occurred over the past couple of weeks. We have lost two registered subjects, including a member of a sasquatch clan." Voss's voice sounded much more pleasant than her partner. "In addition to these subjects, three members of the Griffin Family were killed under what we understand to be mysterious circumstances. Our team's primary mission is to identify and eliminate whatever is attacking our subjects."

Flynn stepped back to the front. "Our secondary mission is to monitor Griffin activity in the area. The Board does not anticipate any retaliatory strikes, but we can't be too careful."

Chuck could hear murmurs coming from the crowd. Flynn held up a hand to quiet them.

"These mission objectives have been agreed upon by both The Board and Site Alpha's Command. We are operating under emergency response protocols. While we carry out our duties over the coming days, I will be in command of Alpha's operations and closely assisted by Chief Hines and his staff." There was another low murmur. Flynn waited for the noise to dim before following up.

"Your supervisors will be debriefing any of you unfamiliar with these protocols as soon as we dismiss. Allow me to personally assure you, Delta has only the safety and security of our staff and subjects in mind with this operation."

Sally coughed.

A hand went up. Flynn seemed to debate whether he wanted to accept questions, but finally nodded in the direction of the raised hand.

Cole stood. "Thank you for the information you have provided thus far, Warden, but I do have a question. It was my understanding that we have a truce of sorts with the Griffins. Does Delta have evidence that there is in fact a possibility of retaliation?"

Flynn nodded. "CIT Cole, is it? Your understanding of relations with the Griffins, while genuinely optimistic, is a bit flawed. I am not authorized to speak specifically on matters of diplomacy with regards to the Family, however, I can assure you that the Griffins are no less a threat today than they were thirty or forty years ago. If anything, they may be more dangerous due to their scattered nature."

More murmuring. A second hand went up. This one was an admin that Chuck knew by face but not by name. Flynn pointed to her.

The admin remained seated. "And Delta believes these attacks are all related?"

Flynn smiled, but Voss answered the question. "Phantom Kangaroo and CIT teams from several different sites, including yours here at Alpha, are currently sorting through the evidence we have. In addition, we are gathering evidence compiled by non-Family agencies. We have ruled nothing out..." She paused. Flynn looked in her direction, but she didn't look at him. "This operation has been undertaken through an overabundance of caution. I'm sure that everyone in this room is aware of the dangers that some of our subjects can pose to not only the general population, but other subjects as well."

Several more hands shot up, but Flynn now ignored them. "We are all grateful that you have been so immediately accommodating of us and our team, and we look forward to completing this operation in as expedient a manner as possible. We ask that you each return to your operational hubs to receive your debriefings." Flynn then looked straight up at where Chuck and DeRosa were sitting. "Agents DeRosa and Barnes, would you please stay here in the auditorium?"

Chuck had been studying the Wardens hard and forgotten about her friend. Sally, who kind of grunted at hearing her name, sat up but said nothing. Most of the crowd looked back at them, then started to get up as the members of Command stood and headed towards the doors.

"Yep, glad I wore my waders today." DeRosa kept her voice low.

"Voss seems genuine enough," Chuck replied, trying not to speak too loudly.

Sally bit off a bit of bagel. "The best liars always do."

"Do you think we should get up?"

"Nah, if they want us, they can bring their asses up here."

As the two visiting agent teams filed out, the Wardens began walking towards them. They entered the row ahead of where she and DeRosa were sitting. Chuck felt inclined to get up and offer to shake hands or perform some other sociable greeting, but Sally stayed glued to her chair, so she did too.

The gesture didn't seem to bother Flynn as he moved all the way up to stand in front of them. "Agent DeRosa, it's a pleasure to finally meet you. You're a bit of a legend around Delta." He extended a hand towards her.

DeRosa looked at the outstretched hand for a moment before finally shaking it. "I think the word you were looking for is 'pariah.'"

Flynn nodded. "In some circles I suppose that's true." He turned to face Chuck. "Agent Barnes, Chief Hines has spoken very highly of you. He also told me you were close with one of the deceased subjects."

Chuck felt a pang of resentment towards Flynn. "I first met Sparkles while I was still in training. I've—I had grown close with her and her group."

DeRosa took a drink of her coffee and leaned forward. "Okay, now that you have the formalities out of the way, wanna tell us what bullshit assignment Delta has in mind for us?"

Flynn furrowed his brow. "The only instructions Delta gave me concerning the two of you is that I should use you as I see fit."

Sally chuckled. "Cut the crap, Warden. You didn't ask us to stay behind after class for nothing."

Flynn smiled. "You've got me there. I was hoping that Ruby and I could hear your stories concerning the recent events. Unfiltered."

DeRosa's face contorted into an odd half-smile, and she pointed at Voss. "Wait, is your name actually Ruby, or is that the name the Family gave you?"

Voss gave DeRosa a quizzical look. "No, my mom named me Ruby. Voss is my assigned name."

DeRosa nodded, her half smile becoming a full one. "That's my grandma's name. My dad wanted to call me Ruby in her honor. Apparently my mom wasn't on board with it though."

Voss smiled warmly. Unlike when her partner tried to smile, the expression on Voss's face looked genuine. "My mom thought it would be funny because I had red hair when I was born. My nickname in school was Jo, like Jolene from the Dolly Parton song. I went by that until I graduated, but when I joined the Family they made me drop it."

Flynn held up his hands. "Okay ladies, can we get back to the matter at hand?"

Sally rolled her eyes. "What exactly *is* the matter at hand, Warden? And don't give me that line about the Griffins retaliating. What was that you said at the end Ruby? Something about the dangers our subjects can pose to other subjects and the public as well."

Flynn gave Voss a withering look. "It's my understanding you two recently encountered a former member of the Family while retrieving the Mog."

Chuck felt way out of her element, sitting among this group. They all spoke with a familiarity that she couldn't relate to.

"We sure did." Sally took a sip of her coffee. "An old friend of the Family, you might say."

Flynn crossed his arms. "Yes, we've been briefed concerning former Agent McFadden and his treachery. The Board feels as though his arrival in Arizona is no coincidence."

"Well, he sure as hell wasn't out in those woods sightseeing."

Flynn tilted his head. "No, he wasn't. When was the last time you spoke with Hank McFadden?"

The corners of Sally's mouth dropped into a scowl. "Flynn, the last time I saw McFadden before that morning was the picture of him I lit on fire, right before burning the bastard's house down."

Flynn's eyes widened as Sally finished speaking. Voss cleared her throat then responded before her partner recovered. "Would it be safe to assume that McFadden may have some personal vendetta against you, Agent?"

Sally rolled her eyes. "Are you implying he was out there looking for me?"

"The thought he came out here because of you had crossed my mind." Voss replied.

Chuck didn't like the way the Wardens were talking to Sally. She began speaking before really knowing what she was going to say. "Agent DeRosa handled that encounter about as well as I think anybody could have, under the circumstances."

Flynn gave Chuck a long, measured look. He continued to look at her as he spoke. "Agent DeRosa, we know you served alongside McFadden around the time he defected. And I'm sure you're aware of Hank's familiarity with the occult." Chuck blinked in surprise at his words, ending the staring match with Flynn.

Sally took in a deep breath. "Where exactly is this going, Warden?" She nearly spat the final word.

"The chatter we picked up from the Griffins—they mentioned rituals and enchantments. We think there's a chance McFadden may have brought something over. Facilitated an entity crossing into our world."

The last sentence sounded odd to Chuck. Even a couple of years into interacting with cryptids, the notion of something 'crossing into our world' gave her goosebumps.

"Do you think we're dealing with a Revenant, Warden?" Chuck asked Flynn.

"Personally, Agent Barnes, I don't. The numbers don't add up. But that Mog and your sasquatch friend weren't killed by wolves. Something got to them, the question is what."

Chuck looked at Sally, who nodded. Turning back to Flynn, she swallowed a lump in her throat then spoke. "Warden, I saw something while trying to recover Sparkles from the ravine she fell into. Something I didn't mention in my report."

Flynn raised his eyebrows. "What exactly did you see, Agent?"

"Someone, or something, was down there with us. I saw a pair of glowing red eyes."

The Wardens stood for a moment in silence. Chuck got the feeling she was being judged. After an uncomfortable amount of time, Flynn looked at Sally and then back at Chuck. "I take it you're familiar with the Fitchburg Incident, Agent Barnes."

Chuck nodded.

"And I'm guessing you're also aware of the fallout and backlash it caused for Agent DeRosa."

Again, she nodded.

Flynn sighed. "Considering all the extra work the two of you have been forced to do here, I can't say I blame you for not wanting to add to your stress. I think it'd be a good idea for you to give a statement to Ruby about what you saw." Chuck let out a breath she hadn't consciously been holding upon hearing this.

He then turned to Sally. "Agent DeRosa, would you mind meeting with the visiting agents? Maybe let them pick your brain a bit."

DeRosa finished off her coffee then plastered a big, eat-shit grin on her face. "Sure thing! Not that there's that much brain left to pick."

Flynn ignored her sarcasm. "Let's all meet up in the cafeteria, say in an hour?"

They all voiced their agreement. Flynn and Voss then turned and left, leaving DeRosa and Chuck alone in the big room. A strained silence settled over them.

"God, I need a drink," DeRosa finally said.

Chapter Twenty-Six:

Strength in Numbers

For an eternity, the great oceans stood as a barrier to those who once walked this land now known as America. And yet they also sheltered the ancient peoples and creatures native to this side of the world. Thanks to the voices, I can feel, see, and hear the magnificent storm birds and hulking arachnids of ages past, even though they are now no more than dust and ash.

My kind were once worshipped in the mountains and canyons the voices now guide me through. The rocks still bear witness of the prayers the inhabitants of this land once spoke in honor of these long past beings. And yet, in this age of man, we are relegated to being myths and boogiemen.

Instead of being worshipped, we are merchandised.

The truth has been made plain to me. The reason we are no longer worshipped is because we are no longer feared. The three buffoons who freed me certainly felt fear, as did my deceased friend Bradley. Humans, like most prey, are easy to dispatch when singled out or separated from their pack.

But in large numbers, when provoked or forced to fight, they can quickly turn the tables. Many of my ilk learned this the hard way over the years. In fact, it was the reason I fled to this godforsaken continent in the first place.

I had my run of London for years, manipulating men of power and feeding on the poor and downtrodden who had no one to miss them when they were gone. I grew complacent and careless, attacking people not just in the darkened alleyways that I normally frequented, but in their own homes, or openly in the street. This folly led the city to take notice. Newspapers ran stories. The constabulary warned citizens and patrolled in larger numbers.

They could not hurt me, but slowly the populous starved me of my sustenance, both mental and physical. I tried for a time to adopt different aliases, even tried blending into their world. In the end these measures only served to delay my decline.

Ultimately I set out for New York and, for a time, enjoyed a new life preying on a populous who did not yet know, or understand me. Until I encountered Maraleen Rogers and her insufferable society.

They didn't fear me, seeing me instead as a new exotic creature to study and tame. I could have submitted to them, as others of my kind had, but my pride got the best of me. I rebuffed them, and when that didn't drive them away, I killed several of their representatives.

I can hear their screams in my memories. The cries as I tore arms and legs from their sockets. Soon, I will add new members to this chorus of the damned.

Chapter Twenty-Seven:

The Occult and Red Eyes

Sally started to stand, but Chuck grabbed at her arm. "Not so fast. We need to talk about McFadden, like now."

DeRosa gave her a rather hateful look, then sat back down. "Well then, talk."

"What the hell was all that about McFadden being into the occult?" Even though they were alone she kept her voice at barely a whisper. "And could he really be capable of summoning something?"

"Listen, when I knew McFadden I wouldn't exactly say he was *familiar* with the occult. But he did have a fascination with it. He read a few books, even studied Latin at some point to speak these ritual words. Sometimes we'd get high, and he'd start spouting all kinds of bullshit about summoning and binding spirits. I spent most of the time laughing my ass off because it sounded absolutely ridiculous."

"Jesus Sally, that doesn't sound ridiculous. It sounds terrifying."

"Yeah, in retrospect it kind of was. But like I said, he never actually made anything happen. Maybe he's perfected his craft." Sally shrugged; a reaction Chuck couldn't comprehend. The thought of a person like McFadden wielding otherworldly powers scared her deeply.

"You think he opened that box?" Chuck asked, not entirely sure she wanted to know the answer.

"I really don't know. And frankly, the Wardens aren't telling us everything they know either. For now, I say we keep McFadden and his pictures to ourselves. God only knows why he really gave them to us, but I'd be surprised if that was just him trying to show off. That's extreme, even for a narcissistic prick like him."

Chuck shook her head. "I don't like this."

"I don't either, Chuck my dear, but until we know what cards

168

we're actually holding, I'd rather not show our hand."

***

An hour later Chuck sat across from Voss at the far end of the cafeteria. The Warden seemed more relaxed now that her partner wasn't standing next to her.

"When was the last time they upgraded the décor around here?" Voss asked, looking at the murals and TV's.

"Probably before either of us were born," Chuck replied, listening to the voice drone on about how the Family now had four whole bases operating—three short of the current number.

Voss giggled, an odd sound coming from the otherwise serious Warden. "Rumor has it Delta's gonna shut this place down when Iota goes online."

Chuck nodded. "Worst kept secret in the Family at the moment."

Pulling out a pen and notebook from her jacket, Voss leaned forward. "Well, I don't guess we're sitting here just to shoot the shit. Let's get down to business, tell me about these eyes you saw."

Chuck took a breath to steady herself as she played the encounter back in her mind. "They looked human—except for the fact they glowed red."

"How close did you get to them?"

"Twenty, thirty feet maybe. Close enough that I could see the pupils." Envisioning those eyes again, set apart so starkly in the darkness, caused Chuck to shudder.

Voss made a series of chicken scratches across her paper. "Did you see anything else behind them? An outline, a shape, something?"

"Nothing but darkness." Chuck paused, not wanting to miss anything. "It bounced away after I looked at it."

"Bounced?"

"That's the best way I can describe it."

Voss tapped the pen against her cheek. "But it didn't fly? It appeared to be earthbound?"

"It didn't look like flying, no."

Voss put her pen down. "I mean, glowing red eyes doesn't eliminate the possibility of it being a Revenant. But the fact it didn't

169

kill you on sight would suggest it isn't one. Hopefully, we can find it quickly."

"What happens when you do find it?" Chuck hadn't heard any actual plans yet concerning what all these visitors intended to do about the mysterious being.

"Delta's working on that right now. If it's a Revenant, we'll pray we destroy it before it can get one of us. But if what you saw is a Class One, then who knows. Hopefully, we can neutralize or reason with it." Voss spoke rather nonchalantly, as though this was all very routine.

"That sounds like an awful lot of maybes," Chuck said, with a bit more sarcasm than she'd intended.

"Maybe. Kind of comes with the territory." Voss replied. She put down her pen then looked Chuck in the eyes and got very still.

After an uncomfortable moment of silence, Chuck finally asked, "What, do I have something in my teeth?"

"Sorry, it's just you." Voss sat back. "You remind me of my sister, that's all."

The statement caught Chuck off guard. She responded with the first question that came to mind. "Were the two of you close?"

"Yeah, sorry. I'm still kind of adjusting to this whole Double O Seven vibe they have us get into."

Chuck's curiosity kicked in. "You do look a lot younger than most of the Wardens I've seen before. How long have you been in?"

"I could say the same about a training agent. I joined the Family right out of school, just like you. They approached me the summer after I became a full-fledged agent. I finished Warden School less than a year ago."

Chuck didn't really know what the regs were on becoming a Warden, meaning she still wasn't sure about the woman's age. "Is it hard? Being a Warden?"

Voss rested her chin on her hand, a wistful look passing across her face. "The work is mostly fun. It's just… isolating, I guess. My family thinks I died in a car crash." She shrugged.

Chuck really thought Sally was joking when she talked about telling their families they were dead. "But they don't change your name? Aren't they afraid someone might find you?"

"You keep one of your names. They tell us it helps to anchor our minds. I guess they learned that if you go totally witness protection on people, they eventually rebel in some way."

"Are all Wardens former agents?"

Voss shook her head. "No, they take Kangaroos, even CITs in some cases. They make it out to be a big honor around Delta, but really, I think they pick the people they believe can handle the detachment the best."

"And you really turned your back to your family? Just like that?"

Voss sighed then looked Chuck in the eyes. "I love my sister, my mom, all of them. I'll always miss them, but I felt like I'd miss saving the world more."

The statement felt overly dramatic. Saving the world? But Voss looked and sounded dead serious.

The Warden checked her watch. "Hey… maybe we can talk again another time?"

"As much as I'd enjoy that, I'm hoping you don't have to be here for too long." Chuck replied, attempting to sound as friendly as possible, while at the same time rebuffing the Warden's offer.

Voss laughed. "See you around, Agent."

Chuck headed back to her apartment and cleaned the place up a bit. Minutes before noon, someone knocked on her door. She opened it and found her recruits standing outside. She placed her hands on her hips as she guessed at the reason for the surprise visit.

Rita spoke first. "Hi, Agent Barnes! We were wondering if you'd be joining us for lunch today."

Chuck smiled. "Because you want to ask me questions about the Wardens?"

Marcy shook her head as she smirked. "We missed you this morning, that's all."

"Funny. Bullshit, but funny. Head for the cafeteria. I'll be there in a minute."

She watched them leave, then swung through her place one last time before joining them. They'd taken over one of the larger tables in the hall, allowing everyone to sit together.

"What are the Wardens like?"

"Are we going to get to meet them?"

"Do they all dress the same?"

"Nigel told me that he heard from one of the Kangaroos that heard it from Smalls' secretary, that the Wardens are, like, genetically enhanced with cryptid DNA. Is that true?"

Chuck had to do a double take at Josh after he'd asked this question. "I highly doubt they're enhanced with cryptid DNA."

Josh tapped his fingers together. "So, you're saying there's a chance?"

Chuck's watch rang. Looking down she saw DeRosa's name. "I've got to take this. I'll see you this afternoon." They frowned as she got up to take the call.

Chuck swiped at her watch and Sally's face appeared. "Hey, what's up?"

"Flynn wants to meet with us at five in the Command Center."

"Really, why?"

"I'm not entirely sure, but he's acting squirrelly. I'll see you then." Sally's voice dripped with irritation.

"Gotcha, I'll be there."

***

Chuck walked into the Command Center a minute before five. Sally and the Wardens were already there, along with Hines, Smalls, and Tillman.

Flynn started speaking as soon as Chuck sat down. "I'd like to thank everyone for attending on such short notice. I don't wish to take up too much of your time, so we'll get right to the matters at hand."

He tapped a tablet that sat next to him on the central table, and several screens around the room came to life, showing a red headed, bearded man. "Early this morning, Bradley Osborn was found dead at his campsite in the Juniper Mesa Wilderness Area."

The screens switched, now showing a dimly lit camp. Chuck's stomach flipped as the image became clear.

Next to a fire pit lay an eviscerated body. The picture changed again, showing a close-up image of his abdomen. The man hadn't simply been gutted. His organs looked to have been arranged, with several pulled out and placed in the dirt at his sides.

Flynn continued. "The local authorities are blaming the attack on an animal, a mountain lion being their primary suspect."

"Since when does a mountain lion make a display of its victim's organs?" Hines asked.

The screen changed one more time, revealing a picture of Bradley's face. His bright red beard was streaked with blue around his mouth and nose.

Voss spoke up. "I believe that all of you in this room are familiar with the blue powder found on the Mog's face a couple weeks ago. We have also been informed by Delta that very trace amounts of the same substance were found in the lungs of Subject 100701. We think it's a good bet that whatever killed our subjects, also killed Mr. Osborn."

Sally leaned forward. "I don't suppose Delta has any suggestions about what kind of cryptid throws blue powder in people's faces?"

Flynn shook his head. "They are working on it, though there is the possibility it may be a new species we haven't encountered before. The one thing we are certain of is that we aren't dealing with a Revenant. It would appear we have a predator moving in a generally westerly direction, possibly headed for the Pacific Ocean."

"Why do you think it might be headed for the ocean?" Chuck asked.

"The ocean is the largest geographical feature in the direction this creature is moving. There is still a lot of desert and mountains between where this attack occurred and any major population centers. We're hoping to contain the entity before it gets very far." Voss explained.

Sally turned towards Flynn. "Where does that leave us exactly?"

"Delta has requested that you, Agent Barnes, and the recruit team be activated for limited use. You'll only be sent into the field if an issue arises close to Site Alpha."

Sally frowned. "Isn't that a bit… unorthodox, Warden?"

"These are unorthodox times, agent. Your team will answer directly to Chief Hines, and he will answer to me. My understanding is that at least two of your recruits have experience in the field?"

"Josh and Marcy went out with us to retrieve the Mog." Chuck replied.

Voss shrugged. "That will have to do. We're hoping to have this whole thing resolved quickly. Mr. Osborn's death does give us a good search vector, which is a positive, at least on our end."

"And you want us to sit around until this whole thing blows over?" Chuck asked.

"Operationally, it makes the most sense." Flynn said, standing up.

Chuck would have preferred to be one of the people bringing this monster to justice, but also understood that at this point, it was out of her hands.

DeRosa didn't hide her displeasure. "When do we need to inform our new *team* of their assignments?"

"I'll leave that up to your discretion, agent. Thank you for all of your assistance today." With that, Flynn turned and headed for the exit, Voss in tow.

Hines rubbed his head. "I'll make sure your team has gear, Sally."

"Thanks boss. Any other nuggets of advice?" Sally's words were laced with contempt.

Ignoring her, Hines stood and started for the exit. The rest of those present followed, Tillman giving Chuck a little wave as he kept pace with Smalls.

Chuck and Sally sat alone for the second time that day. After a long pause, the senior agent spoke. "Tell the kids I want to meet with them at breakfast tomorrow. I'm going to need a couple of drinks tonight to sort this bullshit assignment out."

Chuck nodded, thinking she may join Sally for those drinks.

***

The next morning, Alpha's new team sat assembled to eat breakfast. The recruits turned their attention to DeRosa as she started the conversation.

"Listen up. All of you are in a rather extraordinary position at this point. Agent Barnes and I are trusting you to have each other's backs. Our *assignment*, if you can call it that, is to be ready to respond to local issues, whatever those may be. This is just a fancy way of saying that we can be assigned to handle normal missions that may come up while the emergency protocols are in place. Site Alpha is still responsible for fulfilling its normal responsibilities."

Josh raised his hand, and DeRosa nodded to him. "Are we still in training? I mean, like, when this… whatever it is, is over?"

"Yes. Your status as recruits will go unchanged." DeRosa paused. "However, you will each receive bonus compensation, if we are sent on a mission."

Greg's ears perked up. "Wait, how much is this bonus?"

DeRosa shrugged. "I don't know that off the top of my head, but it'll work like all your other pay does."

Jess raised her hand. "Are they still going to hold some back until we graduate?"

Chuck had to smile. These five had just been told they may be called upon to work as agents, and the thing causing the most questions was their pay?

"Yeah, they'll still withhold," DeRosa confirmed.

Rita raised a hand, but DeRosa batted it down. "You don't have to raise your hands. If you have a question, ask it."

Rita folded her arms, as if trying to keep them down. "When you say *normal missions*, what kind of missions are we talking about?"

Chuck answered, giving DeRosa a break. "It is entirely possible we won't ever get sent out. But if something comes up, within reason, then our group will handle it."

The recruits all seemed to accept this answer. DeRosa spent a few more minutes explaining that they would each need to report to the admin building for any additional field gear they might need. By the time DeRosa dismissed them, Chuck was feeling better about the whole affair.

As the recruits disappeared out of the cafeteria, DeRosa turned to her. "Okay, now we go and pray to whatever God is out there that we don't have to answer a single damn call."

Chapter Twenty-Eight:

Scout's Honor

Three long days had passed since the team's formation.

Chuck hadn't seen the Wardens since Sunday around lunch time. She'd barely seen Tillman, for that matter. Other than an all too brief meal shared in the romantic hub of the cafeteria, her only interactions with him had been texts where he shared tiny bits of information, like the fact another camper had been killed, much further west of the previous victim. Otherwise, it'd been mostly sitting around and training.

This morning, DeRosa had chosen to take them all to the gym for some sparring practice. Sally even spent some one-on-one time with Marcy, showing her close quarters disarming moves.

Chuck went over defensive techniques with Rita and Jess while Greg and Josh practiced taking each other down or shooting, as it was sometimes called by MMA fighters.

"Man, you had me sweating, bruh," Greg said to Josh as they were gathering up their gear.

Josh faked a punch. "Same."

Greg picked up his bag, then stopped. A funny look crossed his face, and at first Chuck couldn't tell what he was doing. Then she heard it. A faint beeping.

Rita pulled her watch out of her bag. Chuck could see the LED light on the top of the face strobing. She hurried over to her own bag and rummaged for her watch. The beep wasn't one of the emergency signals. The face instead read "REPORT", in big green letters.

Sally walked up, toweling off sweat. "Looks like we've got something to do now."

Chuck turned to the recruits. "Okay. Get back, get cleaned up, and get your asses to Command."

Everyone hurriedly gathered their gear and headed for the exit.

Chuck listened to the excited chatter of the recruits until the point they separated and headed for the barracks.

Once within her own apartment Chuck rinsed off the sweat of the gym and pulled on her uniform with her hair still wet. Unsurprisingly, Sally had reached the Command Center first, though Chuck was still ahead of her recruits.

As they entered, Chuck saw Hines, Smalls, and Tillman sitting at the long table. A much smaller group of admins than normal hurried about the room.

"Where are the others?" Hines asked, sounding a bit perturbed.

DeRosa pulled her chair out as she responded, "They'll be here soon, Chief. You paged us while we were at the gym."

As Chuck took her seat, Jess entered and sat next to Tillman. The recruit gave her an excited wave. Within five minutes, the others all arrived. They were decked out, looking every bit like a group of nervous, nearly hired employees.

Hines grumbled something under his breath then stood. "Okay, now that you're all here, we have a pair of sasquatches that have left their range. Specifically, they've moved closer to a state recreation area."

He tapped a button on the table, bringing up a satellite image of one of the endless tracks of patchy woods and sagebrush so prevalent in Arizona. A box near the bottom of the image read *Horsethief Basin Recreation Area*. Several other smaller landmarks were given yellow dots.

Smalls picked up a tablet and began speaking. "Subjects 100633 and 100649, Buddy and Octavia, are a mated sasquatch couple. They've moved approximately twenty miles over the course of three days. Last night, vitals indicated that the two had begun actively mating. It appears that both subjects' transmitters may have been damaged due to vigorous exertion."

Chuck would've paid good money right then to hear Smalls read a romance novel. She could literally make anything sound boring and insufferable.

Hines continued. "We had to move this same couple last year; it seems they have a history of wandering. As the weather is getting warmer, their proximity to potential human contact is now becoming an issue. To complicate matters further, they appear to be sheltering on a property that has a pair of summer homes located on it. Records show this property is currently for sale and listed as vacant, but we don't want them to get comfortable there."

Chuck had only met these two a couple of times. Octavia had been a rogue sasquatch until meeting up with Buddy. He'd left his parents about a month prior to him and Octavia getting together.

A closer view of a wooded area with a small patch of open land appeared on the monitor. Half of a building could be seen jutting from under some of the trees.

"Are they actually in one of the buildings?" Chuck asked.

Hines looked around the room. "It is not clear at this time. That satellite pass was from around two this morning. Our stationary satellite is currently being employed for a separate operation."

"I've never worked with Buddy or Octavia. Are they *amicable* to moving?" DeRosa asked.

Hines nodded. "They were last year. If the readings are correct and the two are—well, then they're likely looking for a birthing place also. Today we are sending your team out simply to investigate. We can fit Octavia with an ABC and assess the damage to Buddy's transmitter. You will also inform them that they'll either need to return to their current range, or we will have to relocate them."

Smalls looked up from her tablet. "Your team will need to inspect the property and check for any damage. You'll also need to confirm that there are no security cameras on site."

Sally studied the map. "Are we getting a bird for this mission?"

"Negative. All pilots are involved in ongoing ops. We're sending you via MTV for this one. This assignment falls well within the safe zone designated previously by the Wardens. We believe you can reach, complete, and return from this mission before nineteen hundred hours."

Chuck looked at Sally who shot her a quick glance before speaking. "And Flynn signed off on this?"

It seemed like a fair question to Chuck, but Hines' cheeks turned red in response.

"Warden Flynn is rather busy with other operations at this time. I'm overseeing this mission, and I have his and Delta's full backing."

It wasn't exactly a 'yes', but it wasn't exactly a 'no.' Chuck continued to watch DeRosa's face but couldn't read anything on it.

Sally suddenly stood. "Great! Then let's get going, huh?"

The red in Hines' face lessened. "Your vehicle is already loaded."

"Even better," DeRosa said without looking at him.

Everyone filed out of the center before making a quick stop at their quarters to confirm they had everything they'd need. Soon they were grouped up, ready to load into the elevator.

"What were all those letters?" Greg asked from behind Chuck.

"Letters?"

"MTV?" Greg clarified.

"Oh, ABC is an Advanced Biometric Communicator, and MTV is Medical Transport Vehicle. It's a fancy way to say ambulance."

"Oh, okay."

Ding!

They went up in two shifts to keep the elevator from being elbow to elbow. As the first group boarded, Jess hung back and got close to Chuck.

"I can't believe I get to go out into the field. It's like I manifested it," she half-whispered.

Chuck smiled. "I guess you could say that."

"I won't let you or Agent DeRosa down, I promise."

"Scout's honor?"

Jess nodded, then smiled. "You know Tilly... erm Agent Moseby says that a lot," Jess said, flinching instinctively at Chuck's glare.

She thought about it for a second. "Yeah, I think I picked it up from him."

"That's not the only thing of his you've picked up." Jess half whispered, half giggled the sentence.

Chuck drew back a fist this time, silencing the recruit, who still wore a huge smile on her face.

Soon, the rest of them piled into the elevator. The transport already had its lights flashing as they walked out into Warehouse 2. Chuck saw Walt had again been assigned to drive for them. She hoped he was up to the challenge of hauling ass down a dirt road in that thing.

"Ms. Charlotte! Good to see you again!" Walt shouted from the cab of the transport.

"Hey, Walt! Don't shake us around too much going up that mountain," she called back.

He gave her a thumbs up. They loaded into the rear of the vehicle. Rita and Greg sat next to each other, the young woman looking on excitedly at the various compartments marked with red crosses. Within moments the transport jumped forward, and soon they were cruising along on the freeway.

"Linking comms!" Jess said enthusiastically. She had a tablet like the one Tillman used. Watches flashed various colors then uniformly turned to a GPS view showing their destination ETA. Jess played with a few more things on the screen before putting the tablet down. She was handling things like a seasoned veteran sitting among the other recruits.

"Agent DeRosa, it's an honor to be serving with you on this mission!" Jess said beaming.

"Just keep your nose clean, kid," DeRosa said. "We wouldn't be out here if I didn't think you all could handle yourselves."

The recruits lit up like Christmas trees. DeRosa sat up and cleared her throat. "Here's the deal. When we get up there, we get out, we do our jobs, and we get the hell back home. Understood?"

Every head bobbed yes.

"Nobody goes anywhere alone. Marcy, Josh, you two check any buildings we can see for cameras or damage. Jess and Rita, you two will come with Agent Barnes and me. We're going to find those sasquatches and check their monitors and health. Roberts, you stay with Walter and the vehicle. If for some reason anyone spots trouble, I want you available to help."

Greg looked disappointed but wisely kept his mouth shut.

Chuck looked over the group. "You all know how to use your comms?"

Marcy leaned forward. "Are you worried something's going to go wrong?"

Sally answered. "Not really, but I am worried about running into other people. There are a lot of cabins up in that area."

"Someone said the sasquatches' transmitters were broken. How do we know they're even still there?" Josh asked.

Jess perked up as she answered him. "The transmitters all have a short-range beacon, kind of like a flight recorder box on an airplane. Even if it can't transmit vital signs and other data, the beacon gives us a general idea of where they are." She held up a padded box with two short antennae. "I'll use this to find them once we're on site!"

Her exuberance was welcome, but it couldn't dissolve the tension Chuck felt building among the vehicle's occupants. There was an uneasy air in the cabin as they ascended in elevation. Conversation dropped to nil. The van, which had been hurrying along, suddenly began to decelerate, before taking a long, lazy turn.

Not long after they'd left the freeway, Chuck noticed the red lights on everyone's body cams turn to green. She adjusted her own camera and checked the ETA on her watch. Thirty-five minutes to go.

The speed of the vehicle stayed low as it took a series of sharp turns. Soon they left paved roads altogether. Her teeth rattled as the transport now swerved and bounced, violently at times. The back of the transport lacked windows, denying them the mountain views as the vehicle climbed ever higher in elevation.

Walt's voice came from the intercom. "We are passing into the recreational area now."

"Here we go," Chuck heard Sally whisper.

Chapter Twenty-Nine:

Horsethief Basin

The vehicle slowed and finally came to a stop fifteen minutes later. They'd all held tight to their gear through the long, jarring assent. After a final check, they piled out of the transport.

The air felt colder than it did in the valley. Walt had parked inside the cleared yard area shared by the two homes. A grand two-story house sat to the south, and a log-cabin-style home sat a bit further back into the woods to the north. Chuck tapped DeRosa on the shoulder then pointed at the bigger house. Up near the roof, pointing directly at the clearing, was a security camera.

Sally nodded. "Okay, that answers one question." She motioned everyone to gather up.

"We've got cameras so here's how we're going to play this. First, minor change in plans. Greg, you're coming with Agent Barnes and me. Once Jess has helped us track down the subjects, you'll escort her back here so she can deal with the security cameras. Marcy and Josh, since we can already see security, give that two-story house a quick circling to make sure it's undamaged. As soon as you're done there, book it over to that log cabin. Make sure to keep an eye out for any detached buildings. Sasquatches don't often invade homes, but I wouldn't put it past them to break into a garage or tool shed."

Greg smiled upon hearing this development. Chuck smirked as he and Josh exchanged a bro clap of approval.

Sally turned to Walt. "You think you can hold down things here?"

He reached over and turned up the talk radio show he'd been listening to. "I'll keep everything four by four, Agent."

Chuck reported into Command as Jess calibrated her tracking device. With the plans settled, they separated into their groups.

Jess took the lead, indicating that the transmitters were due east. They marched across the field and under the canopy of the tall pines.

Their footsteps were the only sound in the forest as the underbrush crunched loudly beneath them. It didn't help that this area of woods was choked with tangled bushes and smaller trees, some already showing signs of their spring buds.

They'd been trampling through the brush for several minutes when Sally paused, looking at the canopy. "Jess, how much farther does it say we have?"

Jess stopped and turned around. "We're close, less than fifty yards."

Sally looked back at Chuck, concern evident on her face. "Have they moved at all since you started tracking them?" It was a good question. Another good question was what the hell were they doing way out here when there were perfectly good porches or awnings just up the hill.

Jess shook her head. "I don't think so."

"Maybe they're sleeping?" Rita suggested.

Chuck put a hand on her sidearm. "Maybe, but you'd think they would've heard us with all the noise we're making."

Dropping in unannounced on sasquatches, or any cryptid really, was a bit of a gamble. At this point, if Octavia or Buddy had chosen to run, Chuck doubted any of the humans would've had much chance of catching them.

The underbrush lessened as Jess's tracker started making several quick beeps. The funk that normally announced the presence of a sasquatch hung thick in the air. The hairs on Chuck's neck started to rise. Something was wrong.

Jess turned to Sally. "It says they should be here, like, within ten feet."

DeRosa took up a defensive posture and began taking measured steps towards the northern edge of the clearing. Chuck unclipped her holster. The recruits, their senses not as finely tuned, simply stood in place.

A loud burst of static emitted from the group's watches. Chuck turned up her arm to see the face of the device. A grainy image that may have been Tillman revealed itself for a moment before going dark. She was about to turn to Jess concerning the tech when something caught her eye. A large hand lay next to the base of a pine tree. The ruddy fur caused it to blend in with the dead needles and leaves that covered the forest floor.

"Agent DeRosa," her eyes followed an almost indiscernible line of blood that trailed around the tree. Chuck heard Sally moving closer to her now, but she didn't look back at the senior agent.

Chuck pulled her gun out, hearing DeRosa do the same. Taking slow, deliberate steps, she moved out to give the tree a wide berth.

"Talk to me, Agent," Sally's words were calm.

In response, Chuck held up her left hand. A few more steps brought her completely around the edge of the tree, where she came upon a horrifying sight.

The two sasquatches sat propped against each other, heads on one another's shoulders. Buddy's right arm had been severed at the elbow, and Octavia's left leg was missing. Both creatures had been eviscerated, their intestines and other organs laying in piles in their laps.

Chuck took a couple of steps back. Another burst of noise sounded from the watches, but she ignored it, instead looking towards Sally and shaking her head.

A pair of gunshots rang out from back in the direction of the homes. Sally spun to face the noise. Greg pulled his firearm as both Rita and Jess stood like statues.

"I'm on it!" Chuck called as she turned and broke into a sprint.

"Greg, go with her!" Sally yelled from behind.

Chuck didn't wait to see if Greg followed. She moved as fast as she could through the brush and fallen trees. Within moments the noise of Greg's footfalls told her he was right on her heels.

They burst into the grassy field only a few minutes after they'd heard the shots. The first thing Chuck noticed was the absence of Walt. He might have been in the back of the vehicle or behind it, but all thought of their driver was obliterated as a third gunshot sounded. This gunshot came from the direction of the log cabin. She started to move with caution towards the home, but her watch made a new noise and suddenly she was sprinting again.

The pulsing alarm that rang out from both their wrists meant one of their team was flatlining.

Sally's voice suddenly sounded, "Command, we have shots fired!"

Chuck flicked her wrist, turning the watch's sound off. She ran as hard as she could, her lungs burning, but still the cabin felt like it was taking forever to reach.

Finally, they arrived at the edge of the building. She paused for a second, deciding to circumvent the home to the left around its garage. She placed her back against the log structure, Greg stepping up directly beside her.

Chuck made a hand motion to him, indicating which way they were going. Greg nodded his understanding. They carefully moved along the side of the home, passing by the garage door. Once they reached the corner, she held up three fingers and counted them down to one. She turned and took a few steps into the open with her pistol held out in front of her. Greg was right at her shoulder.

"Marcy?"

What Chuck saw was difficult to process. Marcy had her back turned to them, her pistol in her left hand. She appeared to be looking down at Josh, who was lying on a patch of loose stone and decorative cacti. The next few moments rolled out like a slow-motion scene in a movie.

Marcy turned, a stiff, unnatural motion. As she came to face them, Chuck saw something was wrong with the recruit's face. The pupils of her eyes were rolled up into her head and it looked like she had something smeared across her cheeks—something colored blue. The sight was so startling that Chuck failed to process Marcy's raised pistol. She had a split second of realization before the weapon fired.

Pain exploded at the center of Chuck's chest. She staggered and fell, hearing at least two more shots whizzing by around and over her. She crashed hard onto the bed of pine needles. The pain ripping through her body was intense, but somehow it didn't feel as bad as she'd envisioned getting shot would be. Opening her eyes, she saw Greg had turned slightly to look down at her. Raw fear seized her as she looked past her companion.

Standing on top of the cabin, right above where she and Greg had been moments ago, was a figure. It resembled a man, but in shape only. The details were infinitely more disturbing. It had pale white skin and deep red eyes that she knew all too well. Its whole face was framed by a pitch-black hood. This dark covering extended down the length of the creature's arms, ending at the wrist, leaving its clawed hands exposed. Its torso matched this blackness, and Chuck could only assume the same could be said for its legs, which were oddly covered by a pair of black pants.

It jumped down to land in front of Greg. The recruit must have realized she'd seen something because he crouched and swept his leg forward. The kick landed, unbalancing the creature whose head angled up as a burst of blue fire and smoke spewed forth. With inhuman quickness, the thing threw an uppercut that clipped Greg's forehead. He fell back, landing close to where Chuck was lying.

The creature was on him swiftly, lifting Greg up with both hands. She could see its nails were grey, metallic-looking, and jagged like broken glass. The recruit threw a punch, which connected with the thing's face. Another burst of blue flame engulfed Greg's arm. Letting out a guttural sound, the creature swiveled and threw Greg, who smashed into the garage door, creating a huge indentation. The recruit crumpled into a pile on the driveway.

Chuck kicked out and connected with the thing's leg, the quick movement causing a burst of pain to run through her body. The monster jumped back, a fluid, effortless motion for such a lanky figure. She sat up and shifted, looking on as it casually landed next to Marcy, whose gun was still raised.

"Would you look at that! Three shots and still willing to fight. You must reveal your secrets to me, Agent!"

The creature's voice made Chuck's blood run ice cold. It sounded like it was coming out of an echo chamber, reverberating from high to low. And there was something else—it spoke with an accent.

Marcy's mouth moved as if she were talking, but Chuck couldn't hear any words. The creature lowered its head, bringing his face close to the recruit's.

"What's that, love? You want me to let you go. Now where would the fun be in that?"

It ran a finger down Marcy's cheek. The motion made Chuck nauseous.

"Don't you worry, little lamb. You'll learn to enjoy it, I promise."

Chuck shifted her weight around. The pain in her chest was awful, but she realized now that the bullet hadn't hit her. It had hit her body cam.

The thing turned to face her full on then grinned. The mismatched, pointed teeth, along with the look of realization on its face, froze her in her place.

The glow behind the creature's eyes intensified. "Hello, little bird. I've seen you before, haven't I? Inside that canyon, with the daft beast. You and your flying friends." As it said these words, the monster moved its arm in a flapping motion.

Her extremities tingled as the initial shock of the gunshot wore off. Chuck felt the adrenaline pumping through her veins as she got up on one knee. Suddenly Marcy raised the gun and pointed it at her own head.

"Tsk, Tsk, little bird. You might be bulletproof, but I'm betting your friend here isn't."

Chuck's muscles seized. It was controlling Marcy! She stared into the creature's eyes, challenging it, needing to keep his attention focused on her.

"Let her go, you son of a bitch, or I swear to God," she said loudly, buying time.

"God, eh?" The creature laughed, a hollow, disturbing sound. "Oh, little bird, God and I go way back. Way back—"

It was cut off as Walt brought a tire iron down across its head. The creature fell, and Marcy screamed out in pain, her head snapping forward. Chuck heard a noise to her right and turned to see Greg, who was making sickening gasping noises. There was blood running down the front of his face and out of his ears.

It had taken her only a moment to check on Greg, but that moment had been costly. Turning back, she saw with horror what was about to happen. She screamed, a primal, panicked noise.

Walt hit the creature with the tire iron again and was raising his arm for another strike. He was so focused that he didn't notice Marcy training her gun on him. Chuck saw Marcy's muscles flex, firing the gun once, twice, three times. She continued to pull the trigger, even though the gun's magazine was now empty. Walt had absorbed all three bullets, blood exploding from his left side to paint the decorative rocks and wood of the home's front porch.

Chuck was pulling out her own weapon as the monster shifted, using the momentum of Walt's body to push itself away from the man. The creature stood, bounding to stand behind Marcy as Chuck trained her pistol. It pulled Marcy up to create a human shield. The recruit's hand was still squeezing the trigger repeatedly.

The creature's eyes blazed with anger. "We've had our fun, little bird, but I'll be running now. You tell your Family ole Jack is back, won't you?"

He reached around and cut Marcy's throat open with one jagged claw. Blood gushed from the right side of her neck, and her pupils rolled back down. The creature pushed Marcy forward and then launched backwards in two big jumps before disappearing up into the woods. Chuck squeezed off half a dozen shots before racing forward to try and help Marcy.

Her temples pounded with blood, her anger and fear boiling over. She ripped a bandage from one of her arm pockets as she closed the yards between her and her recruit. Crashing hard on her knees, she flipped Marcy over. The woman's eyes were wide with terror as Chuck pressed the bandage down on her neck.

"Stay with me, Marcy, just stay." She tried to sound comforting as tears flowed down her cheeks. The sound of footsteps approaching caused her muscles to tense, but she didn't move.

Sally was suddenly at her side. Chuck looked at her through watery eyes. She could hear Jess behind them, screaming for immediate extraction.

DeRosa placed an open medical kit on the ground. "I've got her, Chuck. Go see if Walter is still with us," she instructed, her voice eerily soothing.

The senior agent's hand pressed firmly over the spot where the bandage had quickly turned red. Chuck pulled back her hand and placed her gun on the ground. She nodded and got up to go check on Walt.

He was laying on his left side, his right arm extended out with the tire iron still firmly grasped. She could see three separate wounds: one on his right arm, a second near the back and base of his neck, and a third near the front curve of his right temple. Blood had pooled beneath him, but to Chuck's amazement, she could see Walt's chest still moving.

She pulled him over and blanched as the exit wounds came into view. The one in his arm looked like a clean through and through, but both his neck and head were gruesome. She ripped out more bandages, tying them around the wounds. Jess approached and kneeled beside them. The younger woman's face was pale, and her eyes were full of fear, but she was there.

"Can—can I help?" Jess stammered.

Chuck placed Jess's hands over the two more egregious wounds. Once she was confident the bandages were secure, she pulled out the small emergency kit each agent was equipped with and broke the seal. Chuck removed the one thing she hoped could save her friend: a syringe with red liquid in it. She had no idea what the stuff was, but they'd been taught it was only to be used in true life or death situations.

While Jess kept pressure on the wounds, Chuck ripped the cap off the needle. She felt for Walt's sternum, found the top of it, and administered the solution. She'd never seen the stuff demonstrated and was shocked when Walt's face instantly turned a deep purple color like someone choking to death. Jess's eyes somehow got bigger, but to her credit she kept the pressure firm. After a moment, the color faded, and Walt's face seemed to relax.

Chuck looked down at Walt's arm, the one wound she'd not yet tended to, and could see the blood looked darker and had begun to flow much slower.

"Stay with him!" she yelled, not really meaning to. Jess nodded.

Chuck returned to DeRosa's side. There were two of the same syringes lying empty near Marcy's head. Her eyes were now closed, her face calm. Sally had wrapped bandages carefully around the young woman's neck.

Chuck stood there a moment, then went to pick up her pistol. For the first time she noticed the blood covering not only her hands, but her gear, her boots. Even her gun had blood on it. She holstered it without trying to remove a single crimson stain.

"The thing from the canyon. It did this?"

DeRosa's question sounded more like a statement of fact. Chuck kneeled to look the senior agent in the eyes.

"It… Jesus Christ, Sally it made her kill them," she struggled to make her voice work.

"Agents!" Jess called, her voice sounding far away. "Chopper ETA is five minutes!"

For a moment, Chuck had an urge to wipe the blue substance from Marcy's face. She didn't. CIT might have some use for it.

"Ole Jack is back," she whispered.

Sally looked at her. "What?"

"The thing, it—he. He said to tell my family ole Jack is back." Even the memory of its voice caused her to shudder.

A look of confusion crossed DeRosa's face. "Jack?"

Chuck didn't have a response. Instead, she stood and walked over to where Josh's body lay. He'd been shot, execution style, and had a blue streak running across his face. She didn't know about Marcy and Walt, but there would be no cryptid-made wonder drugs for Josh Lamont.

She wanted to look up and scream at the sky. She wanted her emotions to erupt out of her like a volcano, to spew the sorrow, the hate, the terror directly into the atmosphere. Pain threatened to overwhelm her, and she wiped away an errant tear with the back of her blood-soaked sleeve.

Exhausted, Chuck turned stiffly and went back to make sure Jess was okay. The young woman's hands were pale from exertion.

Chuck pulled a fresh bandage out of Jess's sleeve, then moved her hand so that both were attending to just the one wound. She pulled away the blood-soaked bandage on Walt's head. The wound still looked ugly, but the blood had stopped flowing freely. Chuck applied the fresh bandage, then tried to check for a pulse. She wasn't sure that she could feel one.

"Josh?" Jess asked weakly, tears streaming from her eyes. Chuck shook her head.

"Marcy?"

"I—I don't know. Is Rita with Greg?"

Jess nodded meekly. "Agent Barnes... what the hell attacked us?"

A helicopter flew low over the house. "Jess, I need you to go direct whoever is in that helicopter. Get their asses over here. You got me?"

The recruit stood and bolted away. Chuck wiped away another tear as the sound of a second helicopter rattled through the forest. She placed her hand over Walt's. His skin now felt cold and lifeless.

Chuck closed her eyes, and red glowing points looked back at her in the dark.

Chapter Thirty:

Jack's Back

The white light reflecting off the tile floor made her head hurt, and a stray length of hair hung across her face, but Chuck didn't care. She sat, bent over, waiting for Cole or anyone to come out and give an update about Marcy.

She heard the doors to the medical wing open and close far down the long entry hall. Even as the footsteps approached, she didn't look up. Finally, a pair of blood-spattered boots stopped in front of her, and a hand holding a cup of coffee lowered itself into her field of vision. She reached out and accepted the cup from Sally, who sat down beside her. She took a few sips, but otherwise they sat in silence. Neither of them had washed off since returning to Alpha.

Chuck hadn't left Marcy's side until they reached this room. Cole had forcefully sat her down and then rushed into what functioned as the site's ER. A promise that he was going to save Marcy was the only thing she had to hold onto.

"Walter didn't make it," Sally said after several long minutes.

Chuck had already assumed that. The only other person to have come through on a stretcher was Greg. A nurse had been with him, and they didn't seem to be in quite as much of a rush.

Chuck nodded as a tear ran down her cheek. She didn't bother stopping it, letting it fall to the floor to join the others already there. More time slipped away in silence.

The sound of the door echoed through the hall again. This time she could hear multiple footsteps. Alpha was on lockdown, so she expected it to be the Wardens. By all that was holy if one of them asked her a question right now…

"Um, Agent Barnes?" Jess spoke timidly.

She looked up; thankful it wasn't Voss and Flynn.

Tillman stood next to Jess and Rita. The poor recruits looked completely out of sorts. Jess's eyes were puffy from crying, and her makeup had become smeared. Rita's hair was messy, and her hands were still caked in blood. Chuck stood and took a few steps towards them before embracing both in a hug. The younger women broke down, their bodies shaking while crying onto Chuck's shoulders.

"Thank you, Tillman," she whispered bringing her head to rest on Jess's.

"Have they said…"

He stopped. Chuck guessed Sally had cut him off with a look. Tillman stood awkwardly next to the gathered women for a moment before moving and sitting down.

"You were damn good up there, ladies," DeRosa said. Both Jess and Rita seemed to be regaining their composure. Soon they gave Chuck one last good hug, then stepped back a little.

The double doors opened, and Doc came out, still wearing his scrubs. His smile gave away the news before he even had a chance to deliver it. "Ms. Nelson is stable and resting comfortably."

There were no cheers or high fives. Just relieved sighs and a few more tears.

Doc adjusted his glasses. "She was incredibly lucky. An eighth of an inch more and her jugular would have been severed.

"Young Mr. Roberts will require some physical therapy, but he will be back to fighting form soon enough."

Chuck smiled at the others. The news brought the tiniest bit of good to the day, but it didn't bring comfort.

Sally rose from her seat. "We should probably all go clean ourselves off and get some rest."

Doc shook DeRosa's hand. "You all run along. They should be ready for visitors by this evening."

Chuck put an arm over each of the younger women's shoulders. "Come on, I'll walk you two back to the dorms."

Tillman stayed behind, talking quietly to Doc. As the women approached the double doors, Flynn and Voss entered the hall.

The Wardens had been on the first helo that landed. Chuck almost hadn't recognized them. They'd ditched the MIB get ups for their field gear, which made them look like future soldiers. The padded mesh suits and gadgets hanging from their belts would be right at home in a Sci-Fi movie.

Sally didn't break stride or slow down for a moment. Voss stepped to the side, but Flynn stood his ground, partially blocking the senior agent's path.

"Excuse us, Warden," Sally said calmly, though coldly.

"Actually, Agents, if we could get a word."

DeRosa swiveled and in one stride stood within an inch of Flynn. Much like when she'd been staring down McFadden, Sally's quiet fury seemed to make her about a foot taller than she was.

"Sir, I say this from a position of respect. But if the next words you plan to say aren't 'We got the son of a bitch,' then you should just let us pass. We all know good and damn well you want a report, but right now we need some time to collect ourselves."

Sally turned and continued through the doors.

Chuck pulled her destroyed bodycam off the front of her uniform and slapped it into Flynn's hand. She knew the Wardens had a job to do, and she fully intended to help them do it, but not right now. She kept her arms around the recruits, shielding them from any blame the Wardens may try and target her and Sally with later.

She did as she'd promised and walked them back to the dorms. They looked shell-shocked, and Chuck gave them another long hug before leaving.

"Agent Barnes, the Wardens are going to get the thing that did this, right?" Rita asked, her voice barely more than a whisper.

Chuck nodded. "If they don't, I will."

She patted them each on the shoulder before turning and leaving. During the walk back to her room, all she could think about was the creature's look and voice. Sasquatches and Chupacabras could pass as something from the natural world; the thing they'd encountered was otherworldly.

She got into her apartment and immediately stripped naked. Unlike when she'd returned the morning of Sparkles's death, she dropped her gear, clothes, and all on the floor in a pile. She made it into the bathroom, opening the shower door and turning the hot water knob all the way up. She spun, meaning to go to the bathroom, but her image in the mirror stopped her.

Smeared blood mixed with tears looked like war paint across her cheeks. The blood had stained her skin halfway up her arms, and right in the center of her chest an ugly purple bruise had formed. She stood there staring for a time, all other needs forgotten.

The mirror had started to steam over before she stepped into the shower. She watched as red flecks splashed all over the interior tiles. Red, like the creature's eyes. Grabbing her bar of soap, she began to scrub and continued scrubbing, even after the water in the basin had turned completely clear.

Chuck had a passing urge to sit down, cry, and let the water wash away the tears. But that wouldn't soothe the burning anger she felt. She wanted to punch holes in the shower tiles or beat that red-eyed face so badly her own hands would be bloody and broken.

She got out of the shower, not even bothering with a towel, and wiped away the steam from the mirror with her palm. There in the blurry reflection her skin was clean except for the bruise, her own personal reminder of the events of the day.

She wanted answers, and now she was better equipped to get them.

Walking back out into her living area, Chuck pulled her watch from within the blood-stained pile of clothing. She hit the general com function. A random Kangaroo was waiting on the other end.

"I need to be connected to Warden Flynn."

"Um, I'll check the Warden's status, Age—"

"Right now, damn it!"

"One moment," came the irritated reply.

After a few seconds Flynn's face flashed onto her screen.

"Yes, Agent Barnes. Are you—"

"I'm ready to give that report."

"Okay, ah, can you meet us in command? Say thirty minutes."

"I'll be there."

"And can you see about bringing Agent DeRosa?"

Chuck cut off the com without answering him. She went to her kitchen and grabbed McFadden's envelope. No more secrets, no more lies.

She got dressed and headed for the Command Center. Sally was already sitting on the steps, just as Chuck had suspected she would be.

"You lasted longer than I was giving you credit for," DeRosa said as Chuck approached.

"I had to take a shower."

"That would explain it I suppose." She glanced at the envelope then back to her face. "You sure you're ready for this?"

Chuck held out a hand and helped her up.

"Ready as I'll ever be."

They entered the room and sat down at the table. They waited in silence until the Wardens finally entered, they'd returned to the trench coat and tie look.

Voss sat across from them. She looked like she wanted to say something but remained silent. Flynn sat next to his partner.

"Thank you for meeting with us, Agents."

"What the hell was that thing, Flynn?" Sally asked bluntly.

"Delta is reviewing what footage we were able to retrieve, which sadly wasn't much. We're combing the recruits' cameras to see if anyone actually got a good look at it." Flynn paused as he glanced at Chuck's face. "Camera-wise."

Voss jumped in, probably trying to redeem her partner. "Agent Barnes, obviously you're the most reliable witness we have concerning this subject. What can you tell us?"

"Well first off, I'd say he knew we were coming. That was a trap from the get go." Voss nodded, though in agreement or simply to placate her, Chuck wasn't sure. "The *subject* looks like a man in a deranged Halloween costume. He's about the same height as Greg, red eyes. I've never heard of a Class One, or any cryptid for that matter, like him before, even in our books."

Flynn leaned towards her. "Based on the scene we are in full agreement that your team walked into a trap. You say 'he'? Did it speak to you? The comms picked up some strange sounds, but nothing we've been able to define as a voice."

"He spoke to me alright. He had an accent."

Flynn shared a confused look with Voss, who had been recording the interview on a tablet. "Wait, an accent?"

"Yes, an accent. It sounded English maybe, but like someone trying *not* to sound like they have an accent. And he knew about the Family, or at least I think that's what he was trying to get at."

Voss frowned. "What exactly did he say that made you think that?"

"He told me to tell my family Jack is back."

Flynn sat up in his seat, a questioning look on his face. "Jack?"

"Yeah, he said Jack. How many Class Ones do you know that have first names?"

Voss stood and pulled a phone from her pocket. "Pardon me for a moment."

Flynn shot a disapproving glance at Voss, then turned back to face Chuck. "Recruit Nelson shot a fellow recruit, Walter Johnson, and you. Dr. Cole tells me you think this subject was controlling her? Can you give me some details concerning that?"

Voss had stopped by the entrance across from them, just out of earshot if you were quiet. She stood with a hand cupped over her mouth as she spoke into her phone.

Chuck looked Flynn in the eyes. "Marcy had already killed Josh by the time we reached her. She shot me without saying anything. After that thing appeared and attacked Greg, it moved back and stood next to Marcy. I don't know how, but it was linked to her. It made her hold the gun to her own head, and she freaked out when Walt attacked the monster."

Sally leaned over, effectively stepping between Chuck and Flynn. "Why isn't Hines here? This was his decision."

Flynn glanced at DeRosa. "Hines has been relieved of his command post and is, at this moment, on a plane to Delta to answer for this incident. He was told to postpone this op, regardless of the chances of subject discovery. Your team should've had backup. I'm sorry."

The tone of his voice and look on his face made the apology feel entirely ungenuine to Chuck.

Sally grunted and Chuck thought a smart remark would be forthcoming, except Voss suddenly spoke, "Yes, I'll patch you through now."

Voss picked her tablet up and made a couple of swipes, causing several of the big monitors in the room to flash on. After a moment, a young woman wearing glasses and a lab coat came into view. The image was crystal clear; Chuck could even make out the freckles on the bridge of the woman's nose.

"Dr. Micha, these are Agents DeRosa and Barnes," Voss announced. "Agents, this is Dr. Melody Micha, Lead Investigator for CIT Delta."

"Good evening, Agents." The doctor's voice was soft but held an authority Chuck felt didn't exactly match the rather childlike face. She looked younger than Voss even.

"Agent Barnes had the interaction with the subject," Voss stated. Chuck wasn't exactly sure which monitor she was supposed to be looking at. She concentrated on the largest one directly behind the Wardens.

"Agent Barnes, you indicated the subject spoke with an accent and stated his name was *Jack*?" Micha asked.

Chuck nodded. "Yes, he made a point of it."

Micha appeared to be typing something on her end. Suddenly the monitors all changed to a strange drawn image. In it two men stood aghast, looking at a third figure. It was a cartoony version of the thing Chuck had seen, with pale skin, a black outfit, and even the ridiculous looking pants. In block print over the drawing read the words, "SPRING HEELED JACK."

"The thing I saw looked way more insidious, but yeah, I'd say that's him."

Micha's face returned to the screens. "Wow, Spring Heeled Jack," she said with awe.

"Is that name supposed to mean something to us?" Sally asked.

"No, no, I don't guess it would. Give me a moment." She turned to the side and began typing again. "ENOS, please sync with Site Alpha's command center."

A deep robotic voice responded, "Of course, doctor."

After a few seconds, the display on the table came to life. A projected 3D image of this Spring Heeled Jack appeared.

The robot voice now came through the command center's speakers. "Spring Heeled Jack. Class One Cryptid, hostile, first actively recorded in England. Known to be capable of jumping long distances, gliding, and possessing a flaming breath weapon. Defenses: Regenerating carapace, ability to appear human. Last encountered August 25th, 1902, in Buffalo, New York State. Status: redacted."

Chuck frowned as she remembered the blue smoke and flame the creature had tried to use against Greg. "Dr. Micha, what exactly does that breath weapon do?"

Micha sat up in her chair. "Oh! Did Jack employ it during your encounter?" She sounded genuinely pleased.

"Yes, when he first attacked us. Marcy and Josh also had a blue substance all over their faces. This Jack was controlling Marcy's actions, like he had a link with her."

Micha leaned forward. "When you say he was *controlling her actions*, how exactly did that manifest? And what kind of a link did he have?"

Chuck took a breath before answering. "Her eyes were rolled up into her head, and she attacked several of us. They must have had a mental link because he never gave commands out loud, she just did things. He even threatened to have her..." Chuck paused, swallowing a lump in her throat. "He implied that he could make her kill herself."

She wiped away a tear, annoyed to be sharing the memory for a second time.

Micha adjusted her glasses. "Fascinating!"

Chuck's jaw dropped. "Fascinating? That son of a bitch made my recruit waste two of my friends and you're calling it *fascinating*?"

Sally put a hand on her shoulder and squeezed, obviously intending to calm Chuck, which it did somewhat.

Micha sat back, clearly surprised. "My apologies, Agent Barnes. It was a poor choice of words."

Flynn, who'd also looked a bit surprised by Chuck's outburst, spoke up. "Doctor, why did it say this creature's status was redacted?"

Micha paused as if weighing her words. "Jack was one of the first *hostile* Class Ones the Family ever encountered. Truthfully, we didn't even call them Class Ones back then. Stories about him go back to 1837 in England, but he didn't get on our radar so to speak until about 1895. Tragically, our record keeping at the time was not what one would call, *good*. Most of the records we do have were pieced together after Jack had been dealt with."

"Excuse me doctor, but we're not looking for a history lesson. We want to know why the hell this thing is putting our team in body bags," Sally said tersely.

"Yes, certainly, Agent. DeRosa... I like that name." Micha brushed her bangs back from her face. "Again, I can't stress the foibles of our historical records enough. We're not precisely sure why Jack came to America, but it must have changed him. In London he was a prankster and lecher. In New York, our records suggest he became murderous and aggressive. After several encounters and battles with Jack, the Family was able to trap him by some means, though what happened to him after that is a bit of a mystery."

Chuck looked down at the envelope and then at DeRosa. "Damn."

Flynn and Voss turned to her as Micha cocked her head to the side on the monitor.

"Could you trap a Class One inside something like this?" Chuck raised the envelope and dumped its contents onto the table. Straightening out the paper, she slid it towards the Wardens. Flynn snatched the page up, looking over it suspiciously. He then handed it to Voss, who frowned as she examined it.

Flynn sat side-saddle on the table as Voss held the paper up to give Micha a view. He motioned to the pictures. "Where did you get these?"

Chuck leaned back. "Hank McFadden. He tracked me down during our last Media Day, spouted a bunch of stuff about the Family and the Griffins not wanting a war. He seemed to think someone in our organization sent that note to a group of unsuspecting Griffins."

The color in Flynn's face rose. "How long were you planning on keeping *this* a secret!"

Sally stood in Chuck's defense. "Don't yell at her. If you want to get mad at someone, get mad at me. I told her to keep this under wraps. Besides, you've been feeding us half-truths since you got here."

Flynn stood but Voss was right at his side, a hand on his shoulder, mimicking what Sally had done to Chuck moments before. He looked from Sally to his partner, then back to Sally before taking a step back.

"I should charge you both with treason! Was this your plan all along? To conspire with McFadden?"

"Stand down, Warden," Micha said. The strength behind her words resonated through the room.

Flynn frowned, then looked past Chuck and Sally to a different monitor. "What?"

"You heard me, Flynn. You are not to reprimand either of these agents. We don't know what this McFadden character was up to, and frankly it shouldn't matter. At this point we need to buckle down and figure out where Jack is. Too much blood has already been shed."

Flynn clenched and unclenched his fists. He turned, took a few steps, then sat down. Voss took a seat next to him as Sally returned to her own chair.

Micha typed something on her end. "Ruby, I'll need you to send me scans of everything from that envelope. Flynn, I'm going to recommend calling in a disposal team to the Board. Jack is clearly a danger to the Family and our operatives."

Chuck looked to Sally. "What's a disposal team?"

The senior agent gave a sarcastic smile. "It's a team of nothing but Wardens. In the mafia they'd probably call it a hit squad."

Voss nodded. "Pretty much."

"Wait! You want us to sit on our asses while that piece of shit kills how many more people?" Chuck realized how dumb the statement was before it even finished leaving her mouth. Micha had just announced plans for bringing in a group to go out and straight-up murder this thing.

Flynn looked like he was about to respond when she corrected herself. "Sorry, that was uncalled for. I'm stressed, that's all."

Flynn dipped his head slightly. "We all are, Agent."

Micha cleared her throat. "I'm sending over all the information I have on Spring Heeled Jack."

Voss nodded. "Thanks, Melody."

The doctor's face disappeared from the monitors.

The Wardens excused themselves and left through the command exit, taking McFadden's envelope and its contents with them. Chuck sat with Sally in silence for a bit before her friend reached over and squeezed her hand. "You good?"

Chuck nodded. "I am, actually. Thanks."

They both stood and walked out of the Command Center side-by-side.

Chapter Thirty-One:

Washing Out

The double entry doors leading into the medical wing rang loudly in the otherwise quiet hall. Chuck led Marcy, Rita and Jess towards the reception area, her pace slow and deliberate. The plain yellow walls felt strange, like she was seeing them for the first time.

As Chuck walked, her thoughts took a hard-left turn. It wasn't their fault, but she couldn't help but think it. She wished Will Smith and Tommy Lee Jones would fall in a fire or have some other manner of pain and suffering inflicted upon them.

Her disdain for the men was entirely unfounded. They were playing a part. She should've been mad at some dipshit writer, not the guys that played the role given them. But she didn't know the writer's name, and instead it was the two sharply suited, sunglasses-wearing leading men that she focused her disgust on at this moment.

In the movies it was *so* easy. You hold up a little stick. Tell the person to look at the green flashing light, then erase the last minute, hour, year of their memories. Bada Bing, Bada Boom. All better. That alien you just saw? Oh, don't worry, it was a dog with mange.

She didn't know if that movie had been an influence or not, but there was no denying it. A gimmick created by some Hollywood hack had been brought ineloquently into the real world by the brain trust at Delta.

The Family called it washing out, probably because *mind erasing,* and *brain wiping* didn't sound as pleasant. Apparently, they hadn't started broad use of the process until sometime in the late nineties. How long it had been going on before that, no one seemed sure.

Washing out was the ultimate deterrent for someone leaving the Family. Those who received it most frequently however were recruits. Some people didn't want to live a solitary life, even if that life meant getting to see exotic and fantastic things.

It was the very last thing a recruit learned their first day with the Family. You were welcomed to leave at any point, but if you did, the Family would reset (as they put it) your memories. You would become a regular, ordinary, exceptionally smart college student. When Chuck heard this as a recruit, she'd thought *yeah right*. She suspected most recruits did. But now, years into her time with the Family, she knew how real this process was.

Aided by some cryptid byproduct, or possibly many of them, the Family could in fact erase your memories. But they didn't use some flashy light, and if the rumors were true, it wasn't a painless process. It also wasn't flawless.

The full list of rumored side effects was long and appalling. Complete amnesia, lifetime migraines, paralysis, and like any good drug, death. The one *positive* as her training agent had put it: the chance of catastrophic side effects became exponentially lower the younger you were.

For older members of the Family, it was considered one of the harshest punishments. If you did something that could warrant it, you were usually given an ultimatum: gamble with being washed out, or we'll throw you in a cell and leave you there until you die of old age. It was what Chuck often thought of as being forced to wash out. Did the person technically make their own choice? Sure, but the alternative wasn't exactly a walk in the park.

Her group reached the waiting room and took their seats. Just three days previous, she and DeRosa had been sitting in this exact spot, waiting to see Marcy and Greg. That night, waiting to see her injured recruits, she had no idea the difficult conversation she'd be having hours later.

***

The morning after the attack on Horsethief Basin, Chuck had gone to the gym, mostly wanting an excuse for kicking the shit out of something. She felt powerless against the storm that was Spring Heeled Jack. Years of training meant nothing during the encounter with the Class One. Had it not been for a luckily placed camera, she would've joined Walt and Josh in the morgue.

She'd been working out for fifteen minutes when a voice

startled her. "Agent Barnes, can I talk with you?"

She turned to see Jess, looking pale and sickly. "Hey Jess, sure. How are you feeling?"

"Like shit. Sorry, I can wait, or whatever."

"No, I probably need to take a break." Chuck grabbed a towel while walking with Jess to a bench in the corner. "What's up?"

Jess looked at her, opened her mouth, then closed it again and rushed towards the bathroom.

She followed the younger woman a moment later, hearing a toilet flush. Jess was sitting on the floor of the stall, head hung over the rim. Chuck placed a hand on her shoulder.

"Here's some water." Jess took the bottle. She swished a bit of liquid around in her mouth before spitting it out.

"I want out." Jess's voice was shaky.

It took Chuck a moment to process what the recruit had said. "Jess, I don't—"

"I can't do this." She looked up, tears streaming down her face. "I'll never unsee all that blood. I just—" Jess shook her head before drinking down the remaining water.

"The Family has psychologists if you want some counseling."

"I don't want counseling! I want my goddamned mind erased! Every time I close my eyes I see Walt, or Josh, and so much blood. I'm... I'm done." Jess's head whipped around, and she spat into the toilet.

The anguish in her voice left little doubt Jess had already made up her mind.

Chuck patted the younger woman's shoulders. "Then we'll go talk to Cole."

Jess nodded her head, then accepted Chuck's hand lifting her up off the floor.

***

As Chuck had suspected, Cole wasn't exactly fond of the idea.

He sat back in his chair, hands behind his head. "Jess, I want to again suggest taking some time off. The Family offers several programs for members who have experienced a traumatic event, especially while in the line of duty."

Jess sat balled up in her chair, head resting on her knees. "And I want to *again* say, no thank you."

Cole looked to Chuck, but she only shook her head. She could very much sympathize with Jess. Hell, she'd thought about it a few times herself over the last couple of days. Her desire to see Spring Heeled Jack brought down was currently keeping her from going that route.

Cole sighed then sat forward. "Alright, Jess. I'll submit the paperwork to Delta."

Jess slowly uncoiled, then stood. "One thing. Can we wait until Marcy's out of the infirmary? I'd like a chance to say a proper goodbye."

Cole nodded. "I'm sure that can be arranged."

***

And so, on this otherwise nondescript morning, Chuck had accompanied Jess, Rita, and the newly released Marcy to the waiting room. No one should have to make the final walk down that hall on their own, and today, no one had.

The infirmary doors opened, and Doc walked in wearing a smock and looking every bit the mad scientist. He had a packet of papers for Jess to fill out. Many of the pages sounded like repeats of previous ones. The part where Jess signed off on what would replace her wiped memories gave Chuck chills. It all sounded so routine, and it sickened her.

Doc flipped to the final page and took in a deep breath, holding it for a moment before continuing. "There are a number of possible side effects. The most common being recurring headaches, though these seem to fade after a couple of months. There is the possibility you will lose all memory of these last several months, or maybe longer, permanently. The new memories don't always take, which has been known to cause other psychological trauma. And of course, you'll need to initial here to show you absolve the Family of any responsibility should the process lead to your death."

Jess had powered through the rest of the paperwork, but finally paused. She looked to the other women, then back at Doc. "How many people have died from this?"

Doc frowned. "More than should have."

The ominous answer hung in the air for several long moments.

Jess looked down at the paper, then quickly scrawled her initials on the final line.

Doc stood slowly. "I'll give you a moment to say goodbye," he said before taking up a position next to the double doors.

They all stood, tears streaming down their cheeks. Together Chuck, Rita, and Marcy enveloped Jess in a hug. The three of them remained there, holding her for a long time, offering words of encouragement to their soon to be gone friend.

Chuck thought back to the day on campus where Jess had lobbied to become a field agent. It felt like a hundred years had passed since that moment. Jess wanted to get off-site, to be on the ground with the agents. She had, and now she knew in her heart this wasn't the life she wanted.

The dreams Chuck had been having gave her an extra bit of understanding for Jess's decision. There were some things you couldn't unsee, at least not without help.

When they finally released each other, Chuck was touched to see the smile on Jess's face.

The recruit sniffed, "I'm gonna miss you, bitches."

"No, you won't," Marcy whispered.

Jess gave Marcy and Rita one last hug, and they all wiped away a few final tears. With a sigh, she walked over to join Doc.

"Let's do this," Jess said.

Doc nodded and the two disappeared through the double doors.

Chuck placed an arm around both Marcy and Rita. They turned as one, heading back down that long hallway.

Jess was leaving on her own terms.

It was better than the terms Josh and Walt had been given.

Chapter Thirty-Two:

On The Inside

Fear.

It is not at all a sensation I am used to. Even while inside the damnable box I don't believe I truly felt it. But I do now.

I am afraid my mind may never fully be restored. My difficulty at sorting out the beast's mind. The kindness I showed the camper. Even the voices. I shrugged them all off, confident it was only a passing phase. That my mind, as my body before it, would heal. Would regenerate. Would be whole again. And yet I am still broken on the inside.

The voices led me to my targets, more of the bipedal creatures that Bradley thought of as being called Bigfoot, a stunningly dull name if ever I have heard one. I stalked them as the voices instructed, following their meandering path. On the second night, the voices told me the time had arrived to make them my thralls.

Overcoming them while they slept proved almost too easy, though these beasts were of stouter mind than the young Bigfoot had been. Their understanding of what would and wouldn't summon the Rogers made it easy for me to sort out a simple trap. The voices did the rest by revealing a suitable location to me.

Killing the beasts brought me a proper dose of satisfaction, as did watching the arrival of the Rogers. Sadly, this feeling was short lived.

As I observed them from my perch in the nearby trees, I was immediately struck by how young these members looked. They split up, which made my plan all the easier. Rather than attack their main group, I followed the two individuals who broke from the others. As soon as the voices willed it, I struck.

Humans have advanced and evolved during my long captivity, and the Rogers have evolved right alongside them. As I struck the female with my toxins, I was assaulted by a flood of complex thoughts, emotions, and outright rebellion as my mind looked for purchase within hers. This girl, Marcy, had been conditioned to solve problems and think independently from a young age, requiring me to fight exceptionally hard to cull her.

The other agent, though stunned by my initial appearance, mustered a counterattack. A second dose of my toxins was required before I could control Marcy. I attempted to strike the boy, Josh, but only caught him with a glancing blow. Realizing the strength of the female, and not wishing to risk losing her, I simply commanded her to dispatch the boy.

Over one hundred years later, and the Rogers are still confounding me. Those who imprisoned me are long dead. Their children's children are likely dead as well. Not a single member of this group bears any relation to the actual Rogers Family. Instead, they work for them, taking on the name collectively, and thus becoming my enemy.

My revenge feels hollow, and the anger this raises within me has muddled my motivations. I want these modern Rogers to suffer as I have, more so actually. But I likewise want to control some of them. None more than my little bird.

She took a bullet and survived. She distracted me as her geriatric companion snuck up from behind. She is a leader among them, and I can see why.

Two dead is a good start, but this taste of revenge has only piqued my desire for more. Thankfully, I now have eyes on the inside, and I know where they are gathered. The Rogers think they are hidden in their underground shelter; they think they are protected.

They do not suspect the horrors I intend to visit upon them. I hunger for their flesh and their minds. As luck would have it, the voices are hungry too.

Chapter Thirty-Three:

Can We Talk

Marcy leaned back against the wall, idly brushing her hair. "He doesn't deserve you," she stated matter of factly.

Rita clapped, nodding enthusiastically. "I mean, you're so right! How the hell can he be my *man* if he won't even post pics with me in them?"

Marcy focused on a particularly tough snag. "You can pull any guy you want."

"Damn right I can! He *knows* how multi-talented I am. I play guitar, for God's sake!" Rita threw her hands in the air for emphasis. "You know what? I'll record a couple of songs, slide into a few DMs. It'll be one thirsty boy after another!"

Despite actively hooking up with Greg, Rita evidently had a boyfriend, or something, back in Boston. He'd committed the cardinal sins of A) not liking several of Rita's TikTok's from a few weeks prior and B) not posting a picture of her on Instagram in the past few months.

Chuck sat nearby, trying to read her book but having a hard time concentrating. Campus visits had been suspended until the death squad could find and deal with Jack, which led to her and the recruits holding a modified Media Day.

Marcy continued to feed the dragon. "You should write a song about how much he disrespected you."

Rita jumped up from her seat. "Oh my God! Can you imagine? I'm doing it!"

"You don't think that maybe the fact you live half a continent away now might be why he isn't posting pictures of you?" Chuck questioned. "Have you even asked?" Considering it had never crossed her own mind to juggle multiple relationships, whatever kick Rita was on now held next to zero interest for her.

Over the last few weeks Chuck's attitude towards Rita had changed a lot. Regardless of how she managed her love life, the recruit had the potential to be a great member of the Family.

"Ask him? Come on, Agent Barnes. You don't ask. He's supposed to know!" Rita flipped her hair, then went back to her phone.

"Wow, yeah, what was I thinking," Chuck replied.

"God, I should've known he was a dick. That selfie I took by the fountain, where my hair was all messed up? He said it was one of his favorites. Hello! There were a bunch of bitches in the background wearing booty shorts! Is that trashy or what?"

Marcy nodded, though her passion for the conversation seemed to finally be waning.

Rita gave Marcy a look, clearly unsatisfied by the lack of enthusiasm her friend was now showing for her plight. She huffed, then returned her attention to her screen.

Five long days had passed since what was now being referred to as the Horsethief Ridge Incident. The whole base was still on edge. Jack being on the loose wasn't helping matters.

Greg was in rehab for injuries suffered when he slammed into the garage door. This meant that Chuck was spending most of her time with Rita and Marcy. Normally this wasn't bad. However, when Rita decided she needed to be the focus of the world's attention, while simultaneously requiring the world's pity because of how tough it was to be young, talented, and good looking, that was Chuck's signal to try and find greener pastures.

Her main concern now revolved around Sally and Tillman all but disappearing. She assumed they were both busy, probably helping Flynn in Hines' absence.

"Hey, am I interrupting anything?"

Chuck looked up from her book past the recruits to see Tillman standing in the doorway, as if summoned by her thinking about him. Rita and Marcy gave him a glance but must have noticed he was looking most directly at Chuck.

She put the book down. "Not really, what's up?"

Tillman rubbed the back of his neck. "Actually, I was hoping I could talk with you, in private if that's okay."

Both Marcy and Rita looked at her; Rita closed her eyes and poked her tongue into her cheek.

Chuck rolled her eyes. "You bet," she said, all too happy to have an out from the situation.

She left the younger women behind, following Tillman across the hall into one of the smaller meeting rooms that littered the area below Warehouse 1. She closed the door behind her, then took a seat across from Tillman at the room's small central table. "What's up?"

Tillman looked at her for a moment, then closed his eyes. He clasped his hands together in front of him and took a deep breath.

Chuck leaned forward. "Um, are you okay?"

He sighed. "I... I need to tell you something. It's just that, well, I'm not particularly good with stuff like this." He looked incredibly uncomfortable.

"Tillman, we've all been through a lot lately, maybe this could wait."

"No, if I don't do this now, it's going to... I need to say this now or never."

Chuck didn't know exactly what he was getting ready to say, but things already felt weird. She interlocked her hands, not wanting to hurt his feelings with an unflattering response.

Tillman exhaled, then looked her straight in the eye. "Charlotte, this last week or so has been like, really messed up. And it made me realize that I don't want to miss out on something that could be incredible. I know I told you I wanted this to go slow, but a couple inches in either direction and you'd never have come down off that mountain. I don't want to look back on us six months from now and think, *what if.*" He stopped there, continuing to stare into her eyes.

Sweat broke out along Tillman's hairline as Chuck tried to play back what he'd said in her mind. Their relationship had taken a backseat to all the other emotions she'd been dealing with since the attack. The losses of Josh, Walt, and Jess left raw, angry scars. The bruises now fading on her chest were a reminder that she herself could easily have joined them. But she hadn't even stopped to process what that would've meant to others. Her mother, her brothers, and yes, even Tillman.

He put a hand over hers, a look of concern on his face. "Oh, shit. I'm sorry. I shouldn't talk about dying, and I'm not trying to put you on the spot, it's just…"

Chuck shook her head. "No, Tillman, you didn't say anything wrong." She closed her eyes and pulled his hand to her lips, kissing his fingers gently as moisture welled up at the edges of her eyes.

Tillman opened his hand and caressed her cheek, wiping away the single tear that escaped. His touch was comforting, even if his hand was shaking.

She stood, going around the table and lifting Tillman up to wrap him in a hug. He put a hand on her head, and she pulled him closer to her, taking in everything. The feel of his clothing, the smell of his deodorant, the sound of his breath. Tillman wasn't perfect, and neither was she, and maybe that was for the best.

He sighed. "Um, I know enough to know that saying I love you right now would be stupid, and disingenuous, so is there like a better phrase?"

Chuck leaned back a bit, shook her head, and then kissed him. She couldn't help but feel as though it was the best kiss she'd shared with anyone, ever. When they finally separated she looked him right in the eyes. "Keep saying that for now, okay?"

Tillman looked absolutely confused for a moment. "Say wha— Wait, the kiss?"

Chuck laughed then kissed him again, to make sure he understood. "I don't want to wonder *what if* either. Are you free tonight?"

In true Tillman fashion, he looked to his watch. "Like for dinner? Yeah I should be."

"And after dinner?"

He let go of her to scroll his watch. "Um, I guess as long as—"

Chuck grabbed his cheeks and kissed him aggressively, making sure to press herself as closely to him as was possible. "After dinner?"

Tillman's eyes widened, a look of utter shock crossing his face. "Yeah, uh, I'll be free after dinner."

She kissed his neck. "Good."

Blushing, Tillman pointed over his shoulder. "I should probably get back and make sure Smalls isn't having a meltdown."

"Okay, I'm done with the ladies at five, you wanna meet at the cafeteria around six?"

"How about Warehouse 2 at say five-thirty."

Chuck scrunched up her face. "You want to eat in the warehouse?"

"I was thinking Gegi's, you know, in honor of our first *date*."

"I didn't think we were allowed off site."

Tillman waved his hand. "The security and admins still go home every day. I think if we're back before the sun goes down, we'll be fine."

"If you can pull the strings, then yes, Gegi's would be lovely."

He smiled, looking truly pleased with himself. "It's a date. I mean, like for real this time."

"Go on, I'll see you tonight."

He kissed her one more time, then made his way to the door. "Awesome. I'll see you later."

Chuck stepped to the doorway, seeing Rita nearly fall over herself trying to scramble back into the other room. Chuck was about to go give Rita a piece of her mind when her phone rang.

Looking down, she saw it was her mom. She swiped the accept button.

"Hey, Mom. How's it going?"

"Hi, Charlotte. I'm good. How's the weather?"

"Same as always, Mom. Dry and mild."

"That's good. I was calling because I hadn't talked to you in a while."

"Yeah, I'm sorry. Things with work have been... kind of crazy. I've been meaning to call."

"Oh, of course. I didn't want to fuss. I'm not interrupting anything, am I?"

Chuck's voice caught in her throat. She really had been meaning to call her mother, but something had been stopping her. Now, hearing the love and sorrow thinly veiled in her mom's voice, made her wish she hadn't waited.

"No, Mom. I'm glad you called."

"Charlotte, what's wrong honey?"

"I'm... it's really good to hear your voice, Mom. I'm sorry I haven't been back in a long time."

Silence, then a ragged breath. "Charlotte, I've missed you so much."

"I've missed you too."

Her mom's voice was strained as she continued. "I'm proud of you for pursuing your dreams. For going out into the world. You're fearless and beautiful, and I'll always be rooting for you."

Chuck wiped away a fresh tear. "Thanks, Mom. I promise I won't let you down."

"Honest Abe?"

Smiling, she nodded. "Sure thing. Honest Abe."

"I love you, and I miss you. We all miss you, Charlotte."

"I miss all of you too, Mom. And I'm going to get back your way as soon as I can."

Her mother sniffed loudly. "I can't wait for that day to come. Listen, I don't want to keep you from your work for too long, so I'll let you go. It's so good to hear your voice, Charlotte. Goodbye."

"Bye mom."

She put the phone back in her pocket, and sat down, trying to regain her composure. The back-to-back emotional rollercoasters had taken a lot out of her.

Once she had herself back together, she let Rita and Marcy know they were going to have to behave without her because she needed to go lay down. They nodded, then went right back to working on Rita's diss track.

Chuck didn't even look at her watch as she entered her sanctum. She grabbed her bottle of ibuprofen, gulped down a thousand milligrams, then laid down. Sleep wasn't easy to find, but once she had, her dreams were wracked with the dead stares of Josh and Walt. And always in the background, the other eyes: bright, red, hateful.

***

Chuck woke up with DeRosa's voice filling her room.

"Charlotte!? Where are you?"

She pulled her arm out from under her pillow, seeing Sally's face on her watch. "There you are! What's going on? I've been trying to reach you for an hour."

"Sorry, I fell asleep." Not fully awake yet, she yawned as she spoke.

"No worries, I'm coming back to your place, stay there," Sally pressed on. Evidently she'd already been to her room once. How hard had she been sleeping?

Chuck blinked a few times. "Did something happen?"

"I just need to talk to you."

"Um, sure, sounds good."

At least she had clothes on for this DeRosa visit. Hopefully, the Wardens had finally made some headway with killing Jack.

"See you in a second." DeRosa's face disappeared.

Chuck shook her head, trying to clear the cobwebs. She got up and went into the bathroom to freshen up. Sally was knocking on her door within three minutes.

"Sorry, I wanted to catch you earlier. Did you take a sleeping pill or something?"

"No. The ladies were in rare form, and Tillman and I had a heart-to-heart, so it's been a bit of a day already."

"Okay, maybe we need to talk about that first?"

"We're good. I'm just being dramatic."

She moved to the little counter that had become their spot for talks. "You want some water or something?"

Sally shook her head. "Nothing to drink today."

"Well then, what's up?"

"I know I haven't been around much the last couple of days, but I've been meeting with Flynn and Delta," Sally started out.

Chuck nodded. "I kind of figured you'd be busy getting things caught up with Hines not being back yet."

"Yeah, that's kind of the reason I came to talk to you." Sally had a funny glint in her eye.

"So?"

"I was meeting with them because I'm being promoted. I'm taking over Alpha."

Chuck's mouth dropped open. "Are you shitting me?"

"Nope, they're moving me up next week. I wanted to let you know about it before, you know, they made it official." Sally had always been tough to read unless she was angry, and this moment was no exception.

Chuck chose her next words carefully. "And you're sure this is what you want to do?"

Sally clasped her hands behind her neck. "I mean, for fear of saying I'm getting too old for this shit, I actually feel like I might be getting too old for this shit."

"Being a field agent, you mean?"

Sally nodded.

"Working with Delta and Smalls. You're not going to turn all politician and shit?" Chuck was needling but Sally seemed happy enough.

"I know the Board and I have our issues, but this way I'll be able to keep in close contact with them. And I'm definitely not going to turn all politician!" Sally giggled, something Chuck couldn't remember ever seeing her do. "Once Iota goes online, this place might be shut down, so I'm not getting any delusions of grandeur or anything."

"Chief Agent DeRosa, wow. Congrats!" Chuck moved over and gave Sally a hug. The future head of Alpha returned it warmly.

A thought occurred to her as she leaned back. "Wait, who is going to be evaluating me now?"

"Silverman," Sally replied sheepishly.

"Oh, come on. Seriously?" Silverman was what Chuck's father would've called a stick in the mud. She didn't think she'd seen the woman smile in three years. Silverman was a perfectly good admin, but ouch.

"She'll do fine, and besides—you only have like a year and change left."

Sally's defense was flimsy. But Chuck knew there wasn't anything she'd be able to do about it in the short term. For now, she'd be happy for her friend.

Chapter Thirty-Four:

Gegi's Italian Kitchen

Stepping off the elevator an hour later, Chuck was startled to find the disposal team loading gear into a transport. Flynn was directing the other Wardens, all of whom were dressed in their full trench coat and sunglasses regalia.

"Agent Barnes, it's good to see you," Voss said as she noticed Chuck approaching. "You're looking good tonight, who's the lucky guy?"

Chuck looked down at the dress and sweater combination she'd chosen, smiling. "Thanks, actually…"

"Tillman Moseby," Flynn interrupted, appearing suddenly close to her. "I had to sign off on the two of you leaving the site for your little *date*."

"Yes, Tillman," Chuck replied, casting a suspicious eye towards Flynn.

Voss nodded approvingly. "Nice. Well, you two have a good time and be safe."

Chuck's curiosity got the better of her. "Where are you all off to this evening?"

Flynn coughed. "That is a need-to-know matter."

Voss punched him in the arm prompting a frown from Flynn. "God you're annoying sometimes." She turned to Chuck. "Don't mind him. We're going to see if we can find that box from the pictures you gave us. Delta's thinking Jack may have returned to it so he can recharge." She glanced at Flynn. "Or some shit like that."

Flynn rolled his eyes and walked away. Voss shook her head. "Go on, have a good time. I think your ride just pulled up." She pointed towards the bay doors.

Chuck turned to see Tillman getting out of a blue car. She brushed her hair back, getting a good look at him. He'd worn a burgundy sweater and lightly faded jeans. A scarf really set the look off though, and she smiled despite herself as she approached him.

"Yellow looks good on you," Tillman said, taking her hand. He opened the door for her as she got into the car.

"You're looking good yourself," she said as he slid into the driver's seat.

"What's up with them?" Tillman asked, pointing to the Wardens.

"Work, and as of right now we aren't allowed to talk about work." She leaned over and kissed him.

"Understood."

***

Walking into the restaurant, Chuck had butterflies in her stomach. It wasn't a rational sensation at all. She'd dated people in high school, including a guy who was going to the local community college. This felt different though, like she was starting a new chapter in her life.

"Do you miss Florida?" Tillman asked her as their drinks arrived.

"I didn't used to, but the next time I get a proper break I want to go back, if for no other reason than to see my mom and brothers. I've got a niece on the way that I look forward to meeting."

"Do you like having siblings?"

Chuck tilted her head. "Did I enjoy having two older brothers? Let's see. They pretty much hated me when I was little because my dad doted on me so much. As we got older they were useful for keeping away creepy guys though. All in all, not a bad trade off."

"Interesting. I always thought it would've been fun to have a younger brother or sister to pick on." He looked out the window. "My parents acted like spoiling me was a competition. I'm shocked they stayed together as long as they did."

Chuck wasn't all that enthused about getting into a conversation about parents. She was debating mentioning this when Tillman looked back at her. "I know you said work was off the table, but can I ask a really quick question about how Marcy is doing? I honestly thought she was going to join Jess in washing out."

She blinked. "Wow, that may be the mother of all subject changes. Um, good, I guess. She doesn't remember anything about the attack. Cole explained what she'd done, and they set her up with a counselor, but she's seemed pretty upbeat to me."

Tillman shrugged. "That's probably for the best. I wouldn't want to remember any of that either." He shook his head then reached out and grabbed her hand. "Sorry... you were there, you do remember I'm sure. I'll—I mean, do you want to talk about it?"

Chuck squeezed his hand, trying to control her tone so as not to sound overly upset. "Currently, no. Someday, with you, maybe. Can we talk about something else?"

Tillman looked crestfallen as he nodded. "I'm sorry, Charlotte. God, I suck at this."

"Look at me, Tillman." He obliged. "Us, here. I want this. Okay? Stop trying to be what you think I want, and just be you, which *is* exactly what I want."

His grip relaxed slightly, and he sat up a bit straighter in the booth. "Charlotte, for the purposes of full disclosure, I should probably mention I've kind of been infatuated with you for a while now. As in, way before you kissed me."

Chuck raised her eyebrows and took a breath, suppressing what would likely have been an embarrassing laugh. "It's okay Tillman. If we're being honest, part of the reason I said yes to being a trainer is because it meant I'd get to spend more time with you." She paused as a thought passed through her mind like a bolt. Before she could talk herself out of it, she spoke. "And, if it's not too weird for you, would you mind calling me Chuck?"

Whatever concerns Tillman might've had concerning his feelings for her before they became a couple, appeared to disappear. He sat back, studying her. "Chuck?"

"Yeah, it was kind of my dad's nickname for me. After he died I adopted it, in my own mind at least, like a secret way of keeping his memory alive." She frowned, not wanting to make it sound any weirder than she already had. "It's just, to everyone else at Alpha, I'm Agent Barnes. But to those close to me, I'd like to be Chuck."

He leaned over the table, as if to kiss her, and nearly spilled his drink. They laughed together until the food arrived.

***

218

The orange and purple sky that signified the Arizona sunset was fading as they pulled back into Alpha. Chuck's side hurt from the laughter they'd shared throughout the night. She smiled while walking back towards the warehouse, hand in hand with Tillman. The scene made for a wonderful end to a wonderful date.

As they were rounding the exit gate from the parking lot, Tillman stopped suddenly.

Chuck followed his gaze. "What's wrong?"

"Sorry, I thought I saw something moving along the fence there. Probably just lights from the interstate." He shrugged. Chuck pulled his arm, hurrying him towards the elevator and its warmth.

Chapter Thirty-Five:

One Hell of A Night

Chuck and Tillman stepped out of the elevator, still hand in hand, and turned left towards the apartments. She leaned against him, giggling as she forced him into the wall and pressed her lips against his.

"Ahem—Agent Barnes?" Rita's voice rang out through the hall, startling them.

Chuck turned, releasing Tillman. "Rita, hey."

The recruit gave Tillman a sideways look before approaching Chuck. "I think something's wrong with Marcy."

"What? Where is she?"

"We were hanging out in the dorm when she just stood up and started walking away, like mid-conversation. I asked her what was up, and she mumbled something about needing to go to the infirmary."

Chuck looked over her shoulder. "How long ago was this?"

Rita shrugged. "Ten, maybe fifteen minutes. It felt off. I went to see if you were in your apartment, and when you didn't answer I decided to go and check on her myself."

Tillman checked his watch. "There should be a nurse on duty. I'll call down to medical and see if she made it."

Chuck bent, removed her heels, then turned and began walking in the direction of the medical wing. "I'm going to see if I can catch up to her."

"I'll come with you." Rita said, falling in behind Chuck.

They moved hurriedly through the halls, currently bereft of staff, most of whom would've gone home or retired for the night. As they passed the cafeteria, the droning of the TV's drifted out from the giant empty space. For some reason, the sound made the hairs on Chuck's arm stand on end. She quickened her pace.

As they made the last turn before entering the medical wing, a loud siren began blaring within the complex. Chuck froze for only a moment as she processed what was happening, before breaking into a full sprint.

Site Alpha was under attack.

She burst through the hallway doors, hearing Rita close behind her. The alarm's echo, combined with the flashing red and blue lights located above the distant elevator doors, made the hall feel foreign and sinister.

Chuck instinctively reached for her weapon, which wasn't there. The sound of her bare feet hitting the floor echoed loudly through the hall, adding to the disorienting atmosphere. She turned towards the infirmary doors as she entered the waiting area.

"Agent Barnes!" Rita screamed from directly behind her. Chuck turned towards Rita, then continued along the recruit's sight line until she saw a woman's body in scrubs slumped against the far wall.

Chuck didn't have her watch, and a quick glance back at Rita confirmed the younger woman wasn't wearing hers either. She grabbed the recruit by the shoulder. "Rita, get back to the dorm. I'm—"

Ding.

The sound of the elevator was almost inaudible over all the other noises, yet it sent a bolt of fear through Chuck's body. She spun on her heel, facing the doors as they opened. Two security team members came spilling out, their uniforms drenched in blood.

A bright red glow shone within the elevator, but it wasn't Spring Heeled Jack that followed the security member's bodies out. The smaller form of Marcy, strode into the waiting area carrying a rifle. Her pupils were rolled up into her head, just as they'd been back on the mountain.

"Rita! Fall back!" Chuck yelled as she turned, intending to dive into the infirmary. Two shots rang out and holes exploded in the door inches from Chuck's outstretched arms.

"Ah, ah, ah, little bird." Jack's voice caused her muscles to tighten, and she turned her head to look in the direction of the elevator.

Marcy was pointing the gun directly at her now, advancing slowly. Jack entered the waiting area, his countenance dripping with malice. They took several steps toward her before Jack placed a hand on Marcy's shoulder. "That will do, my dear. We need her in one piece."

He suddenly pivoted as a bedpan came flying across the waiting room, striking the wall as it missed him by inches. Marcy swiveled to face this new threat and Chuck took advantage of the distraction, kicking up and causing the recruit to fire two shots into the ceiling.

A second bedpan struck Jack in the chest as Chuck grabbed the gun, pulling Marcy in close to her. Three more shots popped off into the infirmary doors before Chuck forced a finger behind the trigger, cutting off Marcy's ability to fire the weapon, at least temporarily.

Pain erupted along the right side of Chuck's head, and she suspected the close proximity of the gunshots had burst her eardrum. Through the pain she continued to push back against Marcy.

Chuck saw Jack launch himself in the direction the bedpans had flown from, suspecting Rita was his target. Marcy's mouth opened as though she were screaming in frustration, yet no sound came out. Chuck pulled her head back and delivered a hard headbutt to Marcy's nose, feeling the cartilage snap under the force of the blow. Marcy's hold on the gun slackened, allowing Chuck to slam her knee hard into the recruit's arm. The weapon clattered uselessly to the floor.

Rita screamed, but Chuck couldn't divert her attention, instead slipping her free arm up and under Marcy's own and turning the smaller woman around. "I'm sorry," Chuck whispered as she put Marcy in a choke hold, cutting off the blood and oxygen to her brain.

Jack's voice rose over the sound of the alarm. "Unleash her, you damnable bitch!"

Chuck rolled, taking Marcy with her as she saw the shadow of Jack out of the corner of her eye. He crashed into the wall they'd been standing near a moment earlier. The recruit's body went limp, and Chuck used the momentum of their fall to push Marcy back towards the elevator.

"You think you can beat me little bird?" Jack asked as Chuck continued her roll, putting a bit more space between her and the cryptid.

"I'll give it my best shot, asshole," she said, getting her feet under her and adopting a fighting stance.

"Aye." Jack said. He crouched, and Chuck's body tensed, expecting him to pounce at her.

Instead, a fire extinguisher smashed into the side of Jack, knocking him off balance. Tillman followed the thrown object and tackled the lanky monster, sending both sprawling. Jack clearly had a strength and weight advantage, which allowed him to recover more quickly.

He threw a punch at Tillman, which caught him in the cheek. Jack pulled back to deliver another blow, but Chuck landed a spinning kick to his head, smashing it against the wall. Jack's eyes blazed and his jaw unhinged in a ghoulish way as a blast of blue smoke and flames escaped. Chuck spun away, barely avoiding the attack. Panic began to creep into her mind, as she tried to figure out a way to defeat Jack, or at least slow him down.

"Time to end this charade *Agent Barnes*." Jack spit as he kicked away from the wall. Not waiting, Chuck somersaulted backwards, stopping in a crouch, and scooped up the rifle. Bringing it to bear, she fired. The first two rounds hit Jack square in the chest, but his arm came up for the third, and she saw a spark as the bullet deflected. Tillman cried out in pain and Jack let out a guttural laugh.

"Now that's something I haven't felt in a long time," Jack said, focusing his red eyes on her. Chuck could see Marcy moving again near the elevator, and rather than fire another shot, she threw the weapon in the direction of the recruit. It seemed to work, as Jack's gaze followed the flying gun.

Chuck immediately turned and crashed through the infirmary doors, her dress catching on an exposed screw and tearing, tripping her slightly. She recovered quickly, again hearing Jack scream, and rushed towards the back of the room.

"All these years! Trapped in a tiny box, while the Rogers grew fat and happy!" Jack bellowed behind her. "All that time buried in a bloody hole!" She heard the doors crack from the force of being thrown open.

"I've come to deliver some vengeance little bird! And you're going to help me!"

Chuck grabbed the end of a hospital bed and used it like an emergency break, spinning to face Jack. "You'll have to catch me first you son of a bitch!"

"Oh, I fully intend to," he replied casually. His jaw unhinged again, and a blue glow emanated from behind his crooked, pointy teeth. Chuck inhaled a quick breath and rolled backwards over a bed.

Jack coiled up, eyes ablaze and leapt towards her. Chuck had chosen her spot carefully, waiting until the last second to grab an IV stand which she thrust like a spear. It caught Jack on the chin, forcing his face sideways. Another gout of blue smoke and flame sprayed the wall.

The momentum of Jack's jump, combined with Chuck's attack, sent him careening into the nearby nurse's station. Chuck rolled back over another bed as supplies rained down upon the crumpled form of her attacker.

She didn't wait for him to recover, instead jumping over the final bed in the row and running for the doors at the back of the infirmary leading to the staff offices. She heard a crash that might have been a hospital bed being shoved out of the way. Chuck ducked instinctively as Jack landed close to her. Kicking out her left leg, she tripped him as a metallic claw tore open the flesh of her arm.

Chuck smashed into one of the swinging doors as Jack rammed into the wall of the infirmary, separating them briefly. She rolled, pain radiating out from her torn arm. She stumbled towards the first office on the left.

She grabbed the door handle, turned, and pulled. Thankfully, it opened. She stepped in, then immediately turned, and forced the door to open back into the hall. Her instincts paid off. The door smashed into Jack, who'd taken one great leap down the hallway. She pulled the door closed and twisted the lock, hoping things hadn't changed since the last time she'd been in this room.

There was an explosion of glass as Jack punched through the window on the door. Running around the desk, she looked up, eyes scanning. She reached up and pulled down her target, spinning fast and turning with her hands.

Jack was there. He shoved the desk aside. She struck out with her wounded left arm, but he batted it away. In one smooth motion he grabbed her shoulder and squared his face with hers, mouth agape. Blue smoke and flames engulfed her head, the acrid substance filling her nose and mouth.

It was like someone stabbed a thousand needles into Chuck's skull. She could feel Jack's mind encroaching on hers. Claws rent at her subconscious, exposing layer after layer of Chuck's most private personal thoughts. Jack's power left her feeling naked and exposed.

Except, the power seemed to work both ways, and Jack's mind began to reveal memories to her.

She saw everything: The years of darkness in the box, the Griffins freeing him, Jack killing them in return, him killing Sparkles, Jack watching her and Greg from atop the house, and underlying all of it, she could hear voices. They cried out with a burning hatred and a deep thirst for revenge—feelings that too closely resembled those she'd been feeling herself.

Suddenly she could see through Marcy's eyes. The recruit was being held down by a pair of security guards. Chuck saw DeRosa entering the infirmary with her weapon drawn. Marcy turned slightly and she caught a glimpse of Tillman, propped up against the wall, with his head down. The front of his sweater was covered in blood. She clung to that image, trying to keep her own mind under possession for just a few seconds more.

"The harder you fight the worse it will be for you, little bird." Jack's voice rang within her head. He saw the others as well, and it didn't worry him in the least. He was supremely confident that nobody currently within Site Alpha could cause him harm.

"You're going to be mine n—" There was a pause, his crawling fingers pulling back from within her mind ever so slightly. "What's that odor?"

Her right hand darted up, smearing a great glob of Doc's pink stuff across Jack's face. Inside her mind, she watched herself through his eyes, praying her plan would work. Jack forced her away, and she felt the tendrils of his mind withdraw from her own.

"The hell?"

Jack barely finished the phrase when a bright purple flash erupted around his face. Within her head, Marcy and Jack screamed simultaneously. He fell back against the wall, pink flames erupting from the area where she'd smeared the goo. Jack's presence in her mind lessened further.

Jack's face from his nose down started dripping away like melting candle wax. In his burning red eyes, she saw something that filled her with joy. Those eyes showed fear. He extended an arm outward, as if he were going to try and grab her again. For just a moment, Jack was once more in her mind.

"Damn you!"

His head violently exploded, spraying the office with gore. She lifted her arm to try and shield herself and screamed in horror.

Her right hand was gone. At the point where her wrist should have been there was only a burning stump, her own skin and bones mimicking what had moments before been the lower half of Jack's face. Pain exploded through her entire body.

The door to the office nearly broke off its hinges as DeRosa slammed it open. Chuck saw Sally entering the room as she passed out, pain and exhaustion overcoming her.

Chapter Thirty-Six:

Within A Void

I underestimated my little bird...

The ghastly substance she used to destroy my shell was swift and terrible in its effectiveness.

As the realization of my fate dawned on me, I reacted in desperation, forcing my conscious into the closest available vessel... Charlotte Barnes.

Unfortunately, I could not complete the process before my body succumbed to the effects of the vile weapon. Fragmented and broken, what was left of my spirit came to rest within my little bird's mind, and the voices came with me.

Freed from my physical form, I now understand what they are and why they have stayed with me.

The Rogers, in their haste to imprison me, turned to inauspicious rituals—sacrificial rituals. They killed others like me, to power the enchantments that bound me and kept me powerless within that damnable box.

The spirits of those beings exist within a void, somewhere between the physical world and the spiritual. And now, in the quite hidden places of Charlotte's mind, they speak to me, whispering their secrets.

Gorgons, as they were called by some, slaughtered by the Rogers for their poisoned blood and unbreakable bones. These ancient souls hunger for revenge against the family that murdered them, a desire I happen to share.

But at present, without my precious body, I am too weak, too wounded to do more than linger within the fragile frame of the woman that killed me, listening to the voices, and replaying my brief time between prisons, over and over again.

There are still those that dabble in the mystic arts; Charlotte has encountered such a person. The voices assure me this state need not be permanent, that a solution will present itself.

Until then I must watch and wait, knowing only one thing for certain.

I will not underestimate my little bird again.

Chapter Thirty-Seven:

Bedside Manner

The iridescent glow of the fixture hanging over her stung Chuck's eyes. She blinked, feeling pain radiate across her whole body. As her eyes adjusted to the light, she saw Sally's face come into focus. The Chief Agent was sitting close by. As she tried to turn her head to get a better view, she felt pressure from a tube inserted into her nose.

Sally sat up. "Hey, sister. No sudden movements."

Chuck returned to her original position, the pressure lessening. "How long have I been out?"

"Four days, but don't let Cole know I told you."

"Four days! Shit, what about Marcy? Tillman?"

Images flashed in her head. She could see through other eyes... Jack's eyes.

Sally stood up. "They're alive, and so is Rita. All thanks to you."

"What about the guards and the nurse?"

A shadow passed across her friend's face. "They didn't make it. Marcy killed them all; well, Jack killed them, but you get what I mean."

Closing her eyes, Chuck could see the recruit's body as it lay on the floor. She'd done what she could to stop Marcy without killing her but choking someone out was dangerous. She hoped the young woman would make a full recovery.

DeRosa patted her shoulder. "Now, you need to get some rest."

"I just slept for four days."

"Doc would probably argue that a medically induced coma isn't the same as sleeping. I'm going to go let Cole know that you're up. I'm sure he's gonna want to ask you a few questions." Sally smiled and then headed out the door.

Chuck stretched, her legs felt stiff, and her right hand tingled. She raised her arm.

"Oh God."

Tears welled up, then overflowed from her eyes. The whole encounter came rushing back into her mind. She looked at her wrapped arm, which ended a couple of inches above where her elbow had once been. She wanted to scream, to lash out at the creature responsible for this. Instead, she quietly cried, letting the tears run down her face to fall freely on her pillow.

Minutes passed before Cole entered her room, followed closely by Sally, who took one look at her and rushed to the bedside. Chuck took a sharp intake of breath, trying to get her emotions under control. Sally gently wiped away Chuck's tears. Cole stood back a few feet, giving the women some space. As Chuck began to calm down, he stepped forward.

"I'm sorry, Charlotte. We saved as much of it as we could. It was just—" He grasped her left hand.

"I know. It was the only thing I could think of to stop him."

"Well, it did. You saved a lot of lives, Agent." He smiled warmly. "Oh! And Delta is sending their best Prosthetist out. They're going to be making you a new arm."

She appreciated that Cole was trying to cheer her up and forced a smile back. "You're the one that gave me the idea. The morning that Sparkles died."

Cole looked at her quizzically for a moment before recognition dawned on his face.

He gave her hand a final squeeze. "I'm glad you're awake. Obviously, there are going to be a lot of people who will want to talk to you. But we can worry about all of that once you feel better." He left her and Sally alone.

Her friend switched to the other side of the bed, then sat down. She reached out and took the hand that Cole had been holding. Sally was still there when Chuck fell asleep.

***

The next time she woke up, Chuck was startled to see that her room had been filled with balloons and flowers. Doc was sitting at her bedside, looking over her equipment and jotting down notes on a small pad of paper.

"Agent Barnes! How're you feeling this fine morning?"

"Tired and sore." Her stomach gurgled audibly. "And hungry."

"I bet you are. I'll let Cole know you're up and see if he thinks you're ready for real food." Doc leaned in closer to her bed. "Listen, what you did, the way you handled yourself the other night? That was some hero level stuff, you hear me. Very few people possess the kind of courage you and your friends showed fighting that nightmare."

"Thanks Doc."

He smiled before scribbling down a few more notes and heading out the door.

After what felt like an hour, Cole arrived. "Good morning, Charlotte. Doc tells me you're hungry."

"Starving would be a more appropriate term."

He walked around to the right side of her bed. Lifting her arm, he pulled out a small, pointed instrument. "I want you to tell me on a scale of one to five, five being the most painful, how much it hurts each time I touch this to your arm."

She nodded, and he pressed the small end against her shoulder. "One."

A press about halfway down her arm.

"Oh, like three."

He pushed the rod down on the tip of the remainder of her arm. She winced and pulled away from him. "Five, maybe six."

"Good."

He ran a couple more tests before finally asking her if she would prefer boiled chicken or boiled chicken. She went with option two.

***

When the meal arrived later that morning, the entire thing was bland and tasteless. It was also the most exquisite food Chuck had ever eaten. Her stomach lurched more than once, but she ate every bite. The hardest part was trying to eat with only her left hand.

Not long after she'd finished, there was a knock at her door. Sally came in along with Greg. His arm was still in a sling, and he was wearing the goofy smirk Chuck no longer hated.

He stepped to her bedside. "I heard you kicked all the ass the other night. I'm sorry I missed it."

"Trust me when I say you shouldn't be." She pointed at the sling. "How's the therapy going?"

"Better. Doc says I've only got a couple more weeks. How's your arm?"

The question stung a bit, but she understood there was no malice behind it. "It hurts worse than the punch you hit me with." He smiled. "I'm glad you're healing up. The Family can use a few more good agents."

"I'll count myself lucky if I'm even half the agent you are."

The compliment was surprising, and felt a bit forced to Chuck, but she smiled all the same.

Sally cleared her throat. "Okay champ, I snuck you in here against doctor's orders, so head on back to therapy before Cole finds out."

He nodded then pointed at Chuck. "You still owe me a rematch."

Chuck held up the stump of her right arm. "Trust me you'll get one, eventually."

Greg gave her a thumbs up then headed for the door.

Sally smiled as he passed by. "I thought you might want a distraction before the whole agency descends on you."

Chuck sighed. "Thanks." She adjusted her bed, reclining to take some of the pressure off her back. "Sally, I know how it ended, but how did Jack get in here?"

"Well, we don't know everything but from the looks of it, Jack still had a link with Marcy. Even all those days later. He was spying on us through her head the whole time. That night he used her to get into Warehouse 3."

Chuck shook her head. "He really didn't think there was anything we could do to stop him. He came here wanting to kill everybody because we are part of the Family. He'd been plotting his revenge the whole time he was buried."

"I wish he'd stayed buried."

"Sally, I saw them free him. The Griffins. They had to use some type of ritual to break him out of that container."

A dark look crossed over her friend's face. "Yeah, Delta's still sorting it all out. Whenever the Wardens come to see you, tell them everything."

"Trust me, I've learned that lesson."

Sally took her hand. "The others are still recovering themselves. Tillman and Rita lost a lot of blood. It was real touch and go for both. Marcy got her memory back, and… well it's got her pretty twisted up."

Chuck slumped in her bed. The bastard had been dead for days and he was still making people suffer. "When can I see them?"

Sally smiled. "I was wondering when you were going to ask that. Cole says soon."

Chuck smiled and laid her head back. Eating had made her tired and soon she was sleeping again.

***

The next morning, Doc came to her room. He gave her a big hug, then began removing her IVs. "I told Cole he couldn't keep you down for long! You're looking healthier every day!"

"I'm sure it's all because of your wonderful bedside manner, Doc."

He smiled, then turned as someone knocked at the door. Flynn and Voss entered Chuck's room, trench coats and ties in full effect. Doc showed himself out.

Flynn walked up to her bed. "Agent Barnes, how are you doing today?"

"I'm feeling better, stronger."

Voss smiled at her. "That's good to hear."

Chuck sat up. "What do you say we get this over with?"

The Wardens sat down on either side of her. Voss pulled out a notepad as Flynn scooted his chair closer to her bed. He spoke first. "Chief DeRosa told us you gained some information during your fight with Spring Heeled Jack. Can you clarify exactly what that was?"

She sighed. "I got a first-class lesson on those blue flames. They let him get inside your head. But it goes both ways. I could see things in his mind, just like he was seeing things in mine."

Voss scribbled furiously.

"I saw the darkness he'd been trapped in. I saw his rage at us, the Family. And I saw the Griffins. They used magic to open that box. And he killed them,"—she winced at the memory—"slaughtered them in a frenzy actually."

Flynn ran a hand through his hair. "Our team was still out studying the container when a call came in that Alpha was under attack. That thing is a real piece of work. Made my skin crawl after only being around it for a couple of minutes. The code from the paper led the Griffins right to it. Delta's still trying to figure out how anyone even knew about its location."

"Does that mean someone in the Family gave it to them?"

Voss shook her head. "We don't know, but we're sure as shit going to try and find out."

"If you do, I'd like thirty minutes alone with them."

Voss put down her notepad. "You and me both."

Flynn sighed and rubbed his eyes. "Agent Barnes, is there any other insight you can give us concerning your encounter?"

"Jack was angry, furious even. But there was something else, or many somethings else. I could hear voices in his mind, evil voices." Chuck frowned. "That's the only way I can describe them, evil. They all seemed to want the same thing... revenge. The link didn't last long enough for me to make out what they were saying, but I could feel how hateful they were."

Flynn nodded. "Well, thanks to you, Spring Heeled Jack will never again be a problem for the Family." He stood and Voss did likewise.

Flynn placed his hands in his pockets. "Thank you, Agent, for everything you did. If you ever want to join the Wardens, let me know. I'll put in a good word for you."

Chuck shuddered involuntarily, then shook her head. "I don't think you'll have to worry about that. It was nice to meet you both. Hopefully, we don't have to run into each other ever again."

The Wardens left. In the quiet of the room, alone with her thoughts, Chuck shivered as the memory of Jack's voice whispered.

Hello little bird.

Chapter Thirty-Eight:

When Things Got Better

The rest of the day became a blur as high-ranking officials from Delta were paraded through Chuck's room one after the other. They handed her flowers, certificates, awards, pins, and lots and lots of bullshit smiles. She felt like an animal on display. By evening she wanted nothing more than to be left alone.

She sighed when she heard yet another knock.

The door opened a crack before opening fully, revealing Tillman. He flashed her an awkward smile, then stood looking at her, sadness plain on his face. He coughed, as if trying to compose himself. "Hey."

"Hey."

Tillman looked around the room, adorned with flowers and balloons. "You hate this, don't you?"

She chuckled, which felt odd to her now. "I hate this."

He finally moved towards her bed, taking her hand and kissing her gently. "I'm sorry I couldn't come and see you sooner. Cole didn't want me moving around until he was sure the wound was healed up adequately."

"If I'd known the bullet was going to deflect like that."

"No, no. Really, it's not that big of a deal. Cole said it looked worse than it really was. The scar is pretty cool, see." He went to pull down his shirt, but Chuck averted her eyes, and Tillman seemed to realize she didn't share his enthusiasm. "Oh, hey, sorry."

"Tillman, don't apologize."

"Sorry," He winced. "I—I didn't know what to say—what I could say."

Chuck looked into Tillman's eyes. "You being here is perfect right now."

He reached out and took her hand, then motioned to her other side. "Does it hurt?"

"Like hell. The tingling is the worst part. I still feel my fingers."

He gave her hand a gentle squeeze. "You're a hero. You know that don't you?"

Chuck sat back. "Don't you start with that bullshit. If you and Rita hadn't been there I'd never have been able to get to the pink stuff in the first place."

Tillman looked at the wall, then back into her eyes. "Okay, no more bullshit. What are you going to do now?"

"I... I don't know." She looked down at the remains of her right arm. "I didn't sign up for this."

Tillman's face went pale. "Oh God Chuck, you're not thinking of?"

"That monster was in my head Tillman, reading my mind, tearing me apart from the inside. I can't even explain how shitty that is, how violated I still feel all these days later. And the worst part? I can still hear him. Every time I close my eyes I hear him." She choked back tears.

Tillman looked at the floor. "Chuck, I—I can't pretend to understand what that was like. What this *is* like. It's just, Alpha, this job, all of it wouldn't be the same without you around."

"Hey, Tillman, look at me."

He did. "I've had a couple days now, and yes, washing out has crossed my mind. But you know what else has crossed my mind? What it would be like to lose you." She shook her head slowly. "That's not a sacrifice I'm willing to make right now."

He smiled and wiped at the corner of his eye. "In that case, I believe there's something I'm supposed to say." He leaned in and kissed her. Tenderly at first, but when she pulled him closer it became more urgent. Finally, she patted his cheek and he sat back, his face flush.

"Do you know when they're letting you out?"

Chuck sighed. "Tomorrow morning, I think."

"Then I'll be back in the morning. I think Cole said Marcy and Rita will be ready for visitors tomorrow. We can go together."

"Thanks. I'd really like that."

Tillman left when Cole arrived to give Chuck a few final tests. That night was her last in the infirmary, though she hardly slept at all. Every time she tried to rest, tried to close her eyes, Spring Heeled

Jack was there. Hellish red eyes and crooked, fanged grin. Waiting for her in the shadows.

By the next morning all the Deltas had gone, and life at Alpha was slowly returning to normal, for everyone else at least. Chuck's father once told her that tragedy didn't reveal your real friends. Your real friends were the ones that were still there when things got better.

As she sat on her bed, tired, worn out, and still incredibly sore, she thought of those words. Chuck stood and began the long and painful process of dressing herself for the first time, one-handed. Once dressed, she went through some of the cards hanging from the many balloons and bouquets. Most were filled with drivel about how brave she was, or how the sender was praying for her.

The door to her room opened and Sally and Tillman were there. Sally enveloped her in a hug. "Ready to get out of this place?"

"You better believe it. Cole said I could stay in the medical wing if I wanted, but that's not going to happen." Everything in the infirmary reminded her of the final fight with Jack.

Tillman gave her a hug as well. "You still up for visiting Rita and Marcy?"

"Definitely."

The three of them moved two rooms down, to where the recruits were both being kept for observation. Chuck's stomach twisted when she saw Marcy, who had a plastic mask over her face to protect her shattered nose. The young woman also had a cast, likely from when Chuck smashed her knee into Marcy's arm.

Rita looked better, though she had a massive black eye, and a small patch of her hair had turned white at the roots.

"Agent Barnes!" Marcy's eyes lit up as she mumbled through the mask. Chuck approached them.

"Oh my god! Your arm," Rita blurted out.

Chuck raised it as best she could. "Yeah, the price of destroying a Class One I guess."

Marcy's mask fogged up and Chuck could see tears running down the recruit's face. "Agent Barnes, I'm so sorry!"

Picking up the young woman's hand, Chuck smiled. "Marcy, he was in my head too. You have nothing to apologize for. You didn't do any of that. A monster did, and you're not a monster."

Marcy accepted a long hug. Rita was showing Tillman the scar on her scalp left by Jack.

"I don't even remember him hitting me. Doc said I must have a hard head because it didn't crack my skull." Rita said, pulling her hair back to hide the wound.

They talked to the recruits for a bit, but Chuck quickly began to feel tired. Sally and Tillman offered to walk her back to her apartment. Goodbyes were exchanged, along with promises that soon enough, they'd all get back to training.

***

Chuck felt the eyes watching her as they walked their way back across the site. Tillman held her hand the entire time. Having him and Sally with her comforted Chuck and made the walk bearable.

Returning to her own room felt odd, like she was a visitor in someone else's home. Chuck turned to Tillman as they entered. "Would you mind if I have a bit of one-on-one time with the Chief?"

"Sure thing. Can I come back later though?"

"Yeah, I'd like that."

He nodded, then left the room. Sally had wandered over to her usual seat and Chuck turned to her. "Sorry, I guess that was a bit presumptuous of me. Do I need to let you go?"

"No, I've got a few minutes. Was there something particular you wanted to talk about?"

Chuck walked over to the bar. "I just wanted to say you're a great friend Sally. You were the first one there when I woke up, and you're here with me now, when I really need it."

Sally smiled. "And I always will be."

Chuck gave Sally another hug, then waved as Alpha's Chief Agent stepped into the hallway. She walked to the door, locked it, and then collapsed.

Alone in her apartment, without monitors or cameras, shut off even a little from the rest of the site, Chuck curled up on her floor and cried. She cried harder than she ever had before.

When she finally did peel herself off the carpet, she ate a bit of lunch, then spent a while looking at her arm in the mirror. She could still feel the missing limb. In her mind, she wiggled invisible fingers. The whole experience felt surreal. Every act was like doing something for the first time.

As jarring as it was to only have one arm, Chuck could feel other wounds festering within her. Scars every bit as real as the physical ones she bore, lurked within her mind. The tendrils of Spring Heeled Jack had left lacerations, the remnants of which, Chuck worried, might never heal.

***

Early that evening, Tillman returned.

They sat on the side of her bed and talked about nothing and everything, though eventually Chuck's back began to hurt. "Would it be alright if we laid down?" She asked, after holding out as long as she could.

"Yeah, sure."

It took a bit of maneuvering, especially with her learning what was and wasn't comfortable for her arm, but after a bit of trial and error, Chuck lay peacefully in Tillman's arms.

"Tillman, thank you for being here," she whispered, feeling his warmth.

He hesitated. "Am I supposed to say you're welcome? Sorry... I." He stopped talking, possibly as a defensive mechanism.

Chuck shook her head and rolled over so that she was looking into his eyes. "Don't say anything. Just hold me, and don't let go. That's what I need right now."

Tillman smiled and pulled her closer. He was still holding her when she fell asleep. For the first time in days, Chuck slept peacefully.

Chapter Thirty-Nine:

A Lawyer Comes Calling

The Virginia sun warmed her face as she reached up to dust the window frame. The lawyer's imminent arrival caused Andrea to hurry the job so she could move on and clean the mantle. Not that she kept a dirty home. But with everything that had happened over the last couple of weeks, she'd been lax in her routine.

Urgent or not, as her gaze fell upon the pictures on the mantle, she stopped. Picking up the nearest one, Andrea rubbed the faintest hint of dust off its glass. It felt like yesterday they'd all been together and happy. She wiped away a tear, and noticing the time on her watch, immediately got back to the dusting.

As the clock in the hallway chimed two, there came a knock at the front door. Andrea peeked in the dining room to make sure everything was still in order, then hurried to the door. Looking through the peephole, she saw a tall, smartly dressed man, holding a briefcase. She unlocked the deadbolt and opened the door.

The man nodded to her. "Hello, Mrs. Lee I presume?"

"Yes, yes. Please come in."

Andrea directed him to the sofa. He sat, although his long legs made him look a bit awkward.

"Can I offer you some tea?"

"No thank you ma'am." He leaned back, placing his briefcase across his lap. "I must say, you do have a lovely house here."

Taking a seat across from him, she smiled. "You are kind to say that. Now, if I'm not being too forward, how exactly did your office find out about my daughter's condition?"

A wide smile stretched across his face. "Direct and to the point, Mrs. Lee. I like that." He popped the latches to his briefcase. "Well, first off, I'd like to assure you that we're not a bunch of ambulance chasers, if you get my meaning." He stretched the syllables of ambulance so that it sounded like *am-bue-lance*.

"That being said, we found your story in the paper more than a bit intriguing, so we did some research of our own. Much as you yourself indicated in the article, we felt it odd that the so-called *officials* in Arizona didn't provide much in the way of answers concerning your daughter's... what did they call it again? *Accident?*"

She opened her mouth to speak, but a sudden rush of emotion caused the words to catch in her throat. Two months had passed since the whole ordeal started.

Her first indication of something being wrong had been the texts. It had always been Jess's preferred form of communication, but for about two weeks they'd gone silent. She swallowed the lump in her throat.

"I... Jess stopped sending me texts. And then when she finally did, they felt off somehow, like someone trying to imitate my daughter. I spent two straight days trying to call her. When she didn't pick up a single time, I called the State Police and reported her missing."

The lawyer pulled a paper from his case. After scanning it for a moment, he nodded. "The statement you provided to our office spells out how the police gave you the run around for *several weeks*."

"My husband and I felt completely helpless! It took them quite a long time to get back to us. But once they did, the things they said made no sense."

"Is Mr. Lee at work currently?" the lawyer asked.

"This whole terrible business has been incredibly hard on my husband. He's currently staying with his parents, in Illinois."

The lawyer nodded, then continued. "You stated, Mrs. Lee that the police in Arizona claimed they couldn't find any record of your daughter living there? What specifically did they tell you?"

"Where do I begin? They claimed Jess had never been enrolled in school. Claimed she didn't show up in any records as having even applied to ASU. One officer even claimed her mailing address wasn't real. I sent *and* received letters with that address on them. Not once were any sent back." She felt her cheeks getting hot and took a deep breath, attempting to calm her nerves.

Rubbing his mustache, the lawyer continued. "And when did this doctor, Cole, was it? First contact you?"

"It will have been two weeks tomorrow. My caller ID showed an Arizona number, so I answered it. A young sounding man calling himself Dr. Cole said he'd been attending to Jess for several weeks. Several weeks—can you believe that?"

"Did he identify a hospital or care facility of any kind?"

"No, I don't believe so. I must have been in shock. He spoke very quickly, and I only caught some of what he said. In the end, when he mentioned they were arranging for me to pick up my daughter I—I didn't really question it. I was so happy to hear she was alive."

"Completely understandable, ma'am. I'm sure I'd have done the same if I were in your position." He leaned forward a bit. "You know, if it's not too late, I do think I'd enjoy a cup of tea."

"Oh, of course. Just a moment." She went into the kitchen, pausing to look in on the dining room. Satisfied, she retrieved a glass and poured some tea. She turned back towards the living room and nearly dropped the drink, surprised to see her guest standing at the dining room entrance.

"Therapy?" He asked, tilting his head towards the room.

"Yes." She handed him the glass.

"Mrs. Lee, would it be accurate to say your daughter used to be a real whiz when it came to computers?"

Andrea looked at him suspiciously. "Jess was quite good with computers. How exactly did you know that?"

He smiled, a sheepish yet sly expression. "We've got quite the investigative team, Mrs. Lee. Now, not to change subjects too much, but this Cole fella, he never explained the amnesia, or the tremors?"

"I had no warning. None. I didn't realize she was... well, whatever it is, until I met her at the airport." She wiped away fresh tears as she watched Jess struggling to use the laptop set up on their dining room table.

The lawyer took a sip of his tea, leaning against the door frame. "Whoever this Cole was with, they're the ones paying for this therapy and what not?"

"He told me *they* would take care of all Jess's travel, and set her up with a therapist, due to trauma caused by an auto accident. Promising this, promising that!" Andrea paused again. "Always quick, and vague with every response."

He nodded. "That is one part of your story I'm particularly curious about. You claim a few days after Jess returned, your bank account was credited five hundred thousand dollars?"

"It was there one morning, out of the blue. The bank didn't even show a credit, just a massively inflated balance."

"Mrs. Lee, does your husband intend to return, if you don't mind me asking?"

She glanced at her daughter again. "I hope so, to be honest I'm not sure. Jess being back hasn't been easy for him; Rosie either for that matter. I think she remembers how vibrant her sister used to be, and now…" She shook her head. "Martin tried calling that doctor as soon as the airline staff escorted Jess to us. Of course, the number had been disconnected. We called the police, Martin even got in contact with a friend's brother who's in the FBI. No one wanted to help us."

The lawyer leveled a rather stern gaze at her, his eyes locking with hers. "Mrs. Lee, I'm sorry for having to ask this, but you and I both know how important this could be for any lawsuit going forward. Why, if she's really suffering from amnesia and brain fog as you claim she is, did your daughter leave the airport with you that day?"

Andrea stared into the dining room where Jess sat wearing headphones. She felt hot tears running down her cheeks. "Something terrible happened to Jess's mind. Physically, she's fine. Healthy as a horse as my Gran would say. But mentally, it's like someone put her brain in a blender. She can speak as though nothing is wrong, yet can't tell you where she went to school, or who her childhood friends were." She pulled a tissue from her pocket and blew her nose. "My daughter didn't know her own parent's names, just our faces."

She fought back tears, then felt his hand rest on her shoulder. She didn't recoil. Besides Jess's sister Rosie, this man was the first person that hadn't sounded accusatory or disbelieving as he spoke to her.

"The morning your office called, Jess had told me she only knew who my husband and I were because the doctors had shown her a picture of the two of us. I felt so completely broken. When your secretary asked if I'd sought legal representation, I told her no because up to that point I didn't know what, if anything, it would accomplish. We got paid, no questions asked, and seemingly without a paper trail. But somebody knows something. Somebody did this to my Jess, and whoever it is, I want to see them pay."

"And that is precisely what we intend to do." Andrea appreciated the pause he gave her as she collected herself. For the first time in a while, she truly felt like maybe someone was going to get her some answers.

He pulled something from a pocket within his suit coat. "Mrs. Lee, do you recognize the woman in this picture?"

As she studied it, Andrea's anger suddenly grew. "Not the woman on the left, but that's Jess she's sitting with! Where did you get this?"

The lawyer cleared his throat. "From a source we consider reputable. This picture was taken on the ASU campus a few weeks before you reported your daughter missing. We're not sure who the other woman is, as the photograph only captures her profile, but we feel it's a strong lead."

"We have to show this to the police, somebody. This is proof we aren't crazy!"

He waved the statement away. "All in due time, Mrs. Lee. I assure you we intend to do everything in our power to get to the bottom of this, and to make things right for you and your family. To that end"—he pulled out a card and handed it to her—"we want to put you in contact with Pisa Pharmaceuticals. They've had some incredible success in cases which are remarkably similar to your family's own situation."

"That would be wonderful. The therapy they've given us has all come from the internet."

"Mrs. Lee, do you think I might talk with Jess? Just for a moment."

Andrea nodded and stepped into the room. She approached Jess, who often became so focused during her therapy sessions she didn't pay the outside world much mind at all. Andrea tapped her on the shoulder to get her attention.

Jess turned and smiled before removing her headphones. "Hello,"— she concentrated for a moment—"mother."

"Jess, there is a man here who is going to help us find out some more information about your accident. He'd like to speak with you. Would that be alright?"

Jess frowned. "Will you stay with me?"

Andrea's heart melted. "Yes, I will." She motioned to the figure still standing at the dining room entrance. "You can come in. Jess, this is Hank McFadden. Mr. McFadden, this is Jess Lee."

He walked in and sat down. "It's a pleasure to meet you, Ms. Lee. Your mother has told me quite a unique story about your return here to Virginia. She also tells me you don't have any memory of your life prior to a couple of weeks ago."

Jess looked down at the table, trembling. "That's right."

McFadden nodded, putting a finger under Jess's chin and raising her face. "Jess, I know some people who are going to try very hard to change that."

Jess closed her eyes and smiled. "I... I'd like that."

Andrea took her daughter's hand and smiled at Mr. McFadden.

He gave her an awkward wink before turning back to Jess. "So would I, Ms. Jess. So would I."

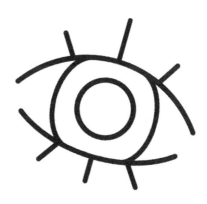

About the Author

Neal Romriell grew up in rural southwest Idaho where he enjoyed spending time outdoors and playing music with friends and family. After graduating high school, he moved to the East Coast where he spent nearly 20 years as a restaurant and retail manager. An avid player of TTRPG's, Neal honed his storytelling abilities while creating countless lands full of magical locations and unique characters. He eventually focused a lifelong fascination with all things paranormal and supernatural into penning his first full length novel. Neal now lives in South Carolina with his wife and children.

CPSIA information can be obtained
at www.ICGtesting.com
Printed in the USA
BVHW031004210622
640285BV00017B/324